Imaginations and Reveries

George William Russell

Contents

IMAGINATIONS
AND REVERIES

BY

George William Russell

PREFACE

The publishers of this book thought that a volume of articles and tales written by me during the past twenty-five years would have interest enough to justify publication, and asked me to make a selection. I have not been able to make up a book with only one theme. My temperament would only allow me to be happy when I was working at art. My conscience would not let me have peace unless I worked with other Irishmen at the reconstruction of Irish life. Birth in Ireland gave me a bias towards Irish nationalism, while the spirit which inhabits my body told me the politics of eternity ought to be my only concern, and that all other races equally with my own were children of the Great King. To aid in movements one must be orthodox. My desire to help prompted agreement, while my intellect was always heretical. I had written out of every mood, and could not retain any mood for long. If I advocated a national ideal I felt immediately I could make an equal plea for more cosmopolitan and universal ideas. I have observed my intuitions wherever they drew me, for I felt that the Light within us knows better than any other the need and the way. So I have no book on one theme, and the only unity which connects what is here written is a common origin. The reader must try a balance between the contraries which exist here as they exist in us all, as they exist and are harmonized in that multitudinous meditation which is the universe.--A.E.

PREFACE TO SECOND EDITION

To this edition four essays have been added. Two of these, "Thoughts for a Convention" and "The New Nation," made some little stir when they first appeared. Ireland since then has passed away from the mood which made it possible to consider the reconciliations suggested, and has set its heart on more fundamental changes, and these essays have only interest as marking a moment of transition in national life before it took a new road leading to another destiny.

NATIONALITY OR COSMOPOLITANISM

As one of those who believe that the literature of a country is for ever creating a new soul among its people, I do not like to think that literature with us must follow an inexorable law of sequence, and gain a spiritual character only after the bodily passions have grown weary and exhausted themselves. In the essay called The Autumn of the Body, Mr. Yeats seems to indicate such a sequence. Yet, whether the art of any of the writers of the decadence does really express spiritual things is open to doubt. The mood in which their work is conceived, a distempered emotion, through which no new joy quivers, seems too often to tell rather of exhausted vitality than of the ecstasy of a new life. However much, too, their art refines itself, choosing, ever rarer and more exquisite forms of expression, underneath it all an intuition seems to disclose only the old wolfish lust, hiding itself beneath the golden fleece of the spirit. It is not the spirit breaking through corruption, but the life of the senses longing to shine with the light which makes saintly things beautiful: and it would put on the jeweled raiment of seraphim, retaining still a heart of clay smitten through and through with the unappeasable desire of the flesh: so Rossetti's women, who have around them all the circumstance of poetry and romantic beauty, seem through their sucked-in lips to express a thirst which could be allayed in no spiritual paradise. Art in the decadence in our time might be symbolized as a crimson figure undergoing a dark crucifixion: the hosts of light are overcoming it, and it is dying filled with anguish and despair at a beauty it cannot attain. All these strange emotions have a profound psychological interest. I do not think because a spiritual flaw can be urged against a certain phase of life that it should remain unexpressed. The psychic maladies which attack all races when their civilization grows old must needs be understood to be dealt with: and they cannot be understood without being revealed in literature or art. But in Ireland we are not yet sick with this sickness. As psychology it concerns only the curious. Our intellectual life is in suspense. The national spirit seems to be making a last effort to assert itself in literature and to overcome cosmopolitan influences and the art of writers who express a purely personal feeling. It is true that nationality may express itself in many ways: it may not be at all evident in the subject matter, but it may be very evident in the sentiment. But a literature loosely held together by some emotional characteristics common to the writers, however great it may be, does not fulfill the purpose of a literature or art created by a number of men who have a common aim in building up an overwhelming ideal--who create, in a sense, a soul for their country, and who have a common pride in the achievement of all. The world has not seen this since the great antique civilizations of Egypt and Greece passed away. We cannot imagine an Egyptian artist daring enough to set aside the majestic attainment of many centuries. An Egyptian boy as he grew up must have been overawed by the national tradition, and have felt that it was not to be set aside: it was beyond his individual rivalry. The soul of Egypt incarnated in him, and, using its immemorial language and its mysterious lines, the efforts of the least workman who decorated a tomb seem to have been directed by the same hand that carved the Sphinx. This adherence to a traditional form is true of Greece, though to a less extent. Some little Tanagra terra-cottas might have been fashioned by Phidias, and in literature Ulysses and Agamemnon were not the heroes of one epic, but appeared endlessly in epic and drama. Since the Greek civilization no European nation has had an intellectual literature which was genuinely national. In the present century, leaving aside a few things in outward circumstance, there is little to distinguish the work of the best English writers or artists from that of their Continental contemporaries. Milliais, Leighton, Rossetti, Turner--how different from each other, and yet they might have painted the same pictures as born Frenchmen, and it would not have excited any great surprise as a marked divergence from French art. The cosmopolitan spirit, whether for good or for evil, is hastily obliterating all distinctions. What is distinctly national in these countries is less valuable than the immense wealth of universal ideas; and the writers who use this wealth appeal to no narrow circle: the foremost writers, the Tolstois and Ibsens, are conscious of addressing a European audience.

If nationality is to justify itself in the face of all this, it must be because the country which preserves its individuality does so with the profound conviction that its peculiar ideal is nobler than that which the cosmopolitan spirit suggests--that this ideal is so precious to it that its loss would be as the loss of the soul, and that it could not be realized without an aloofness from, if not an actual indifference to, the ideals which are spreading so rapidly over Europe. Is it possible for any nationality to make such a defense of its isolation? If not, let us read Goethe, Balzac, Tolstoi, men so much greater than any we can show, try to absorb their universal wisdom, and no longer confine ourselves to local traditions. But nationality was never so strong in Ireland as at the present time. It is beginning to be felt, less as a political movement than as a spiritual force. It seems to be gathering itself together, joining men who were hostile before, in a new intellectual fellowship: and if all these could unite on fundamentals, it would be possible in a generation to create a national Ideal in Ireland, or rather to let that spirit incarnate fully which began among the ancient peoples, which has haunted the hearts and whispered a dim revelation of itself through the lips of the bards and peasant story tellers.

Every Irishman forms some vague ideal of his country, born from his reading of history, or from contemporary politics, or from imaginative intuition; and this Ireland in the mind it is, not the actual Ireland, which kindles his enthusiasm. For this he works and makes sacrifices; but because it has never had any philosophical definition or a supremely beautiful statement in literature which gathered all aspirations about it, the ideal remains vague. This passionate love cannot explain itself; it cannot make another understand its devotion. To reveal Ireland in clear and beautiful light, to create the Ireland in the heart, is the province of a national literature. Other arts would add to this ideal hereafter, and social life and politics must in the end be in harmony. We are yet before our dawn, in a period comparable to Egypt before the first of her solemn temples constrained its people to an equal mystery, or to Greece before the first perfect statue had fixed an ideal of beauty which mothers dreamed of to mould their yet unborn children. We can see, however, as the ideal of Ireland grows from mind to mind, it tends to assume the character of a sacred land. The Dark Rosaleen of Mangan expresses an almost religious adoration, and to a later writer it seems to be nigher to the spiritual beauty than other lands:

And still the thoughts of Ireland brood
Upon her holy quietude.

The faculty of abstracting from the land their eyes beheld another Ireland through which they wandered in dream, has always been a characteristic of the Celtic poets. This inner Ireland which the visionary eye saw was the Tirnanoge, the Country of Immortal Youth, for they peopled it only with the young and beautiful. It was the Land of the Living Heart, a tender name which showed that it had become dearer than the heart of woman, and overtopped all other dreams as the last hope of the spirit, the bosom where it would rest after it had passed from the fading shelter of the world. And sure a strange and beautiful land this Ireland is, with a mystic beauty which closes the eyes of the body as in sleep, and opens the eyes of the spirit as in dreams and never a poet has lain on our hillsides but gentle, stately figures, with hearts shining like the sun, move through his dreams, over radiant grasses, in an enchanted world of their own: and it has become alive through every haunted rath and wood and mountain and lake, so that we can hardly think of it otherwise than as the shadow of the thought of God. The last Irish poet who has appeared shows the spiritual qualities of the first, when he writes of the gray rivers in their "enraptured" wanderings, and when he sees in the jeweled bow which arches the heavens--

The Lord's seven spirits that shine through the rain

This mystical view of nature, peculiar to but one English poet, Wordsworth is a national characteristic; and much in the creation of the Ireland in the mind is already done, and only needs retelling by the new writers. More important, however, for the literature we are imagining as an offset to the cosmopolitan ideal would be the creation of heroic figures, types, whether legendary or taken from history, and enlarged to epic proportions by our writers, who would use them in common, as Cuculain, Fionn, Ossian, and Oscar were used by the generations of poets who have left us the bardic history of Ireland, wherein one would write of the battle fury of a hero, and another of a moment when his fire would turn to gentleness, and another of his love for some beauty of his time, and yet another tell how the rivalry of a spiritual beauty made him tire of love; and so from iteration and persistent dwelling on a few heroes, their imaginative images found echoes in life, and other heroes arose, continuing their tradition of chivalry.

That such types are of the highest importance, and have the most ennobling influence on a country, cannot be denied. It was this idea led Whitman to exploit himself as the typical American. He felt that what he termed a "stock personality" was needed to elevate and harmonize the incongruous human elements in the States. English literature has always been more sympathetic with actual beings than with ideal types, and cannot help us much. A man who loves Dickens, for example, may grow to have a great tolerance for the grotesque characters which are the outcome of the social order in England, but he will not be assisted in the conception of a higher humanity: and this is true of very many English writers who lack a fundamental philosophy, and are content to take man as he seems to be for the moment, rather than as the pilgrim of eternity-- as one who is flesh today but who may hereafter grow divine, and who may shine at last like the stars of the morning, triumphant among the sons of God.

Mr. Standish O'Grady, in his notable epic of Cuculain, was in our time the first to treat the Celtic tradition worthily. He has contributed one hero who awaits equal comrades, if indeed the tales of the Red Branch do not absorb the thoughts of many imaginative writers, and Cuculain remain the typical hero of the Gael, becoming to every boy who reads the story a revelation of what his own spirit is.

I know John Eglinton, one of our most thoughtful writers, our first cosmopolitan, thinks that "these ancient legends refuse to be taken out of their old environment." But I believe that the tales which have been preserved for a hundred generations in the heart of the people must have had their power, because they had in them a core of eternal truth. Truth is not a thing of today or tomorrow. Beauty, heroism, and spirituality do not change like fashion, being the reflection of an unchanging spirit. The face of faces which looks at us through so many shifting shadows has never altered the form of its perfection since the face of man, made after its image, first looked back on its original:

For these red lips, with all their mournful pride,
Troy passed away in one high funeral gleam,
And Usna's children died.

These dreams, antiquities, traditions, once actual, living, and historical, have passed from the world of sense into the world of memory and thought: and time, it seems to me, has not taken away from their power, nor made them more remote from sympathy, but has rather purified them by removing them from earth to heaven: from things which the eye can see and the ear can hear they have become what the heart ponders over, and are so much nearer, more familiar, more suitable for literary use than the day they were begotten. They have now the character of symbol, and, as symbol, are more potent than history. They have crept through veil after veil of the manifold nature of man; and now each dream, heroism, or beauty has laid itself nigh the divine power it represents, the suggestion of which made it first beloved: and they are ready for the use of the spirit, a speech of which every word has a significance beyond itself, and Deirdre is, like Helen, a symbol of eternal beauty; and Cuculain represents as much as Prometheus the heroic spirit, the redeemer in man.

In so far as these ancient traditions live in the memory of man, they are contemporary to us as much as electrical science: for the images which time brings now to our senses, before they can be used in literature, have to enter into exactly the same world of human imagination as the Celtic traditions live in. And their fitness for literary use is not there determined by their freshness but by their power of suggestion. Modern literature, where it is really literature and not book-making, grows more subjective year after year, and the mind has a wider range over time than the physical nature has. Many things live in it--empires which have never crumbled, beauty which has never perished, love whose fires have never waned: and, in this formidable competition for use in the artist's mind, today stands only its chance with a thousand days. To question the historical accuracy of the use of such memories is not a matter which can be rightly raised. The question is--do they express lofty things to the soul? If they do they have justified themselves.

I have written at some length on the two paths which lie before us, for we have arrived at a parting of ways. One path leads, and has already led many Irishmen, to obliterate all nationality from their work. The other path winds upward to a mountain-top of our own, which may be in the future the Mecca to which many worshippers will turn. To remain where we are as a people, indifferent to literature, to art, to ideas, wasting the precious gift of public spirit we possess so abundantly in the sordid political rivalries, without practical or ideal ends, is to justify those who have chosen the other path, and followed another star than ours. I do not wish any one to infer from this a contempt for those who, for the last hundred years, have guided public opinion in Ireland. If they failed in one respect, it was out of a passionate sympathy for wrongs of which many are memories, thanks to them, and to them is due the creation of a force which may be turned in other directions, not without a memory of those pale sleepers to whom we may turn in thought, placing--

A kiss of fire on the dim brow of failure,
A crown upon her uncrowned head.

1899

STANDISH O'GRADY

In this age we read so much that we lay too great a burden on the imagination. It is unable to create images which are the spiritual equivalent of the words on the printed page, and reading becomes for too many an occupation of the eye rather than of the mind. How rarely, out of the multitude of volumes a man reads in his lifetime, can he remember where or when he read any particular book, or with any vividness recall the mood it evoked in him. When I close my eyes, and brood in memory over the books which most profoundly affected me, I find none excited my imagination more than Standish O'Grady's epical narrative of Cuculain. Whitman said of his Leaves of Grass: "Camerado, this is no book. Who touches this touches a man," and O'Grady might have boasted of his Bardic History of Ireland, written with his whole being, that there was more than a man in it, there was the soul of a people, its noblest and most exalted life symbolized in the story of one heroic character.

With reference to Ireland, I was at the time I read like many others who were bereaved of the history of their race. I was as a man who, through some accident, had lost memory of his past, Who could recall no more than a few months of new life, and could not say to what songs his cradle had been rocked, what mother had nursed him, who were the playmates of childhood, or by what woods and streams he had wandered. When I read O'Grady I was as such a man who suddenly feels ancient memories rushing at him, and knows he was born in a royal house, that he had mixed with the mighty of heaven and earth and had the very noblest for his companions. It was the memory of race which rose up within me as I read, and I felt exalted as one who learns he is among the children of kings. That is what O'Grady did for me and for others who were my contemporaries, and I welcome the reprints, of his tales in the hope that he will go on magically recreating for generations yet unborn the ancestral life of their race in Ireland. For many centuries the youth of Ireland as it grew up was made aware of the life of bygone ages, and there were always some who remade themselves in the heroic mould before they passed on. The sentiment engendered by the Gaelic literature was an arcane presence, though unconscious of itself, in those who for the past hundred years had learned another speech. In O'Grady's writings the submerged river of national culture rose up again, a shining torrent, and I realized as I bathed in that stream, that the greatest spiritual evil one nation could inflict on another was to cut off from it the story of the national soul. For not all music can be played upon any instrument, and human nature for most of us is like a harp on which can be rendered the music written for the harp but nor that written for the violin. The harp strings quiver for the harp-player alone, and he who can utter his passion through the violin is silent before an unfamiliar instrument. That is why the Irish have rarely been deeply stirred by English literature, though it is one of the great literatures of the world. Our history was different and the evolutionary product was a peculiarity of character, and the strings of our being vibrate most in ecstasy when the music evokes ancestral moods or embodies emotions akin to these. I am not going to argue the comparative worth of the Gaelic and English tradition. All that I can say is that the traditions of our own country move us more than the traditions of any other. Even if there was not essential greatness in them we would love them for the same reasons which bring back so many exiles to revisit the haunts of childhood. But there was essential greatness in that neglected bardic literature which O'Grady was the first to reveal in a noble manner. He had the spirit of an ancient epic poet. He is a comrade of Homer, his birth delayed in time perhaps that he might renew for a sophisticated people the elemental simplicity and hardihood men had when the world was young and manhood was prized more than any of its parts, more than thought or beauty or feeling. He has created for us, or rediscovered, one figure which looms in the imagination as a high comrade of Hector, Achilles, Ulysses, Rama or Yudisthira, as great in spirit as any. Who could extol enough his Cuculain, that incarnation of Gaelic chivalry, the fire and gentleness, the beauty and heroic ardour or the imaginative splendor of the episodes in his retelling of the ancient story. There are writers who bewitch you by a magical use of words whose lines glitter like jewels, whose effects are gained by an elaborate art and who deal with the subtlest emotions. Others again are simple as an Egyptian image, and yet are more impressive, and you remember them less for the sentence than for a grandiose effect. They are not so much concerned with the art of words as with the creation of great images informed with magnificence of spirit. They are not lesser artists but greater, for there is a greater art in the simplification of form in the statue of Memnon than there is in the intricate detail of a bronze by Benvenuto Cellini. Standish O'Grady had in his best moments that epic wholeness and simplicity, and the figure of Cuculain amid his companions of the Red Branch which he discovered and refashioned for us is, I think, the greatest spiritual gift any Irishman for centuries has given to Ireland.

I know it will be said that this is a scientific age, the world is so full of necessitous life that it is waste of time for young Ireland to brood upon tales of legendary heroes, who fought with enchanters, who harnessed wild fairy horses to magic chariots and who talked with the ancient gods, and that it would be much better for youth to be scientific and practical. Do not believe it, dear Irish boy, dear Irish girl, I know as well as any the economic needs of our people. They must not be overlooked, but keep still in your hearts some desires which might enter Paradise. Keep in your souls some images of magnificence so that hereafter the halls of heaven and the divine folk may not seem altogether alien to the spirit. These legends have passed the test of generations for century after century, and they were treasured and passed on to those who followed, and that was because there was something in them akin to the immortal spirit. Humanity cannot carry with it through time the memory of all its deeds and imaginations, and it burdens itself only in a new era with what was highest among the imaginations of the ancestors. What is essentially noble is never out of date. The figures carved by Pheidias for the Parthenon still shine by the side of the greatest modern sculpture. There has been no evolution of the human form to a greater beauty than the ancient Greek saw, and the forms they carved are not strange to us, and if this is true of the outward form it is true of the indwelling spirit. What is essentially noble is contemporary with all that is splendid today, and until the mass of men are equal in spirit the great figures of the past will affect us less as memories than as prophecies of the Golden Age to which youth is ever hurrying in its heart.

O'Grady in his stories of the Red Branch rescued from the past what was contemporary to the best in us today, and he was equal in his gifts as a writer to the greatest of his bardic predecessors in Ireland. His sentences are charged with a heroic energy, and, when he is telling a great tale, their rise and fall is like the flashing and falling of the bright sword of some great battle, or like the onset and withdrawal of Atlantic surges. He can at need be beautifully tender and quiet. Who that has read his tale of the young Finn and the Seven Ancients will forget the weeping of Finn over the kindness of the famine-stricken old men, and their wonder at his weeping, and the self-forgetful pathos of their meditation unconscious that it was their own sacrifice called forth the tears of Finn. "Youth," they said, "has many sorrows that cold age cannot comprehend."

There are critics repelled by the abounding energy in O'Grady's sentences. It is easy to point to faults due to excess and abundance, but how rare in literature is that heroic energy and power. There is something arcane and elemental in it, a quality that the most careful stylist cannot attain, however he uses the file, however subtle he is. O'Grady has noticed this power in the ancient bards and we find it in his own writing. It ran all through the Bardic History, the Critical and Philosophical History, and through the political books, The Tory Democracy and All Ireland. There is this imaginative energy in the tale of Cuculain, in all its episodes, the slaying of the hound, the capture of the Liath Macha, the hunting of the enchanted deer, the capture of the Wild swans, the fight at the ford, and the awakening of the Red Branch. In the later tale of Red Hugh which, he calls The Flight of the Eagle there is the same quality of power joined with a shining simplicity in the narrative which rises into a poetic ecstasy in that wonderful chapter where Red Hugh, escaping from the Pale, rides through the Mountain Gates of Ulster and sees high above him Sheve Gullion, a mountain of the Gods, the birth-place of legend "more mythic than Avernus"; and O'Grady evokes for us and his hero the legendary past and the great hill seems to be like Mount Sinai, thronged with immortals, and it lives and speaks to the fugitive boy, "the last great secular champion of the Gael," and inspires him for the fulfillment of his destiny. We might say of Red Hugh, and indeed of all O'Grady's heroes, that they are the spiritual progeny of Cuculain. From Red Hugh down to the boys who have such enchanting adventures in Lost on Du Corrig and The Chain of Gold they have all a natural and hardy purity of mind, a beautiful simplicity of character, and one can imagine them all in an hour of need, being faithful to any trust like the darling of the Red Branch. These shining lads never grew up amid books. They are as much children of nature as the Lucy of Wordsworth's poetry. It might be said of them as the poet of the Kalevala sang of himself: "Winds and waters my instructors."

These were O'Grady's own earliest companions, and no man can find better comrades than earth, water, air and sun. I imagine O'Grady's own youth was not so very different from the youth of Red Hugh before his captivity; that he lived on the wild and rocky western coast, that he rowed in coracles, explored the caves, spoke much with hardy natural people, fishermen and workers on the land, primitive folk, simple in speech but with that fundamental depth men have who are much in nature in companionship with the elements, the elder brothers of humanity. It must have been out of such a boyhood and such intimacies with natural and unsophisticated people that there came to him the understanding of the heroes of the Red Branch. How pallid, beside the ruddy chivalry who pass, huge and fleet and bright, through O'Grady's pages, appear Tennyson's bloodless Knights of the Round Table, fabricated in the study to be read in the drawing room, as anemic as Burne Jones' lifeless men in armour. The heroes of ancient Irish legend reincarnated in the mind of a man who could breathe into them the fire of life, caught from sun and wind, their ancient deities, and send them forth to the world to do greater deeds, to act through many men and speak through many voices. What sorcery was in the Irish mind that it has taken so many years to win but a little recognition for this splendid spirit; and that others who came after him, who diluted the pure fiery wine of romance he gave us with literary water, should be as well known or more widely read. For my own, part I can only point back to him and say whatever is Irish in me he kindled to life, and I am humble when I read his epic tale, feeling how much greater a thing it is for the soul of a writer to have been the habitation of a demi-god than to have had the subtlest intellections.

We praise the man who rushes into a burning mansion and brings out its greatest treasure. So ought we to praise this man who rescued from the perishing Gaelic tradition its darling hero and restored him to us, and I think now that Cuculain will not perish, and he will be invisibly present at many a council of youth, and he will be the daring which lifts the will beyond itself and fires it for great causes, and he will be also the courtesy which shall overcome the enemy that nothing else may overcome.

I am sure that Standish O'Grady would rather I should speak of his work and its bearing on the spiritual life of Ireland, than about himself, and, because I think so, in this reverie I have followed no set plan but have let my thoughts run as they will. But I would not have any to think that this man was only a writer, or that he could have had the heroes of the past for spiritual companions, without himself being inspired to fight dragons and wizardry. I have sometimes regretted that contemporary politics drew O'Grady away from the work he began so greatly. I have said to myself he might have given us an Oscar, a Diarmuid or a Caolte, an equal comrade to Cuculain, but he could not, being lit up by the spirit of his hero, he merely the bard and not the fighter, and no man in Ireland intervened in the affairs of his country with a superior nobility of aim. He was the last champion of the Irish aristocracy, and still more the voice of conscience for them, and he spoke to them of their duty to the nation as one might imagine some fearless prophet speaking to a council of degenerate princes. When the aristocracy failed Ireland he bade them farewell, and wrote the epitaph of their class in words whose scorn we almost forget because of their sounding melody and beauty. He turned his mind to the problems of democracy and more especially of those workers who are trapped in the city, and he pointed out for them the way of escape and how they might renew life in the green fields close to Earth, their ancient mother and nurse. He used too exalted a language for those to whom he spoke to understand, and it might seem that all these vehement appeals had failed but that we know that what is fine never really fails. When a man is in advance of his age, a generation, unborn when he speaks, is born in due time and finds in him its inspiration. O'Grady may have failed in his appeal to the aristocracy of his own time but he may yet create an aristocracy of character and intellect in Ireland. The political and economic writings will remain to uplift and inspire and to remind us that the man who wrote the stories of heroes had a bravery of his own and a wisdom of his own. I owe so much to Standish O'Grady that I would like to leave it on record that it was he made me conscious and proud of my country, and recalled to my mind, that might have wandered otherwise over too wide and vague a field of thought, to think of the earth under my feet and the children of our common mother. There hangs in the Municipal Gallery of Dublin the portrait of a man with melancholy eyes, and scrawled on the canvas is the subject of his bitter brooding: "'The Lost Land." I hope that O'Grady will find before he goes back to Tir na noge that Ireland has found again through him what seemed lost for ever, the law of its own being, and its memories which go back to the beginning of the world.

THE DRAMATIC TREATMENT OF LEGEND

The Red Branch ought not to be staged. . . . That literature ought not to be produced for popular consumption for the edification of the crowd. . . . I say to you drop this thing at your, peril. . . . You may succeed in degrading Irish ideals, and banishing the soul of the land. . . . Leave the heroic cycles alone, and don't bring them down to the crowd..." (Standish O'Grady in All Ireland Review).

Years ago, in the adventurous youth of his mind, Mr. O'Grady found the Gaelic tradition like a neglected antique dun with the doors barred, and there was little or no egress. Listening, he heard from within the hum of an immense chivalry, and he opened the doors and the wild riders went forth to work their will. Now he would recall them. But it is in vain. The wild riders have gone forth, and their labors in the human mind are only beginning. They will do their deeds over again, and now they will act through many men and speak through many voices. The spirit of Cuculain will stand at many a lonely place in the heart, and he will win as of old against multitudes. The children of Turann will start afresh still eager to take up and renew their cyclic labors, and they will gain, not for themselves, the Apples of the Tree of Life, and the Spear of the Will, and the Fleece which is the immortal body. All the heroes and demigods returning will have a wider field than Erin for their deeds, and they will not grow weary warning upon things that die but will be fighters in the spirit against immortal powers, and, as before, the acts will be sometimes noble and sometimes base. They cannot be stayed from their deeds, for they are still in the strength of a youth which is ever renewing itself. Not for all the wrong which may be done should they be restrained. Mr. O'Grady would now have the tales kept from the crowd to be the poetic luxury of a few. Yet would we, for all the martyrs who perished in the fires of the Middle Ages, counsel the placing of the Gospels on the list of books to be read only by a few esoteric worshippers?

The literature which should be unpublished is that which holds the secret of the magical powers. The legends of Ireland are not of this kind. They have no special message to the aristocrat more than to the man of the people. The men who made the literature of Ireland were by no means nobly born, and it was the bards who placed the heroes, each in his rank, and crowned them for after ages, and gave them their famous names. They have placed on the brow of others a crown which belonged to themselves, and all the heroic literature of the world was made by the sacrifice of the nameless kings of men who have given a sceptre to others they never wielded while living, and who bestowed the powers, of beauty and pity on women who perhaps had never uplifted a heart in their day, and who now sway us from the grave with a grace only imagined in the dreaming soul of the poet. Mr. O'Grady has been the bardic champion of the ancient Irish aristocracy. He has thrown on them the sunrise colors of his own brilliant spirit, and now would restrain others from the use of their names lest a new kingship should be established over them, and another law than that of his own will, lest the poets of the democracy looking back on the heroes of the past should overcome them with the ideas of a later day, and the Atticottic nature find a loftier spirit in those who felt the unendurable pride of the Fianna and rose against it. Well, it is only natural he should try to protect the children of his thought, but they need no later word from him. If writers of a less noble mind than his deal with these things they will not rob his heroes of a single power to uplift or inspire. In Greece, after Eschylus and his stupendous deities, came Sophocles, who restrained them with a calm wisdom, and Euripides, who made them human, but still the mysterious Orphic deities remain and stir us when reading the earlier page. Mr. O'Grady would not have the Red Branch cycle cast in dramatic form or given to the people. They are too great to be staged; and he quotes, mistaking the gigantic for the heroic, a story of Cuculain reeling round Ireland on his fairy steed the Liath Macha. This may be phantasy or extravagance, but it is not heroism. Cuculain is often heroic, but it is a quality of the soul and not of the body; it is shown by his tears over Ferdiad, in his gentleness to women. A more grandiose and heroic figure than Cuculain was seen on the Athenian stage; and no one will say that the Titan Prometheus, chained on the rock in his age-long suffering for men, is not a nobler figure than Cuculain in any aspect in which he appears to us in the tales. Divine traditions, the like of which were listened to with awe by the Athenians, should not be too lofty for our Christian people, whose morals Mr. O'Grady, here hardly candid, professes to be anxious about. What is great in literature is a greatness springing out of the human heart. Though we fall short today of the bodily stature of the giants of the prime, the spirit still remains and can express an equal greatness. I can well understand how a man of our own day, by the enlargement of his spirit, and the passion and sincerity of his speech, could express the greatness of the past. The drama in its mystical beginning was the vehicle through which divine ideas, which are beyond the sphere even of heroic life and passion, were expressed; and if the later Irish writers fail of such greatness, it is not for that reason that the soul of Ireland will depart. I can hardly believe Mr. O'Grady to be serious when he fears that many forbidden subjects will be themes for dramatic art, that Maeve with her many husbands will walk the stage, and the lusts of an earlier age be revived to please the lusts of today. The danger of art is not in its subjects, but in the attitude of the artist's mind. The nobler influences of art arise, not because heroes are the theme, but because of noble treatment and the intuition which perceives the inflexible working out of great moral laws.

The abysses of human nature may well be sounded if the plummet be dropped by a spirit from the heights. The lust which leads on to death may be a terrible thing to contemplate, but in the event there is consolation; and the eye of faith can see even in the very exultation of corruption how God the Regenerator is working His will, leading man onward to his destiny of inevitable beauty. Mr. O'Grady in his youth had the epic imagination, and I think few people realize how great and heroic that inspiration was; but the net that is spread for Leviathan will not capture all the creatures of the deep, and neither epic nor romance will manifest fully the power of the mythical ancestors of the modern Gael who now seek incarnation anew in the minds of their children. Men too often forget, in this age of printed books, that literature is, after all, only an ineffectual record of speech. The literary man has gone into strange byways through long contemplation of books, and he writes with elaboration what could never be spoken, and he loses that power of the bards on whom tongues of fire had descended, who were masters of the magic of utterance, whose thoughts were not meant to be silently absorbed from the lifeless page. For there never can be, while man lives in a body, a greater means of expression for him than the voice of man affords, and no instrument of music will ever rival in power the flowing of the music of the spheres through his lips. In all its tones, from the chanting of the magi which compelled the elements, to those gentle voices which guide the dying into peace, there is a power which will never be stricken from tympan or harp, for in all speech there is life, and with the greatest speech the deep tones of another Voice may mingle. Has not the Lord spoken through His prophets? And man, when he has returned to himself, and to the knowledge of himself, may find a greater power in his voice than those which he has painfully harnessed to perform his will, in steamship or railway. It is through drama alone that the writer can summon, even if vicariously, so great a power to his aid; and it is possible we yet may hear on the stage, not merely the mimicry of human speech, but the old forgotten music which was heard in the duns of great warriors to bow low their faces in their hands. Dear O'Grady, if we do not succeed it is not for you to blame us, for our aims are at least as high as your own.

1902

THE CHARACTER OF HEROIC LITERATURE

Lady Gregory, a fairy godmother, has given to Young Ireland the gift of her Cuchulain of Muirthemne, which should be henceforward the book of its dream. I do not doubt but there will be a great change in the next generation, for the character of many children will have grown to maturity brooding over the memories of heroes who were themselves half children, half demigods. Though the hero tales will have their greatest power over the young, no one mind could measure their depth. They seem simple and primitive, yet they draw us strangely aside from life, and the emotions they awaken are not simple but complex. Here are twenty tales, and they are so alike in imaginative character that they seem all to have poured from one mind; and to these twenty we could add a hundred others, all endlessly fertile in difference of incident, but all seeming to own the same imaginative creator. It was so for many centuries, and then the maker of the song seems to have grown weary, and distinct voices not overladen with the tradition of the ages were heard; and today every one wanders in a path of his own, finding or losing the way, the truth, and the life of art in the free play of his desires. There was something more to cause this later period of diverse utterance than the interruption of other races and the claims of the world upon us. Surely the ancient Egyptian met in Memphis or Thebes as many strangers as we did, but he wept on through many dynasties carving the same face of mystery and rarely altering the peculiar forms which were his inheritance from the craftsmen of a thousand years before. It was not the introduction of something new, but the loss of something which finally vexed the calm of the Sphinx and marred the Phidian beauty which in Greece was a long dream for many generations. It was not because the Dane or Norman came and dwelt among us that the signature of the Sidhe was withdrawn from the Gaelic mind. I do not know how to express this loss otherwise than by saying we appear to have fallen away from our archetype. We find in all the early stories the presence of one being who may be the genius of our land if that old idea of race divinities be a true one. A strange similitude unites all the characters. We infer an interior identity. The same spirit flashes out in hostile clans, and then Cuculain kisses Ferdiad. They all confidently appeal to; it in each other. Maeve flying after the great battle can ask a gift from her conqueror and obtains it. Fand and Emer dispute who shall make the last sacrifice of love and give the beloved to a rival. The conflicts seem half in play or in dream, and we do not know when an awakening of love will disarm the foes. In spite of the bloodshed the heroes seem like children who fight steadily through a mock battle, but the night will see these children at peace, and they will dream with arms around each other in the same cot. No literature ever had a more beautiful heart of childhood in it. The bards could hate no one consistently. If they took away the heroic chivalry from Conchobar in one tale they restored it to him in another. They have the confident trust--and expectation of goodness that children have, who may have suffered punishment, but who come later on and smile on the chastiser. It is this quality which gives the tales their extraordinary charm. I know no other literature which has it to the same degree. I do not like to speculate on the absence of this spirit in our later literature, which was written under other influences. It cannot be because there was a less spiritual life in the apostles than in the bards. We cannot compare Cuculain, the most complete ideal of Gaelic chivalry, with that supreme figure whose coming to the world was the effacement of whole pantheons of divinities, and yet it is true that since the thoughts of men were turned from the old ideals our literature has been filled with a less noble life. I think a due may be found in the withdrawal of thought from nature, the great mother who, is the giver of all life, and without whose life ideals become inoperative and listless dwellers in the heart. The eyes of the ancient Gael were fixed in wonder on the rocks and hills, and the waste places of the earth were piled with phantasmal palaces where the Sidhe sat on their thrones. Everywhere there was life, and as they saw so they felt. To conceive of nature in any way, as beautiful and living, as friendly or hostile, is to receive from her in like measure out of her fullness. With whatever face we approach the mirror a similar face approaches ours. "Let him approach it, saying, 'This is the Mighty,' he becomes mighty," says an ancient scripture, teaching us that as our aspiration is so will be our inspiration and power. Out of this comradeship with earth there came a commingling of natures, and we do not know when we read who are the Sidhe and who are human. The great energies are all in the heroes. They bound to themselves, like the Talkend, the strength of the fire, the brightness of the sun, and the swiftness of the wind. They seem truly the earth-born. The waves respond to their deeds; the elemental creatures respond and there are clashing echoes and allies innumerable, and armies in the air continuing their battles illimitably beyond: a proud race, who felt with bursting heart the heavens were watching them, who defied their gods and exiled them to have free play for their own deeds. A very different humanity indeed from those who have come to walk the earth with humility, who are afraid of heaven and its rulers, and whose dread is the greatest of all sins, for in it is a denial of their own divinity. Surely the sight heroes is more welcome to the King, in whose heaven are sworded seraphim, than the bowed knees and the spirits who make themselves as worms in His sight. In the symbolic expression of our spiritual life the eagle has become a dove brooding peace. Oh, that it might rebecome the eagle and take to the upper airs!

A generosity and greatness of spirit are in the heroes of the Red Branch, and out of their strength grows a bloom of beauty never fully revealed until Lady Gregory compiled these tales. As we read our eyes are dazzled by strange graces of color flowing over the pages: everywhere there is mystery and magnificence. Procession's pass by in Druid ritual, kings and queens, and harpers who look like kings. When the wind passes over them and stirs their garments a sweetness comes over the teller of the tale, who felt that delight in draperies blown over shapely forms which is the inspiration of the Winged Victory and many Greek marbles. The bards will not have the hands of those proud people touch anything which is not beautiful. "It was a beautiful chessboard they had, all of white bronze, and the chessmen of gold and silver, and a candlestick of precious stones lighting it." The wasting of time has spared us a few things to show that this rare and intricate metal work was not a myth, and we are forced by an inexorable logic to accept as mainly true the narration of the pride, the beauty, the generosity, and the large lovable character of the ancient heroes. We may come to realize that, losing their Druid vision of a more shining world mingling with this, we have lost the vision of that life into the likeness of which it is the true labor of the spirit to transform this life. For the

Tirnanoge is that Garden where, in the mind of the Lord, the flowers and trees blossomed before they grew in the fields, where man lived in the Golden Age before the outer darkness of the earth was built and he was outcast from Paradise. There is no true art or literature which has not some image of the Golden Life lurking within it, and through the archaic rudeness of these legends the light shines as sunlight through the hoary branches of ancient oaks. Lady Gregory has done her work, as compiler with a judgment which could hardly be too much praised, and she has translated the stories into an idiom which is a reflection of the original Gaelic and is full of charm. We are indebted to her for this labor as much as to any of those who sang to sweeten Ireland's wrong.

1902

A POET OF SHADOWS

When I was asked to write "anything" about Yeats, our Irish poet, my thoughts were like rambling flocks that have no shepherd, and without guidance my rambling thoughts have run anywhere.

I confess I have feared to enter or linger too long in the many- colored land of Druid twilights and tunes. A beauty not our own, more perfect than we can ourselves conceive, is a danger to the imagination. I am too often tempted to wander with Usheen in Timanoge and to forget my own heart and its more rarely accorded vision of truth. I know I like my own heart best, but I never look into the world of my friend without feeling that my region lies in the temperate zone and is near the Arctic circle; the flowers grow more rarely and are paler, and the struggle for existence is keener. Southward and in the warm west are the Happy Isles among the Shadowy Waters. The pearly phantoms are dancing there with blown hair amid cloud tail daffodils. They have known nothing but beauty, or at the most a beautiful unhappiness. Everything there moves in procession or according to ritual, and the agony of grief, it is felt, must be concealed. There are no faces blurred with tears there; some traditional gesture signifying sorrow is all that is allowed. I have looked with longing eyes into this world. It is Ildathach, the Many-Colored Land, but not the Land of the Living Heart. That island where the multitudinous beatings of many hearts became one is yet unvisited; but the isle of our poet is the more beautiful of all the isles the mystic voyagers have found during the thousands of years literature has recorded in Ireland. What wonder that many wish to follow him, and already other voices are singing amid its twilights.

They will make and unmake. They will discover new wonders; and will perhaps make commonplace some beauty which but for repetition would have seemed rare. I would that no one but the first discoverer should enter Ildathach, or at least report of it. No voyage to the new world, however memorable, will hold us like the voyage of Columbus. I sigh sometimes thinking on the light dominion dreams have over the heart. We cannot hold a dream for long, and that early joy of the poet in his new-found world has passed. It has seemed to him too luxuriant. He seeks for something more, and has tried to make its tropical tangle orthodox; and the glimmering waters and winds are no longer beautiful natural presences, but have become symbolic voices and preach obscurely some doctrine of their power to quench the light in the soul or to fan it to a brighter flame.

I like their old voiceless motion and their natural wandering best, and would rather roam in the bee-loud glade than under the boughs of beryl and chrysoberyl, where I am put to school to learn the significance of every jewel. I like that natural infinity which a prodigal beauty suggests more than that revealed in esoteric hieroglyphs, even though the writing be in precious stones. Sometimes I wonder whether that insatiable desire of the mind for something more than it has yet attained, which blows the perfume from every flower, and plucks the flower from every tree, and hews down every tree in the valley until it goes forth gnawing itself in a last hunger, does not threaten all the cloudy turrets of the Poet's soul. But whatever end or transformation, or unveiling may happen, that which creates beauty must have beauty in its essence, and the soul must cast off many vestures before it comes to itself. We, all of us, poets, artists, and musicians, who work in shadows, must sometime begin to work in substance, and why should we grieve if one labor ends and another begins? I am interested more in life than in the shadows of life, and as Ildathach grows fainter I await eagerly the revelation of the real nature of one who has built so many mansions in the heavens. The poet has concealed himself under the embroidered cloths and has moved in secretness, and only at rare times, as when he says, "A pity beyond all telling is hid in the heart of love," do we find a love which is not the love of the Sidhe; and more rarely still do recognizable human figures, like the Old Pensioner or Moll Magee, meet us. All the rest are from another world and are survivals of the proud and golden races who move with the old stateliness and an added sorrow for the dark age which breaks in upon their loveliness. They do not war upon the new age, but build up about themselves in imagination the ancient beauty, and love with a love a little colored by the passion of the darkness from which they could not escape. They are the sole inheritors of many traditions, and have now come to the end of the ways, and so are unhappy. We know why they are unhappy, but not the cause of a strange merriment which sometimes they feel, unless it be that beauty within itself has a joy in its own rhythmic being. They are changing, too, as the winds and waters have changed. They are not like Usheen, seekers and romantic wanderers, but have each found some mood in themselves where all quest ceases; they utter oracles, and even in the swaying of a hand or the dropping of hair there is less suggestion of individual action than of a divinity living within them, shaping an elaborate beauty in dream for his own delight, and for no other end than the delight in his dream. Other poets have written of Wisdom overshadowing man and speaking through his lips, or a Will working within the human will, but I think in this poetry we find for the first time the revelation of the Spirit as the weaver of beauty. Hence it comes that little hitherto unnoticed motions are adored:

> You need but lift a pearl-pale hand,
> And bind up your long hair and sigh;
> And all men's hearts must burn and beat.

This woman is less the beloved than the priestess of beauty who reveals the divinity, not as the inspired prophetesses filled with the Holy Breath did in the ancient mysteries, but in casual gestures and in a waving of her white arms, in the stillness of her eyes, in her hair which trembles like a faery flood of unloosed shadowy light over pale breasts, and in many glimmering motions so beautiful that it is at once seen whose footfall it is we hear, and that the place where she stands is holy ground. This, it seems to me, is what is essential in this poetry, what is peculiar and individual in it--the revelation of great mysteries in unnoticed things; and as not a sparrow may fall unconsidered by Him, so even in the swaying of a human hand His sceptre may have dominion over the heart and His paradise be entered in the lifting of an eyelid.

1902

THE BOYHOOD OF A POET

When I was a boy I knew another who has since become famous and who has now written Reveries over Childhood and Youth. I searched the pages to meet the boy I knew and could not find him. He has told us what he saw and what he remembered of others, but from himself he seems to have passed away and remembers himself not. The boy I knew was darkly beautiful to look on, fiery yet playful and full of lovely and elfin fancies. He was swift of response, indeed over-generous to the fancies of others because a nature so charged with beauty could not but emit beauty at every challenge. Even so water, however ugly the object we cast upon it, can but break out in a foam of beauty and a bewilderment of lovely curves.

Our fancies were in reality nothing to him but the affinities which by the slightest similitude evoked out of the infinitely richer being the prodigality of beautiful images with which it was endowed and made itself conscious of itself. I have often thought how strange it is that artist and poet have never yet revealed themselves to us except in verse and painting, that there was among them no psychologist who could turn back upon himself to search for the law of his own being, who could tell us how his brain first became illuminated with images, and who tried to track the inspiration to its secret fount and the images to their ancestral beauty. Few of the psychologists who have written about imagination were endowed with it themselves: and here is a poet, the most imaginative of his generation, who has written about his youth and has told us only about external circumstances and nothing about himself, nothing about that flowering of strange beauty in poetry in him where the Gaelic imagination that had sunk underground when the Gaelic speech had died, rose up again transfiguring an alien language until that new poetry became like the record of another mystic voyager to the Heaven-world of our ancestors. But poet and artist are rarely self- conscious of the processes of their own minds. They deliver their message with exultation but they find nothing worth recording in the descent upon them of the fiery tongues. So our poet has told us little about himself but much about circumstance, and I recall in his pages the Dublin of thirty years ago, and note how faithful the memory of eye and ear are, and how forgetful the heart is of its own fancies. Is nature behind this distaste for intimate self- analysis in the poet? Are our own emanations poisonous to us if we do not rapidly clear ourselves of them? Is it best to forget ourselves and hurry away once the deed is done or the end is attained to some remoter valley in the Golden World and look for a new beauty if we would continue to create beauty?

I know how readily our poet forgets his own songs. I once quoted to him some early verses of his own as comment on something he had said. He asked eagerly "Who wrote that?" and when I said "Do you not remember?" he petulantly waved the poem aside for he had forsaken his past. Again at a later period he told me his early verses sometimes aroused him to a frenzy of dislike. Of the feelings which beset the young poet of genius little or nothing is revealed in this Reverie. Yet what would we not give for a book which would tell how beauty beset that youth in his walks about Dublin and Sligo; how the sensitive response to color, form, music and tradition began, how he came to recognize the moods which incarnated in him as immortal moods. Perhaps it is too much to expect from the creative imagination that it shall also be capable of exact and subtle analysis. In this work I walk down the streets of Dublin I walked with Yeats over thirty years ago. I mix with the people who then were living in the city, O'Leary, Taylor, Dowden, Hughes and the rest; but the poet himself does not walk with me. It is a new voice speaking of the past of others, pointing out the doorways entered by dead youth. The new voice has distinction and dignity of its own, and we are grateful for this history, others more so than myself, because most of what is written therein I knew already, and I wanted a secret which is not revealed. I wanted to know more about the working of the imagination which planted the little snow-white feet in the sally garden, and which heard the kettle on the hob sing peace into the breast, and was intimate with twilight and the creatures that move in the dusk and undergrowths, with weasel, heron, rabbit, hare, mouse and coney; which plucked the Flower of Immortality in the Island of Statues and wandered with Usheen in Timanogue. I wanted to know what all that magic-making meant to the magician, but he has kept his own secret, and I must be content and grateful to one who has revealed more of beauty than any other in his time.

1916

THE POETRY OF JAMES STEPHENS

For a generation the Irish bards have endeavored to live in a palace of art, in chambers hung with the embroidered cloths and made dim with pale lights and Druid twilights, and the melodies they most sought for were half soundless. The art of an early age began softly, to end its songs with a rhetorical blare of sound. The melodies of the new school began close to the ear and died away in distances of the soul. Even as the prophet of old was warned to take off his shoes because the place he stood on was holy ground, so it seemed for a while in Ireland as if no poet could be accepted unless he left outside the demesnes of poetry that very useful animal, the body, and lost all concern about its habits. He could not enter unless he moved with the light and dreamy foot-fall of spirit. Mr. Yeats was the chief of this eclectic school, and his poetry at its best is the most beautiful in Irish literature. But there crowded after him a whole horde of verse-writers, who seized the most obvious symbols he used and standardized them, and in their writings one wandered about, gasping for fresh air land sunlight, for the Celtic soul seemed bound for ever pale lights of fairyland on the north and by the by the darkness of forbidden passion on the south, and on the east by the shadowiness of all things human, and on the west by everything that was infinite, without form, and void.

It was a great relief to me, personally, who had lived in the palace of Irish art for a time, and had even contributed a little to its dimness, to hear outside the walls a few years ago a sturdy voice blaspheming against all the formula, and violating the tenuous atmosphere with its "Insurrections." There are poets who cannot write with half their being, and who must write with their whole being, and they bring their poor relation, the body, with them wherever they go, and are not ashamed of it. They are not at warfare with the spirit, but have a kind of instinct that the clan of human powers ought to cling together as one family. With the best poets of this school, like Shakespeare and Whitman, one rarely can separate body and soul, for we feel the whole man is speaking. With Keats, Shelley, Swinburne, and our own Yeats, one feels that they have all sought shelter from disagreeable actualities in the world of imagination. James Stephens, as he chanted his Insurrections, sang with his whole being. Let no one say I am comparing him with Shakespeare. One may say the blackbird has wings as well as the eagle, without insisting that the bird in the hedgerows is peer of the winged creature beyond the mountain-tops. But how refreshing it was to find somebody who was a poet without a formula, who did not ransack dictionaries for dead words, as Rossetti did to get living speech, whose natural passions declared themselves without the least idea that they ought to be ashamed of themselves, or be thrice refined in the crucible by the careful alchemist before they could appear in the drawing-room. Nature has an art of its own, and the natural emotions in their natural and passionate expression have that kind of picturesque beauty which Marcus Aurelius, tired, perhaps, of the severe orthodoxies of Greek and Roman art, referred to when he spoke of the foam on the jaws of the wild boar and the mane of the lion.

There were evidences of such an art in Insurrections, the first book of James Stephens. In the poem called "Fossils," the girl who flies and the boy who hunts her are followed in flight and pursuit with a swift energy by the poet, and the lines pant and gasp, and the figures flare up and down the pages. The energy created a new form in verse, not an orthodox beauty, which the classic artists would have admitted, but such picturesque beauty as Marcus Aurelius found in the foam on the jaws of the wild boar.

I always want to find the fundamental emotion out of which a poet writes. It is easy to do this with some, with writers like Shelley and Wordsworth, for they talked much of abstract things, and a man never reveals himself so fully as when he does this, when he tries to interpret nature, when he has to fill darkness with light, and chaos with meaning. A man may speak about his own heart and may deceive himself and others, but ask him to fill empty space with significance, and what he projects on that screen will be himself, and you can know him even as hereafter he will be known. When a poet puts his ear to a shell, I know if he listens long enough he will hear his own destiny. I knew after reading "The Shell" that in James Stephens we were going to have no singer of the abstract. There was no human quality or stir in the blind elemental murmur, and the poet drops it with a sigh of relief:

O, it was sweet
To hear a cart go jolting down the street.

From the tradition of the world too he breaks away, from the great murmuring shell which gives back to us our cries and questionings and protests soothed into soft, easeful things and smooth orthodox complacencies, for it was shaped by humanity to whisper back to it what it wished to hear. From all soft, easeful beliefs and silken complacencies the last Irish poet breaks away in a book of insurrections. He is doubtful even of love, the greatest orthodoxy of any, which so few have questioned, which has preceded all religions and will survive them all. When he writes of love in "The Red-haired Man's Wife" and "The Rebel" he is not sure that that old intoxication of self-surrender is not a wrong to the soul and a disloyalty to the highest in us. His "Dancer" revolts from the applauding crowd. The wind cries out against the inference that the beauty of nature points inevitably to an equal beauty of spirit within. His enemies revolt against their hate; his old man against his own grumblings, and the poet himself rebels against his own revolt in that quaint scrap of verse he prefixes to the volume:

What's the use
Of my abuse?
The world will run
Around the sun
As it has done
Since time begun
When I have drifted to the deuce:
And what's the use
Of my abuse?

He does not revolt against the abstract like so many because he is incapable of thinking. Indeed, he is one of the few Irish poets we have who is always thinking as he goes along. He does not rebel against love because he is not himself sweet at heart, for the best thing in the book is its unfeigned humanity. So we have a personal puzzle to solve with this perplexing writer which makes us all the more eager to hear him again. A man might be difficult to understand and the problem of his personality might not be worth solution, but it is not so with James Stephens. From a man who can write with such power as he shows in these two stanzas taken from "The Street behind Yours" we may expect high things. It is a vision seen with distended imagination as if by some child strayed from light:

> And though 'tis silent, though no sound
> Crawls from the darkness thickly spread,
> Yet darkness brings
> Grim noiseless things
> That walk as they were dead,
> They glide and peer and steal around
> With stealthy silent tread.
>
> You dare not walk; that awful crew
> Might speak or laugh as you pass by.
> Might touch or paw
> With a formless claw
> Or leer from a sodden eye,
> Might whisper awful things they knew,
> Or wring their hands and cry.

There is nothing more grim and powerful than that in The City of Dreadful Night. It has all the vaporous horror of a Dore grotesque and will bear examination better. But our poet does not as a rule write with such unrelieved gloom. He keeps a stoical cheerfulness, and even when he faces terrible things we feel encouraged to take his hand and go with him, for he is master of his own soul, and you cannot get a whimper out of him. He likes the storm of things, and is out for it. He has a perfect craft in recording wild natural emotions. The verse in this first book has occasional faults, but as a rule the lines move, driven by that inner energy of emotion which will sometimes work more metrical wonders than the most conscious art. The words hiss at you sometimes, as in "The Dancer," and again will melt away with the delicacy of fairy bells as in "The Watcher," or will run like deep river water, as in "The Whisperer," which in some moods I think is the best poem in the book until I read "Fossils" or "What Tomas an Buile said in a Pub." They are too long to print, but I must give myself the pleasure of quoting the beautiful "Slan Leat," with which he concludes the book, bidding us, not farewell, but to accompany him on further adventure:

> And now, dear heart, the night is closing in,
> The lamps are not yet ready, and the gloom
> Of this sad winter evening, and the din
> The wind makes in the streets fills all the room.
> You have listened to my stories--Seumas Beg
> Has finished the adventures of his youth,
> And no more hopes to find a buried keg
> Stuffed to the lid with silver. He, in truth,
> And all alas! grew up: but he has found
> The path to truer romance, and with you
> May easily seek wonders. We are bound
> Out to the storm of things, and all is new.
> Give me your hand, so, keeping close to me,
> Shut tight your eyes, step forward ... where are we?

Our new Irish poet declared he was bound "out to the storm of things," and we all waited with interest for his next utterance. Would he wear the red cap as the poet of the social revolution, now long overdue in these islands, or would he sing the Marsellaise of womanhood, emerging in hordes from their underground kitchens to make a still greater revolution? He did neither. He forgot all about the storm of things, and delighted us with his story of Mary, the charwoman's daughter, a tale of Dublin life, so, kindly, so humane, so vivid, so wise, so witty, and so true, that it would not be exaggerating to say that natural humanity in Ireland found its first worthy chronicler in this tale.

We have a second volume of poetry from James Stephens, The Hill of Vision. He has climbed a hill, indeed, but has found cross roads there leading in many directions, and seems to be a little perplexed whether the storm of things was his destiny after all. When one is in a cave there is only one road which leads out, but when one stands in the sunlight there are endless roads. We enjoy his perplexity, for he has seated himself by his cross-roads, and has tried many tunes on his lute, obviously in doubt which sounds sweetest to his own ear. I am not at all in doubt as to what is best, and I hope he will go on like Whitman, carrying "the old delicious burdens, men and women," wherever he goes. For his references to Deity, Plato undoubtedly would have expelled him from his Republic; and justly so, for James Stephens treats his god very much as the African savage treats his fetish. Now it is supplicated, and the next minute the idol is buffeted for an unanswered prayer or a neglected duty, and then a little later our Irish African is crooning sweetly with his idol, arranging its domestic affairs and the marriage of Heaven and Earth. Sometimes our poet essays the pastoral, and in sheer gaiety: flies like any bird under the boughs, and up into the sunlight. There are in his company imps and grotesques, and fauns and satyrs, who come summoned by his piping. Sometimes, as in "Eve," the poem of the mystery of womanhood, he is purely beautiful, but I find myself going back to his men and women; and I hope he will not be angry with me when I say I prefer his tinker drunken to his Deity sober. None of our Irish poets has found God, at least a god any but themselves would not be ashamed to acknowledge. But our poet does know his men and his women. They are not the shadowy, Whistler-like decorative suggestions of humanity made by our poetic dramatists. They have entered like living creatures into his mind, and they break out there in an instant's unforgettable passion or agony, and the wild words fly up to the   poet's brain to match their emotion. I do not know whether the verses entitled "The Brute" are poetry, but they have an amazing energy of expression.

But our poet can be beautiful when he wills, and sometimes, too, he has largeness and grandeur of vision and expression. Look at this picture of the earth, seen from mid-heaven:

> And so he looked to where the earth, asleep,
> Rocked with the moon. He saw the whirling sea

Swing round the world in surgent energy,
Tangling the moonlight in its netted foam,
And nearer saw the white and fretted dome
Of the ice-capped pole spin back a larded ray
To whistling stars, bright as a wizard's day,
But these he passed with eyes intently wide,
Till closer still the mountains he espied,
Squatting tremendous on the broad-backed earth,
Each nursing twenty rivers at a birth.

I would like to quote the verses entitled "Shame." Never have I read anywhere such an anguished cowering before Conscience, a mighty creature full of eyes within and without, and pointing fingers and asped tongues, anticipating in secret the blazing condemnation of the world. And there is "Bessie Bobtail," staggering down the streets with her reiterated, inarticulate expression of grief, moving like one of those wretched whom Blake described in a marvelous phrase as "drunken with woe forgotten"; and there is "Satan," where the reconcilement of light and darkness in the twilights of time is perfectly and imaginatively expressed.

The Hill of Vision is a very unequal book. There are many verses full of power, which move with the free easy motion of the literary athlete. Others betray awkwardness, and stumble as if the writer had stepped too suddenly into the sunlight of his power, and was dazed and bewildered. There is some diffusion of his faculties in what I feel are byways of his mind, but the main current of his energies will, I am convinced, urge him on to his inevitable portrayal of humanity. With writers like Synge and Stephens the Celtic imagination is leaving its Timanoges, its Ildathachs, its Many Colored Lands and impersonal moods, and is coming down to earth intent on vigorous life and individual humanity. I can see that there are great tales to be told and great songs to be sung, and I watch the doings of the new-comers with sympathy, all the while feeling I am somewhat remote from their world, for I belong to an earlier day, and listen to these robust songs somewhat as a ghost who hears the cock crow, and knows his hours are over, and he and his tribe must disappear into tradition.

1912

A NOTE ON SEUMAS O'SULLIVAN

As I grow older I get more songless. I am now exiled irrevocably from the Country of the Young, but I hope I can listen without jealousy and even with delight to those who still make music in the enchanted land. I often searched in the "Poet's Corner" of the country papers with a wild surmise that there, amid reports of Boards of Guardians and Rural Councils, some poetic young kinsman may be taking council with the stars, watching more closely the Plough in the furrows of the heavens than the county instructor at his task of making farmers drive the plough straight in the fields. I found many years ago in a country paper a local poet making genuine music. I remember a line:

And hidden rivers were murmuring in the dark.

I went on in the strength of this poem through the desert of country journalism for many years, hoping to find more hidden rivers of song murmuring in the darkness. It was a patient life of unrequited toil, and I have returned to civilization to search publishers' lists for more easily procurable pleasure. A few years ago I mined out of the still darker region of manuscripts some poetic crystals which I thought were valuable, and edited New Songs. Nearly all my young singers have since then taken flight on their own account. Some have volumes in the booksellers and some in the hands of the printers. But there is one shy singer of the group of writers in New Songs who might easily get overlooked because his verse takes little or no thought of the past or present or future of his country: yet the slim book in which is collected Seumas O'Sullivan's verses reveals a true poet, and if he is too shy to claim his country in his verses there is no reason why his country should not claim him, for he is in his way as Irish as any of our singers. He is, as Mr. W. B. Yeats was in his earlier days, the literary successor of those old Gaelic poets who were fastidious in their verse, who loved little in this world but some chance light in it which reminded them of fairyland, or who, if they were in love, loved their mistress less for her own sake than because some turn of her head, or "a foam-pale breast," carried their impetuous imaginations past her beauty into memories of Helen of Troy, Deirdre, or some other symbol of that remote and perfect beauty which, however man desires, he shall embrace only at the end of time. I think the wives or mistresses of these old poets must have been very unhappy, for women wish to be loved for what they know about themselves, and for the tenderness which is in their hearts, and not because some colored twilight invests them with a shadowy beauty not their own, and which they know they can never carry into the light of day. These poets of the transient look and the evanescent light do not help us to live our daily life, but they do something which is as necessary. They educate and refine the spirit so that it shall not come altogether without any understanding of delicate loveliness into the Kingdom of Heaven, or gaze on Timanoge with the crude blank misunderstanding of Cockney tourists staring up at the stupendous dreams pictured on the roof of the Sistine Chapel. These fastidious scorners of every day and its interests are always looking through nature for "the herbs before they were in the field and every flower before it grew," and through women for the Eve who was in the imagination of the Lord before she was embodied, and we all need this refining vision more than we know. It may be asked of us hereafter when we would mount up into the towers of vision, "How can you desire the beauty you have not seen, who have not sought or loved its shadow in the world?" and the Gates of Ivory may not swing open at our knock. This will never be said to Seumas O'Sullivan, who is always waiting on the transient look and the evanescent light to build up out of their remembered beauty the Kingdom of his Heaven:

> Round you light tresses, delicate,
> Wind blown, wander and climb
> Immortal, transitory.

Earth has no steady beauty as the calm-eyed immortals have, but their image glimmers on the waves of time, and out of what instantly vanishes we can build up something within us which may yet grow into a calm-eyed immortality of loveliness, we becoming gradually what we dream of. I have heard people complain of the frailty of these verses of Seumas O'Sullivan. They want war songs, plough songs, to nerve the soul to fight or the hand to do its work. I will never make that complaint. I will only complain if the strife or the work ever blunt my senses so that I will pass by with an impatient disdain these delicate snatchings at a beauty which is ever fleeting. But I would ask him to remember that life never allures us twice with exactly the same enchantment. Never again will that tress drift like a woven wind made visible out of Paradise; never again will that lifted hand, foam-pale, seem like the springing up of beauty in the world; never a second time will that white brow remind him of the wonderful white towers of the city of the gods. To seek a second inspiration is to receive only a second-rate inspiration, and our poet is a little too fond of lingering in his verse round a few things, a face, the swaying poplars, or sighing reeds which had once piped an alluring music in his ears, and which he longs to hear again. He lives not in too frail a world, but in too narrow a world, and he should adventure out into new worlds in the old quest. He, has become a master of delicate and musical rhythms. I remember reading Seumas O'Sulivan's first manuscripts with mingled pleasure and horror, for his lines often ran anyhow, and scansion seemed to him an unknown art, but I feel humbly now that he can get a subtle quality into his music which I could not hope to acquire. I would like him to catch some new and rare birds with that subtle net of his, and to begin to invent more beauty of his own and to seek for it less. I believe he has got it in him to do well, to do better than he has done if he will now try to use his invention more. The poems with a slight narrative in them, like "The Portent" or the "Saint Anthony," seem to me the most perfect, and it is in this direction, I think, he will succeed best. He wants a story to keep him from beating musical and ineffective wings in the void. I have not said half what I want to say about Seumas O'Sullivan's verses, but I know the world will not listen long to the musings of one verse-writer on another. I only hope this note may send some readers to their bookseller for Seumas O'Sullivan's poems, and that it may help them to study with more understanding a mind that I love.

1909

ART AND LITERATURE

A LECTURE ON THE ART OF G. F. WATTS

After the publication of The Gentle Art of Making Enemies the writer who ventures to speak of art and literature in the same breath needs some courage. Since the death of Whistler, his opinions about the independence of art from the moral ideas with which literature is preoccupied have been generally accepted in the studios. The artist who is praised by a literary man would hardly be human if he was not pleased; but he listens with impatience to any criticism or suggestion about the substance of his art or the form it should take. I had a friend, an artist of genius, and when we were both young we argued together about art on equal terms. It had not then occurred to him that any intelligence I might have displayed in writing verse did not entitle me to an opinion about modeling; but one day I found him reading Mr. Whistler's Ten O'clock. The revolt of art against literature had reached Ireland. After that, while we were still good friends, he made me feel that I was an outsider, and when I ventured to plead for a national character in sculpture, his righteous anger--I might say his ferocity--forced me to talk of something else.

I was not convinced he was right, but years after I began to use the brush a little, and I remember painting a twilight from love of some strange colors and harmonious lines, and when one of my literary friends found that its interest depended on color and form, and that the idea in it could not readily be translated into words, and that it left him wishing that I would illustrate my poems or something that had a meaning, I veered round at once and understood Whistler, and how foolish I was to argue with John Hughes. I joined in the general insurrection of art against the domination of literature. But being a writer and much concerned with abstract ideas, I have never had the comfort and happiness of those who embrace this opinion with their whole being, and when I was asked to lecture, I thought that as I had no Irish Whistler to fear, I might speak of art in relation to these universal ideas which artists hold are for literature and not subject matter for art at all.

I must first say it was not my wish to speak. With a world of noble and immortal forms all about us, it seemed to me as unfitting that words without art or long labor in their making should be advertised as an attraction; that any one should be expected to sit here for an hour to listen to me or another upon a genius which speaks for itself. I was overruled by Mr. Lane. But it is all wrong, this desire to hear and hold opinions about art rather than to be moved by the art itself. I know twenty charlatans who will talk about art, but never lift their eyes to look at the pictures on the wall. I remember an Irish poet speaking about art a whole evening in a room hung round with pictures by Constable, Monet, and others, and he came into that room and went out of it without looking at those pictures. His interest in art was in the holding of opinions about it, and in hearing other opinions, which he could again talk about. I hope I have made some of you feel uncomfortable. This may, perhaps, seem malicious, but it is necessary to release artists from the dogmas of critics who are not artists.

I would not venture to speak here tonight if I thought that anything I said could be laid hold of and be turned into a formula, and used afterwards to torment some unfortunate artist. An artist will take with readiness advice or criticism from a fellow-artist, so far as his natural vanity permits; but he writhes under opinions derived from Ruskin or Tolstoi, the great theorists. You may ask indignantly, Can no one, then, speak about paintings or statues except painters or modelers? No; no one would condemn you to such painful silence and self-suppression. Artists would wish you to talk unceasingly about the emotions their pain of making pictures arouse in you; but, under lifelong enemies, do not suggest to artists the theories under which they should paint. That is hitting below the belt. The poor artist is as God made him; and no one, not even a Tolstoi, is competent to undertake his re-creation. His fellow-artists will pass on to him the tradition of using the brush. He may use it well or ill; but when you ask him to use his art to illustrate literary ideas, or ethical ideas, you are asking him to become a literary man or a preacher.

The other arts have their obvious limitations. The literary man does not dare to demand of the musician that he shall be scientific or moral. The latter is safe in uttering every kind of profanity in sound so long as it is music. Musicians have their art to themselves. But the artist is tormented, and asked to reflect the thought of his time. Beauty is primarily what he is concerned with; and the only moral ideas which he can impart in a satisfactory way are the moral ideas naturally associated with beauty in its higher or lower forms. But I think, some of you are confuting me in your own minds at this moment. You say to yourselves: "But we have all about us the works of great artists whose inspiration not one will deny. He used his art to express great ethical ideas. He spoke again and again about these ideas. He was proud that his art was dedicated to their expression." I am sorry to say that he did say many things which would have endeared him to Tolstoi and Ruskin, and for which I respect him as a man, and which as an artist I deplore. I deplore his speaking of ethical ideas as the inspiration of his art, because I think they were only the inspiration of his life; and where he is weakest in his appeal as an artist is where he summons consciously to his aid ethical ideas which find their proper expression in religion or literature or life.

Watts wished to ennoble art by summoning to its aid the highest conceptions of literature; but in doing so he seems to me to imply that art needed such conceptions for its justification, that the pure artist mind, careless of these ideas, and only careful to make for itself a beautiful vision of things, was in a lower plane, and had a less spiritual message. Now that I deny. I deny absolutely that art needs to call to its aid, in order to justify or ennoble it, any abstract ideas about love or justice or mercy.

It may express none of these ideas, and yet express truths of its own as high and as essential to the being of man; and it is in spite of himself, in spite of his theories, that the work of Watts will have an enduring place in the history of art. You will ask then, "Can art express no moral ideas? Is it unmoral?" In the definite and restricted sense in which the words "ethical" and "moral" are generally used, art is, and must by its nature be unmoral. I do not mean "immoral," and let no one represent me as saying art must be immoral by its very nature. There are dear newspaper men to whom it would be a delight to attribute to me such a saying; and never to let me forget that I said it. When I say that art is essentially unmoral, I mean that the first impulse to paint comes from something seen, either beauty of color or form or tone. It may be light which attracts the artist, or it may be some dimming of natural forms, until they seem to have more of the loveliness of mind than of nature. But it is the aesthetic, not the moral or ethical, nature which is stirred. The picture may afterwards be called "Charity," or "Faith," or "Hope"--and any of these words may make an apt title. But what looms up before the vision of the artist first of all is an image, and that is accepted on account of its fitness for a picture; and an image which was not pictorial would be rejected at once by any true artist, whether it was an illustration of the noblest moral conception or not. Whether a picture is moral or immoral will depend upon the character of the artist, and not upon the subject. A man will communicate his character in everything he touches. He cannot escape communicating it. He must be content with that silent witness, and not try to let the virtues shout out from his pictures. The fact is, art is essentially a spiritual thing, and its vision is perpetually turned to Ultimates. It is indefinable as spirit is. It perceives in life and nature those indefinable relations of one thing to another which to the religious thinker suggest a master mind in nature--a magician of the beautiful at work from hour to hour, from moment to moment, in a never-ceasing and solemn chariot motion in the heavens, in the perpetual and marvelous breathing forth of winds, in the motion of waters, and in the unending evolution of gay and delicate forms of leaf and wing.

The artist may be no philosopher, no mystic; he may be with or without a moral sense, he may not believe in more than his eye can see; but in so far as he can shape clay into beautiful and moving forms he is imitating Deity; when his eye has caught with delight some subtle relation between color and color there is mysticism in his vision. I am not concerned here to prove that there is a spirit in nature or humanity; but for those who ask from art a serious message, here, I say, is a way of receiving from art an inspiration the most profound that man can receive. When you ask from the artist that he should teach you, be careful that you are not asking him to be obvious, to utter platitudes--that you are not asking him to debase his art to make things easy for you, who are too indolent to climb to the mountain, but want it brought to your feet. There are people who pass by a nocturne by Whistler, a misty twilight by Corot, and who whisper solemnly before a Noel Paton as if they were in a Cathedral. Is God, then, only present when His Name is uttered? When we call a figure Time or Death, does it add dignity to it? What is the real inspiration we derive from that noble design by Mr. Watts? Not the comprehension of Time, not the nature of Death, but a revelation human form can express of the heroic dignity. Is it not more to us to know that man or woman can look half-divine, that they can wear an aspect such as we imagine belongs to the immortals, and to feel that if man is made in the image of his Creator, his Creator is the archetype of no ignoble thing? There were immortal powers in Watts' mind when those figures surged up in it; but they were neither Time nor Death. He was rather near to his own archetype, and in that mood in which Emerson was when he said, "I the imperfect adore my own perfect." Touch by touch, as the picture was built up, he was becoming conscious of some interior majesty in his own nature, and it was for himself more than for us he worked. "The oration is to the orator," says Whitman, "and comes most back to him." The artist, too, as he creates a beautiful form outside himself, creates within himself, or admits to his being a nobler beauty than his eyes have seen. His inspiration is spiritual in its origin, and there is always in it some strange story of the glory of the King.

With man and his work we must take either a spiritual or a material point of view. All half-way beliefs are temporary and illogical. I prefer the spiritual with its admission of incalculable mystery and romance in nature, where we find the infinite folded in the atom, and feel how in the unconscious result and labor of man's hand the Eternal is working Its will. You may say that this belongs more to psychology than to art criticism, but I am trying to make clear to you and to myself the relation which the mind which is in literature may rightly bear to the vision which is art. Are literature and ethics to dictate to Art its subjects? Is it right to demand that the artist's work shall have an obviously intelligible message or meaning, which the intellect can abstract from it and relate to the conduct of life? My belief is that the most literature can do is to help to interpret art, and that art offers to it, as nature does, a vision of beauty, but of undefined significance.

No one asks or expects the clouds to shape themselves into ethical forms, or the sun to shine only on the just and not on the unjust also. It is vain to expect it, but there is something written about the heavens declaring the beauty of the Creator and the firmament showing His handiwork. If the artist can bring whatever of that vision has touched him into his work we should ask no more, and must not expect him to be more righteously minded than his Creator, or to add a finishing tag of moral to justify it all, to show that Deity is solemnly minded and no mere idle trifler with beauty like Whistler.

I have stated my belief that art is spiritual, that its genuine inspirations come from a higher plane of our being than the ethical or intellectual; and I think wherever literature or ethics have so dominated the mind of the artist that they change the form of his inspiration, his art loses its own peculiar power and gains nothing. We have here a picture of "Love steering the bark of Humanity." I may put it rather crudely when I say that pictures like this are supposed to exert a power on the man who, for example, would beat his wife, so that love will be his after inspiration. Anyhow, ethical pictures are painted with some such intention belief. Now, art has great influence, but I do not believe this or any other picture would stop a man beating his wife if he wanted to. Art does not call sinners to repentance; that is not one of its powers. It fulfils rather another saying: "Unto them that have much shall be given," bringing delight to those that are already sensitive to beauty. My own conviction is that ethical pictures are, if anything, immoral in their influence, as everything must be that forsakes the law of its own being, and that pictures like this only add to the vanity of people so righteously minded as to be aware of their own virtue. We will always have these concessions to passing phases of thought. We have had requests for the scientific painter--the man who will paint nature with geological accuracy, and man in accordance with evolutionary dogmas. He will find his eloquent literary defenders enchanted to find so much learning to point to in his work, but it will all pass. The true artist will still be instinctively spiritual.

Now I have used the word "spiritual" so often in connection with art that you may reasonably ask for some definition of my meaning. I am afraid it is easier to define spirituality in literature than in art. But a literary definition may help. Spirituality is the power certain minds have of apprehending formless spiritual essences, of seeing the eternal in the transitory, of relating the particular to the universal, the type to the archetype.

While I give this definition, I hope no artist will ever be insane enough to make it the guiding principle of his art. I shudder to think of any conscious attempt in a picture to relate the type to the archetype. It is a philosophical definition, solely intended for the spectator. I wish the artist only to paint his vision, and whether he paints this, or another world he imagines, if it is art it will be spiritual. I have given a definition of spirituality in literature, but how now relate it to art? How illustrate its presence? When Pater wrote his famous description of the Mona Lisa, that intense and enigmatic face had evoked a spiritual mood. When he saw in it the summed-up experience of many generations of humanity, he felt in the picture that relation of the particular to the universal I have spoken of. When we find human forms suggesting a superhuman dignity, as in Watts' figures of Time and Death, or in the Phidian marbles, the type is there melting into the archetype. When Millet paints a peasant figure of today with some gesture we imagine the first Sower must have used, it is the eternal in it which makes the transitory impressive. But these are obvious instances, you will say, chosen from artists whose pictures lend themselves to this kind of exposition. What about the art of the landscape painter? Undeniably a form of art, where is the spirituality?

I am afraid my intellect is not equal to talking up every picture that might be suggested and using it to illustrate my meaning, though I do not think I would despair of finally discovering the spiritual element in any picture I felt was art. However, I will go further. We have all felt some element of art lacking in the painter who goes to Killarney, Italy, or Switzerland, and brings us back a faithful representation of undeniably beautiful places. It is all there--the lofty mountains, the lakes, the local color; but what enchanted us in nature does not touch us in the picture. What we want is the spirit of the place evoked in us rather than the place itself. Art is neither pictured botany or geology. A great landscape is the expression of a mood of the human mind as definitely as music or poetry is. The artist is communicating his own emotions. There is some mystic significance in the color he employs; and then the doorways are opened, and we pass from sense into soul. We are looking into a soul when we are looking at a Turner, a Carot, or a Whistler, as surely as when in dream we find ourselves moving in strange countries which are yet within us, contained for all their seeming infinitudes in the little hollow of the brain. All this, I think, is undeniable; but perhaps not many of you will follow me, though you may understand me, if I go further and say, that in this, art is unconsciously also reaching out to archetypes, is lifting itself up to walk in that garden of the divine mind where, as the first Scripture says, it created "flowers before they were in the field and every herb before it grew." A man may sit in an armchair and travel farther than ever Columbus traveled; and no one can say how far Turner, in his search after light, had not journeyed into the lost Eden, and he himself may have been there most surely at the last when his pictures had become a blaze of incoherent light.

You may say now that I have objected to literature dominating the arts, and yet I have drawn from pictures a most complicated theory. I have felt a little, indeed, as if I was marching through subtleties to the dismemberment of my mind, but I do not think I have anywhere contradicted myself or suggested that an artist should work on these speculations. These may rightly arise in the mind of the onlooker who will regard a work of art with his whole nature, not merely with the aesthetic sense, and who will naturally pass from the first delight of vision into a psychological analysis. A profound nature will always awaken profound reflections. There are heads by Da Vinci as interesting in their humanity as Hamlet. When we see eyes that tempt and allure with lips virginal in their purity, we feel in the face a union of things which the dual nature of man is eternally desiring. It is the marriage of heaven and hell, the union of spirit and flesh, each with their uncurbed desires; and what is impossible in life is in his art, and is one of the secrets of its strange fascination. It may seem paradoxical to say of Watts--a man of genius, who was always preaching through his art--that it is very difficult to find what he really expresses. No one is ever for a moment in doubt about what is expressed by Rossetti, Turner, Millet, Corot, or many contemporary artists who never preached at all, but whose mood or vision peculiar to themselves is easily definable. With Watts the effort at analyses is confused: first by his own statement about the ethical significance of his works, which I think misleading, because while we may come away from his pictures with many feelings of majesty or beauty or mystery, the ethical spirit is not the predominant one. That rapturous winged spirit which he calls Love Triumphant might just as easily be called Music or Song, and another allegory be attached to it without our feeling any more special fitness or unfitness in the explanation. I see a beautiful exultant figure, but I do not feel love as the fundamental mood in the painter, as I feel the religious mood is fundamental in the Angelus of Millet. I do not need to look for a title to that or for the painting of The Shepherdess to feel how earth and her children have become one in the vision of the painter; that the shepherdess is not the subject, nor the sheep, nor the still evening, but altogether are one mood, one being, in which all things move in harmony and are guided by the Great Shepherd. Well, I do not feel that Love; or Charity, or Hope are expressed in this way in Watts, and that the ethical spirit is not fundamental with him as the religious spirit is with Millet. He has an intellectual conception of his moral idea, but is not emotionally obsessed by it, and the basis of a man's art is not to be found in his intellectual conceptions, which are light things, but in his character or rather in his temperament. We know, for all the poetical circumstances of Rossetti's pictures, what desire it is that shines out of those ardent faces, and how with Leighton "the form alone is eloquent," and that Tumer's God was light as surely as with any Persian worshipper of the sun. Here and there they may have been tempted otherwise, but they never strayed far from their temperamental way of expressing themselves in art. So that the first thing to be dismissed in trying to understand Watts is Watts' own view of his art and its inspiration. He is not the first distinguished man whose intellect has not proved equal to explaining rightly its sources of power. Our next difficulty in discovering the real Watts arises because he did not look at nature or life directly. He was overcome by great traditions. He almost persistently looks at nature through one or two veils. There is a Phidian veil and a Venetian or rather an Italian veil, and almost everything in life and nature which could not be expressed in terms of these traditions he ignored. I might say that no artist of equal genius ever painted pictures and brought so little fresh observation into his art except, perhaps, Burne-Jones. Both these artists seem to have a secret and refined sympathy with Fuseli's famous outburst, "Damn Nature, she always puts me out!" Even when the sitter came, Watts seems to have been uneasy unless he could turn him into a Venetian nobleman or person of the Middle Ages, or could disguise in some way the fact that Artist and Sitter belonged to the nineteenth century. He does not seem to be aware that people must breathe even in pictures. His skies rest solidly on the shoulders of his figures as if they were cut out to let the figures be inserted. If he were not a man of genius there would have been an end of him. But he was a man of genius, and we must try to understand the meaning of his acceptance of tradition. If we understand it in Watts we will understand a great deal of contemporary art and literature which is called derivative, art issuing out of art, and literature out of literature.

The fact is that this kind of art in which Watts and Burne-Jones were pioneers is an art which has not yet come to its culmination or to any perfect expression of itself. There is a genuinely individual impulse in it, and it is not derivative merely, although almost every phase of it can be related to earlier art. It has nothing in common with the so-called grand school of painting which produced worthless imitations of Michael Angelo and Raphael. It is feeling out for a new world, and it is trying to use the older tradition as a bridge. The older art held up a mirror to natural forms and brought them nearer to man. In the perfect culmination of this new art one feels how a complete change might take place and natural forms be used to express an internal nature or the soul of the artist. Colors and forms, like words after the lapse of centuries, enlarge their significance. The earliest art was probably simple and literal--there may have been the outline of a figure filled up with some flat color. Then as art became more complex, colors began to have an emotional meaning quite apart from their original relation to an object. The artist begins unconsciously to relate color more intimately to his own temperament than to external nature. At last, after the lapse of ages, some sensitive artist begins to imagine that he has discovered a complete language capable of expressing any mood of mind. The passing of centuries has enriched every color, and left it related to some new phase of the soul. Phidian or Michael Angelesque forms gather their own peculiar associations of divinity or power. In fact, this new art uses the forms of the old as symbols or hieroglyphs to express more complicated ideas than the older artists tried to depict.

Watts never attempted, for all his admiration of these men, to follow them in their efforts to realize perfectly the forms that they conceived. They had done this once and for all, and repetition may have seemed unnecessary. But the lofty temper awakened by those stupendous creations could be aroused by a suggestion of their peculiar characteristics. Association of ideas will in some subtle way bring us back to the Phidian demigods when we look at forms and draperies vaguely suggestive of the Parthenon. I do not say that Watt's did this consciously, but instinctively he felt compelled, with the gradual development of his own mind, to use the imaginative traditions created by other artists as a language through which he might find expression peculiar to himself. It is a highly intellectual art to which tradition was a necessity, as much as it is to the poet, who when he speaks of "beauty" draws upon a sentiment created by millions of long-dead lovers, or who, when he thinks of the "spirit," is, in his use of the word, the heir of countless generations who brooded upon the mysteries.

Just as in Millet, the painter of peasants, there was a religious spirit shaping all things into austere and elemental simplicities, so in Watts there was an intellectual spirit, seeking everywhere for the traces of mind trying to express the bodiless and abstract. With Whitman he seems to cry out, "The soul for ever and ever!" It is there in the astonishing head of Swinburne, whom he reveals, if I may use a vulgar phrase, as a poetic "bounder," but illuminated and etherealized by genius. It is in the head of Mill, the very symbol of the moral reasoning--mind. It is in the face of Tennyson, with its too self-conscious seership, and in all those vague faces of the imaginative paintings, into which, to use Pater's phrase, "the soul with all its maladies has passed." In his pictures he draws on the effects of earlier art, and throws his sitters back until they seem to belong to some nondescript mediaeval country, like the Bohemia of the dramatists; and he darkens and shuts out the light of day that this starlight of soul may be more clearly seen, and destroys, as far as he can, all traces of the century they live in, for the mind lives in all the ages, and he would show it as the pilgrim of eternity. Because Watts' art was necessarily so brooding and meditative, looking at life with half-closed eyes and then shutting them to be alone with memory and the interpreter, his painting, so beautiful and full of surety in early pictures like the Wounded Heron, grows to be often labored and muddy, and his drawing uncertain. That he could draw and paint with the greatest, he every now and then gave proof; but the surety of beautiful craftsmanship deserts those who have not always their eye fixed on an object of vision; and Watts was not, like Blake or Shelley, one of the proud seers whose visions are of "forms more real than living man." He seemed to feel what his effects should be rather than to see them, or else his vision was fleeting and his art was a laborious brooding to recapture the lost impression. In his color he always seems to me to be second-hand, as if the bloom and freshness of his paint had worn off through previous use by other artists. It seemed to be a necessity of his curiously intellectual art that only traditional colors and forms should be employed, and it is only rarely we get the shock of a new creation, and absolutely original design, as in Orpheus, where the passionate figure turns to hold what is already a vanishing shadow.

Watts' art was an effort to invest his own age, an age of reason, with the no-

bilities engendered in an age of faith. At the time Watts was at his prime his contemporaries were everywhere losing belief in the spiritual conceptions of earlier
periods; they were analyzing everything, and were deciding that what was really
true in religion, what gave it nobility, was its ethical teaching; retain that, and religion might go, illustrating the truth of the Chinese philosopher who said: "When
the spirit is lost, men follow after charity and duty to one's neighbors." The unity
of belief was broken up into diverse intellectual conceptions. Men talked about
love and liberty, patriotism, duty, charity, and a whole host of abstractions moral
and intellectual, which they had convinced themselves were the essence of religion
and the real cause of its power over man. Whether Watts lost faith like his contemporaries I do not know, but their spirit infected his art. He set himself to paint
these abstractions; and because we cannot imagine these abstractions with a form,
we feel something fundamentally false in this side of his art. He who paints a man,
an angelic being, or a divine being, paints something we feel may have life. But it
is impossible to imagine Time with a body as it is to imagine a painting embody-
ing Newton's law of gravitation. It is because such abstractions do not readily take
shape that Watts drew so much on the imaginative tradition of his predecessors.
Where these pictures are impressive is where the artist slipped by his conscious
aim, and laid hold of the nobility peculiar to the men and women he used as symbols. It is not Time or Death which awes us in Watts' picture, but majestical images
of humanity; and Watts is at his greatest as an inventor when humanity itself most
occupies him when he depicts human life only, and lets it suggest its own natural
infinity, as in those images of the lovers drifting through the Inferno, with whom
every passion is burnt out and exhausted but the love through which they fell.

   Life itself is more infinite, noble, and suggestive than thought. We soon come
to the end of the ingenious allegory. It tells only one story but where there is a
perfect image of life there is infinitude and mystery. We do not tire considering
the long ancestry of expression in a face. It may lead us back through the ages; but
we do tire of the art which imprisons itself within formulae, and says to the spectator: "In this way and in no other shall you regard what is before you." No man is
profound enough to explain the nature of his own inspiration. Socrates says that
the poet utters many things which are truer than he himself understands. The same
thing applies to many a great artist, who, when he paints tree or field, or face, or

form, finds that there comes on him a mysterious quickening of his nature, and he paints he knows not what. It is like and unlike what his eyes have seen. It may be the same field, but we feel there the presence of the spirit. It may be the same figure, but it is made transcendental, as when the Word had become flesh and dwelt among us. His inspiration is akin to that of the prophets of old, whose words rang but for an instant and were still, yet they created nations whose only boundaries were the silences where their speech had not been heard. His majestical figures are prophecies. His ecstatic landscapes bring us nigh to the beauty which was in Eden. His art is a divine adventure, in which he, like all of us who are traveling in so many ways, seeks, consciously or unconsciously, to regain the lost unity with nature and the knowledge of his own immortal being, and it is so you will best understand it.

1906

AN ARTIST OF GAELIC IRELAND

The art of Hone and the elder Yeats, while in spirit filled with a sentiment which was the persistence of ancient moods into modern times, still has not the external characteristics of Gaeldom; but looking at the pictures of the younger Yeats it seemed to me that for the first time we had something which could be called altogether Gaelic. The incompleteness of the sketches suggests the term "folk" as expressing exactly the inspiration of this very genuine art. We have had abundance of Irish folk-lore, but we knew nothing of folk-art until the figures of Jack Yeats first romped into our imagination a few years ago. It was the folk-feeling lit up by genius and interpreted by love. It was not, and is now less than ever, the patronage bestowed by the intellectual artist on the evidently picturesque forms of a life below his own.

I suspect Jack Yeats thinks the life of the Sligo fisherman is as good a method of life as any, and that he could share it for a long time without being in the least desirous of a return to the comfortable life of convention. The name of Muglas Hyde suggests itself to me as a literary parallel. These sketches have all the prodigality of invention, the exuberance of gesture, and animation of "The Twisting of the Rope," and the poetry is of as high or higher a n order. In the drawing called "Midsummer Eve" there is a mystery which is not merely the mystery of night and shadow. It is the mystery of the mingling of spirit with spirit which is suggested by the solitary figure with face upturned to the stars. We have all memories of such summer nights when into the charmed heart falls the enchantment we call ancient, though the days have no fellows, nor will ever have any, when the earth glows with the dusky hues of rich pottery, and the stars, far withdrawn into faery altitudes, dance with a gaiety which is more tremendous and solemn than any repose. The night of this picture is steeped in such a dream, and I know not whether it is communicated, or a feeling arising in myself; but there seems everywhere in it the breathing of life, subtle, exultant, penetrating. It is conceived in the mood of awe and prayer, which makes Millet's pictures as religious as any whichever hung over the altar, for surely the "Angelus" is one of the most spiritual of pictures, though the peasants bow their heads and worship in a temple not built with hands. I do not, of course, compare otherwise than in the mood the "Midsummer Eve" to such a masterpiece; but there is a kinship between the beauty revealed in great and in little things, and our thought turns from the stars to the flowers with no feeling of descent into an alien world. But this mood is rare in life as in art, and it is only occasionally that the younger Yeats becomes the interpreter of the spirituality of the peasant. He is more often the recorder of the extravagant energies of the race-course and the market-place, where he finds herded together all the grotesque humors of West Irish life.

We recognize his figures as distinctly Irish. Here the old rollicking Lever and Lover type of Irishmen reappear, hunting like the very devil, with faces set in the last ecstasy of rapid motion. There is an excess of energy in these furious riders which almost gives them a symbolic character. They seem to ride on some passionate business of the soul rather than for any transitory excitement of the body. And besides these wild horse-men there are quiet and lovely figures like "A Mother of the Rosses," holding her child to her breast in an opalescent twilight, through which the boat that carries her moves. There are always large and noble outlines, which suggest that if Jack Yeats had more grandiose ambitions he might have been the Millet of Irish rural life, but he is too much the symbolist, hating all but essentials, to elaborate his art.

In writing of Jack Yeats mention must be made of his black and white work, which at its best has a primitive intensity. The lines have a kind of Gothic quality, reminding one of the rude glooms, the lights and lines of some half-barbarian cathedral. They are very expressive and never undecided. The artist always knows what he is going to do. There is no doubt he has a clear image before him when he takes up pen or brush. A strong will is always directing the strong lines, forcing them to repeat an image present to the inner eye. In his early days Jack Yeats loafed about the quays at Sligo, and we may be sure he was at all the races, and paid his penny to go into the side-shows, and see the freaks, the Fat Woman and the Skeleton Man. It was probably at this period of his life he was captured by pirates of the Spanish

Main. My remembrance of Irish county towns at that time is that no literature flourished except the Penny Dreadful and the local press. I may be doing Jack Yeats an injustice when hailing him at the beginning of a fascinating career I yet suspect a long background of Penny Dreadfuls behind it. How else could he have drawn his pirates? They are the only pirates in art who manifest the true pride, glory, beauty, and terror of their calling as the romantic heart of childhood conceives of it. The pirate has been lifted up to a strange kind of poetry in some of Jack Yeats' pictures. I remember one called "Walking the Plank." The solemn theatrical face, lifted up to the blue sky in a last farewell to the wild world and its lawless freedom, haunted me for days. There was also a pen-and-ink drawing I wish I could reproduce here. A young buccaneer, splendid in evil bravery, leaned across a bar where a strange, beastly, little, old, withered, rat-like figure was drawing the drink. The little figure was like a devil with the soul all concentrated into malice, and the whole picture affected one with terror like a descent into some ferocious human hell.

In all these figures, pirates or peasants, there is an ever present suggestion of poetry; it is in the skies, or in the distance, or in the colors; and these people who laugh in the fairs will have after hours as solemn as the quiet star-gazer in the "Midsummer Eve." This poetry is evident in the oddest ways, and escapes analysis, so elusive and so original is it, as in the "Street of Shows." Nothing at first thought seems more hopelessly remote from poetry than the country circus, with its lurid posters of the Giant Schoolgirl, the Petrified Man, and the Mermaid, all in strong sunlight; but the heart carries with it its own mood, and this flaring scene has undergone some indefinite transformation by the alchemy of genius, and it assumes the character of a fairy tale or Arabian Nights Entertainment imagined in the fantastic dreams of childhood. The sleepy doorkeeper is a goblin or gnome. Perhaps the charm of it all is that it is so evidently illusion, for when the heart is strong in its own surety it can look out on the world, and smile on things which would be unendurable if felt to be permanent, knowing they are only dreams.

Many of these sketches have a largeness, almost a nobility, of conception, which is, I think, a gift from father to son. "After the Harvest's Saved" is something elemental. The "Post-car" suggests the horses of the sun, or the stage coach in De Quincey's extraordinary dream, when the opium had finally rioted in his brain, and transformed his stage-coach into a chariot carrying news of some everlasting victory. Blake has said "exuberance is genius," and there is an excess of energy or passion, or a dilation of the forms, or a peace deeper than mere quietude in the figures of Mr. Yeats' pictures, which gives them that symbolic character which genius always impresses on its works.

The coloring grows better every year; it is more varied and purer. It is sometimes sombre, as in the tragic and dramatic "Simon the Cyrenian," and sometimes rich and flowerlike, but always charged with sentiment, and there is a curious fitness in it even when it is evidently unreal. These blues and purples and pale greens--what crowd ever seemed clad in such twilight colors? And yet we accept it as natural, for this opalescence is always in the mist-laden air of the West; it enters into the soul today as it did into the soul of the ancient Gael, who called it Ildathach--the many-colored land; it becomes part of the atmosphere of the mind; and I think Mr. Yeats means here to express, by one of the inventions of genius, that this dim radiant coloring of his figures is the fitting symbol of the fairyland which is in their hearts. I have not felt so envious of any artist's gift for a long time; not envy of his power of expression, but of his way of seeing things. We are all seeking today for some glimpse of the fairyland our fathers knew; but all the fairylands, the Silver Cloud World, the Tirnanoge, the Land of Heart's Desire, rose like dreams out of the human soul, and in tracking them there Mr. Yeats has been more fortunate than us all, for he has come to the truth, perhaps hardly conscious of it himself.

1902

TWO IRISH ARTISTS

It is unjust to an artist to write on the spur of the moment of his work--of the just seen picture which pleases or displeases. For what instantly delights the eye may never win its way into the heart, and what repels at first may steal later on into the understanding, and find its interpretation in a deeper mood. The final test of a picture, or of any work of art, is its power of enduring charm. There are many circles in the Paradise of Beautiful Memories, and half unconsciously, but with a justice, we at last place each in its hierarchy, remote or near to the centre of our being; and I propose here rather to speak of the impression left in my memory after seeing the work of Yeats and Hone for many years, than to describe in detail the pictures--some new, some familiar-- which by a happy thought have been gathered together for exhibition. To tell an artist that you remember his pictures with love after many years is the highest praise you can give him; and to distinguish the impression produced from others is a pleasure I am glad to be here allowed.

An artist like Mr. Yeats, whose main work has been in portraiture, must often find himself before sitters with whom he has little sympathy, and we all expect to find portraits which do not interest us, because the interpreter has been at fault, and has failed in his vision. With the born craftsman, who always gives us beautiful brushwork, we do not expect these inequalities, but with Mr. Yeats technical power is not the most prominent characteristic. He broods or dreams over his sitters, and his meditation always tends to the discovery of some spiritual or intellectual life in them, or some hidden charm in the nature, or something to love; and if he finds what he seeks, we are sure, not always of a complete picture, but of a poetic illumination, a revelation of character, a secret sweetness for which we forgive the weakness or indecision manifest here and there, and which are relics of the hours before the final surety was attained.

I do not know what Mr. Yeats' philosophy of life is, but in his work he has been over-mastered by the spirit of his race, and he belongs to those who from the earliest dawn of Ireland have sought for the Heart's Desire, and who have refined away the world, until only fragments remained to them. They have not accepted life as it is, and Mr. Yeats could not paint like Reynolds or Romney the beauty of every day in its best attire. He is like the Irish poets who have rarely left a complete description of women, but who speak of some transitory motion or fragile charm--"a thin palm like foam of the sea," "a white body," or in such vague phrases, until it seems a spirit is praised and not flesh and blood. I remember the faces of women and children in his pictures where everything is blurred or obscured, save faces which have a nameless charm. They look at you with long-remembered glances out of the brooding hour of twilight, out of reverie and dream. It is the hidden heart which looks out, and we love these women and children for this, for surely the heart's desire is its own secret.

His portraits of men have kindred qualities, and the magnificent picture of John O'Leary shows him at his best. It is itself a symbol of the movement of which O'Leary was the last great representative. The stately patriarchal head of the old chief is the head of the idealist, so sure of his own truth that he must act, and, if needs be, become the martyr for his ideal. But the delicate hands are not the hands of an empire-breaker. This portrait will probably find its last resting-place in the National Gallery, where, with a curious irony, the Government places the portraits of the dead rebels who gave its statesmen many an anxious day and many a nightmare; and so it will go on, perhaps, until the contemplation of these pictures inspires some boy with an equal or better head and a stronger hand, and then--.

But to return to Mr. Yeats. Some earlier pictures show him attempting to paint directly the ideal world of romance and poetry; yet interesting as these are, they do not convey the same impression of mystery as the pictures of today. Indeed, the light seen behind or through a veil is always more suggestive than the unveiled light. It may be that the spirit is a formless breath which pervades form, and it is better revealed as a light in the eyes, as a brooding expression, than by the choice of ancient days and other-world subjects, where the shapes can be molded to ideal forms by the artist's will. However it is, it is certain that Millet, the realist, is more spiritual than Moreau or Burne-Jones for all their archaic design; and Mr. Yeats, who, as his King Goll shows, might have been a great romantic painter, has probably chosen wisely, and has painted more memorable pictures than if he had gone back to the fairyland of Celtic mythology.

To turn from Yeats to Hone is to turn from the lighted hearth to the wilderness. Humanity is very far away, or is huddled up under immense skies, where it seems of less importance than the rocks. The earth on which men have lived, where the work of their hand is evident, with all the sentiment of the presence of man, with smoke arising from numberless homes, is foreign to Mr. Hone. The monsters of the primeval world might sprawl on the rocks, for all the evidence of lapse of time since their day, in many of his pictures. He, too, has refined away his world until only fragments of the earth remain to him where he can dream in; and these are waste places, where the salt of the sea is in the wind, and the skies are gray and vapor- laden, or the loneliness of dim twilights are over level sands. Whatever else he paints is devoid of its proper interest, for he seems to impose on the cattle in the fields and on the habitable places a sentiment alien to their nature. He has a mind with but one impressive mood, and his spirit is never kindled, save in the society where none intrude; but in his own domain he is a master, and is always sure of himself and his effect. There is no tentative, undecisive brushwork, such as we often see in the subtle search for the unrevealed, which makes or mars Mr. Yeats' work. He is at home in his peculiar world, while the other is always seeking for it.

"A Sunset on Malahide Sands" shows a greater intensity than is usual even in Mr. Hone's work. There is something thrilling in this twilight trembling over the deserted world. Philosophies may prove very well in the lecture-room, says Whitman, and not prove at all under the sky and stars. Pictures likewise may seem beautiful in a gallery, yet look thin and unreal where, with a turn of the head, one could look out at the pictures created hour after hour by the Master of the Beautiful; but there is some magic in this vision made up of elemental light, darkness, and loneliness, and we feel awed as if we knew the Spirit was hidden in His works. But primitive as this peculiar world is, and remote from humanity, it is just here we find a human revelation; for is not all art a symbol of the creative mind, and if we were wise enough we would understand that in art the light on every cloud, and the clear spaces above the cloud, and the shadows of the earth beneath are made out of the lights, infinitudes, and shadows of the soul, and are selected from nature because of some correspondence, unconscious or half felt. But these things belong more to the psychology of the artist mind than to the appreciation of its work. I have said enough, I hope, to attract to the work of these artists, in a mood of true understanding, those who would like to believe in the existence in Ireland of a genuine art. For ignored and uncared for as art is, we have some names to be proud of, and of these Mr. Yeats and Mr. Hone are foremost.

1902

"ULSTER"

AN OPEN LETTER TO MR. RUDYARD KIPLING

I Speak to you, brother, because you have spoken to me, or rather you have spoken for me. I am a native of Ulster. So far back as I can trace the faith of my forefathers they held the faith for whose free observance you are afraid.

I call you brother, for so far as I am known beyond the circle of my personal friends it is as a poet. We are not a numerous tribe, but the world has held us in honor, because on the whole in poetry is found the highest and sincerest utterance of man's spirit. In this manner of speaking if a man is not sincere his speech betrayeth him, for all true poetry was written on the Mount of Transfiguration, and there is revelation in it and the mingling of heaven and earth. I am jealous of the honor of poetry, and I am jealous of the good name of my country, and I am impelled by both emotions to speak to you.

You have blood of our race in you, and you may, perhaps, have some knowledge of Irish sentiment. You have offended against one of our noblest literary traditions in the manner in which you have published your thoughts. You begin by quoting Scripture. You preface your verses on Ulster by words from the mysterious oracles of humanity as if you had been inflamed and inspired by the prophet of God; and you go on to sing of faith in peril and patriotism betrayed and the danger of death and oppression by those who do murder by night, which things, if one truly feels, he speaks of without consideration of commerce or what it shall profit him to speak. But you, brother, have withheld your fears for your country and mine until they could yield you a profit in two continents. After all this high speech about the Lord and the hour of national darkness it shocks me to find this following your verses: "Copyrighted in the United States of America by Rudyard Kipling." You are not in want. You are the most successful man of letters of your time, and yet you are not above making profit out of the perils of your country. You ape the lordly speech of the prophets, and you conclude by warning everybody not to reprint your words at their peril. In Ireland every poet we honor has dedicated his genius to his country without gain, and has given without stint, without any niggardly withholding of his gift when his nation was dark and evil days. Not one of our writers, when deeply moved about Ireland, has tried to sell the gift of the spirit. You, brother, hurt me when you declare your principles, and declare a dividend to yourself out of your patriotism openly and at the same time.

I would not reason with you, but that I know there is something truly great and noble in you, and there have been hours when the immortal in you secured your immortality in literature, when you ceased to see life with that hard cinematograph eye of yours, and saw with the eyes of the spirit, and power and tenderness and insight were mixed in magical tales. But you were far from the innermost when you wrote of my countrymen us you did.

I have lived all my life in Ireland, holding a different faith from that held by the majority. I know Ireland as few Irishmen know it, county by county, for I traveled all over Ireland for years, and, Ulster man as I am, and proud of the Ulster people, I resent the crowning of Ulster with all the virtues and the dismissal of other Irishmen as thieves and robbers. I resent the cruelty with which you, a stranger, speak of the lovable and kindly people I know.

You are not even accurate in your history when you speak of Ulster's traditions and the blood our forefathers spilt. Over a century ago Ulster was the strong and fast place of rebellion, and it was in Ulster that the Volunteers stood beside their cannon and wrung the gift of political freedom for the Irish Parliament. You are blundering in your blame. You speak of Irish greed in I know not what connection, unless you speak of the war waged over the land; and yet you ought to know that both parties in England have by Act after Act confessed the absolute justice and rightness of that agitation, Unionist no less than Liberal, and both boast of their share in answering the Irish appeal. They are both proud today of what they did. They made inquiry into wrong and redressed it. But you, it seems, can only feel sore and angry that intolerable conditions imposed by your laws were not borne in patience and silence. For what party do you speak? What political ideal inspires you? When an Irishman has a grievance you smite him. How differently would you have written of Runnymede and the valiant men who rebelled when oppressed. You would have made heroes out of them. Have you no soul left, after admiring the rebels in your own history, to sympathize with other rebels suffering deeper wrongs? Can you not see deeper into the motives for rebellion than the hireling reporter who is sent to make up a case for the paper of a party? The best men in Ulster, the best Unionists in Ireland will not be grateful to you for libeling their countrymen in your verse. For, let the truth be known, the mass of Irish Unionists are much more in love with Ireland than with England. They think Irish Nationalists are mistaken, and they fight with them and use hard words, and all the time they believe Irishmen of any party are better in the sight of God than Englishmen. They think Ireland is the best country in the world to live in, and they hate to hear Irish people spoken of as murderers and greedy scoundrels. Murderers! Why, there is more murder done in any four English shires in a year than in the whole of the four provinces of Ireland! Greedy! The nation never ccepted a bribe, or took it as an equivalent or payment for an ideal, and what bribe would not have been offered to Ireland if it had been willing to forswear its traditions.

I am a person whose whole being goes into a blaze at the thought of oppression of faith, and yet I think my Catholic countrymen more tolerant than those who hold the faith I was born in. I am a heretic judged by their standards, a heretic who has written and made public his heresies, and I have never suffered in friendship or found my heresies an obstacle in life. I set my knowledge, the knowledge of a lifetime, against your ignorance, and I say you have used your genius to do Ireland and its people a wrong. You have intervened in a quarrel of which you do not know the merits like any brawling bully, who passes, and only takes sides to use his strength. If there was a high court of poetry, and those in power jealous of the noble name of poet, and that none should use it save those who were truly Knights of the Holy Ghost, they would hack the golden spurs from your heels and turn you out of the Court. You had the ear of the world and you poisoned it with prejudice and ignorance. You had the power of song, and you have always used it on behalf of the strong against the weak. You have smitten with all your might at creatures who are frail on earth but mighty in the heavens, at generosity, at truth, at justice, and heaven has withheld vision and power and beauty from you, for this your verse is but a shallow newspaper article made to rhyme. Truly ought the golden spurs to be hacked from your heels and you be thrust out of the Court.

1912

IDEALS OF THE NEW RURAL SOCIETY

For a country where political agitations follow each other as rapidly as plagues in an Eastern city, it is curious how little constructive thought we can show on the ideals of a rural civilization. But economic peace ought surely to have its victories to show as well as political war. I would a thousand times rather dwell on what men and women working together may do than on what may result from majorities at Westminster. The beauty of great civilizations has been built up far more by the people working together than by any corporate action of the State. In these socialistic days we grow pessimistic about our own efforts and optimistic about the working of the legislature. I think we do right to expect great things from the State, but we ought to expect still greater things from ourselves. We ought to know full well that, if the State did twice as much as it does, we shall never rise out of mediocrity among the nations unless we have unlimited faith in the power of our personal efforts to raise and transform Ireland, and unless we translate the faith into works. The State can give a man an economic holding, but only the man himself can make it into Earthly Paradise, and it is a dull business, unworthy of a being made in the image of God, to grind away at work without some noble end to be served, some glowing ideal to be attained.

Ireland is a horribly melancholy and cynical country. Our literary men and poets, who ought to give us courage, have taken to writing about the Irish as people who "went forth to battle, but always fell," sentimentalizing over incompetence instead of invigorating us and liberating us and directing our energies. We have developed a new and clever school of Irish dramatists who say they are holding up the mirror to Irish peasant nature, but they reflect nothing but decadence. They delight in the broken lights of insanity, the ruffian who beats his wife, the weakling who is unfortunate in love and who goes and drinks himself to death, while the little decaying country towns are seized on with avidity and exhibited on the stage in every kind of decay and human futility and meanness. Well, it is good to be chastened in spirit, but it is a thousand times better to be invigorated in spirit. To be positive is always better than to be negative. These writers understand and sympathize with Ireland more through their lower nature than their higher nature. Judging by the things people write in Ireland, and by what they go to see performed on the stage, it is more pleasing to them to see enacted characters they know are meaner than themselves than to see characters which they know are nobler than themselves.

All this is helping on our national pessimism and self-mistrust. It helps to fix these features permanently in our national character, which were excusable enough as temporary moods after defeat. The younger generation should hear nothing about failures. It should not be hypnotized into self-contempt. Our energies in Ireland are sapped by a cynical self-mistrust which is spread everywhere through society. It is natural enough that the elder generation, who were promised so many millenniums, but who actually saw four million people deducted from the population, should be cynical. But it is not right they should give only to the younger generation the heritage of their disappointments without any heritage of hope. From early childhood parents and friends are hypnotizing the child into beliefs and unbeliefs, and too often they are exiling all nobility out of life, all confidence, all trust, all hope; they are insinuating a mean self-seeking, a self-mistrust, a vulgar spirit which laughs at every high ideal, until at last the hypnotized child is blinded to the presence of any beauty or nobility in life. No country can ever hope to rise beyond a vulgar mediocrity where there is not unbounded confidence in what its humanity can do. The self-confident American will make a great civilization yet, because he believes with all his heart and soul in the future of his country and in the powers of the American people. What Whitman called their "barbaric yawp" may yet turn into the lordliest speech and thought, but without self-confidence a race will go no whither. If Irish people do not believe they can equal or surpass the stature of any humanity which has been upon the globe, then they had better all emigrate and become servants to some superior race, and leave Ireland to new settlers who may come here with the same high hopes as the Pilgrim Fathers had when they went to America.

We must go on imagining better than the best we know. Even in their ruins now, Greece and Italy seem noble and beautiful with broken pillars and temples made in their day of glory. But before ever there was a white marble temple shining on a hill it shone with a more brilliant beauty in the mind of some artist who designed it. Do many people know how that marvelous Greek civilization spread along the shores of the Mediterranean? Little nations owning hardly more land than would make up an Irish barony sent out colony after colony. The seed of beautiful life they sowed grew and blossomed out into great cities and half-divine civilizations. Italy had a later blossoming of beauty in the Middle Ages, and travelers today go into little Italian towns and find them filled with masterpieces of painting and architecture and sculpture, witnesses of a time when nations no larger than an Irish county rolled their thoughts up to Heaven and miked their imagination with the angels. Can we be contented in Ireland with the mean streets of our country towns and the sordid heaps of our villages dominated in their economics by the vendors of alcohol, and inspired as to their ideals by the vendors of political animosities?

I would not mind people fighting in a passion to get rid of all that barred some lordly scheme of life, but quarrels over political bones from which there is little or nothing wholesome to be picked only disgust. People tell me that the countryside must always be stupid and backward, and I get angry, as if it were said that only townspeople had immortal souls, and it was only in the city that the flame of divinity breathed into the first men had any unobscured glow. The countryside in Ireland could blossom into as much beauty as the hillsides in mediaeval Italy if we could but get rid of our self-mistrust. We have all that any race ever had to inspire them, the heavens overhead, the earth underneath, and the breath of life in our nostrils. I would like to exile the man who would set limits to what we can do, who would take the crown and sceptre from the human will and say, marking out some petty enterprise as the limit-- "Thus far can we go and no farther, and here shall our life be stayed." Therefore I hate to hear of stagnant societies who think because they have made butter well that they have crowned their parochial generation with a halo of glory, and can rest content with the fame of it all, listening to the whirr of the steam separators and pouching in peace of mind the extra penny a gallon for their milk. And I dislike the little groups who meet a couple of times a year and call themselves co-operators because they have got their fertilizers more cheaply, and have done nothing else. Why, the village gombeen man has done more than that! He has at least brought most of the necessaries of life there by his activities; and I say if we co-operators do not aim at doing more than the Irish Scribes and Pharisees we shall have little to be proud of. A poet, interpreting the words of Christ to His followers, who had scorned the followers of the old order, made Him say:

> Scorn ye their hopes, their tears, their inward prayers?
> I say unto you, see that your souls live
> A deeper life than theirs.

The co-operative movement is delivering over the shaping of the rural life of Ireland, and the building up of its rural civilization, into the hands of Irish farmers. The old order of things has left Ireland unlovely. But if we do not passionately strive to build it better, better for the men, for the women, for the children, of what worth are we? We continually come across the phrase "the dull Saxon" in our Irish papers, it crops up in the speeches of our public orators, but it was an English poet who said:

> I will not cease from mental fight,
> Nor shall my sword sleep in my hand
> Till we have built Jerusalem
> In England's green and pleasant land.

And it was the last great, poet England has produced, who had so much hope for humanity in his country that in his latest song he could mix earth with heaven, and say that to human eyes:

> Shall shine the traffic of Jacob's ladder
> Hung betwixt Heaven and Charing Cross.

Shall we think more meanly of the future of Ireland than these "dull Saxons" think of the future of their island? Shall we be content with humble crumbs fallen from the table of life, and sit like beggars waiting only for what the commonwealth can do for us, leaving all high hopes and aims to our rulers, whether they be English or Irish? Every people get the kind of Government they deserve. A nation can exhibit no greater political wisdom in the mass than it generates in its units. It is the pregnant idealism of the multitude which gives power to the makers of great nations, otherwise the prophets of civilization are helpless as preachers in the desert and solitary places. So I have always preached self-help above all other kinds of help, knowing that if we strove passionately after this righteousness all other kinds of help would be at our service. So, too, I would brush aside the officious interferer in co-operative affairs, who would offer on behalf of the State to do for us what we should, and could, do far better ourselves. We can build up a rural civilization in Ireland, shaping it to our hearts' desires, warming it with life, but our rulers and officials can never be warmer than a stepfather, and have no "large, divine, and comfortable words" for us; they tinker at the body when it is the soul which requires to be healed and made whole. The soul of Ireland has to be kindled, and it can be kindled only by the thought of great deeds and not by the hope of petty parsimonies or petty gains.

Now, great deeds are never done vicariously. They are done directly and personally. No country has grown to greatness mainly by the acts of some great ruler, but by the aggregate activities of all its people. Therefore, every Irish community should make its own ideals and should work for them. As great work can be done in a parish as in the legislative assemblies with a nation at gaze. Do people say: "It is easier to work well with a nation at gaze?" I answer that true greatness becomes the North Pole of humanity, and when it appears all the needles of Being point to it. You of the young generation, who have not yet lost the generous ardour of youth, believe it is as possible to do great work and make noble sacrifices, and to roll the acceptable smoke of offering to Heaven by your work in an Irish parish, as in any city in the world. Like the Greek architects--who saw in their dreams hills crowned with white marble pillared palaces and images of beauty, until these rose up in actuality--so should you, not forgetting national ideals, still most of all set before yourselves the ideal of your own neighborhood. How can you speak of working for all Ireland, which you have not seen, if you do not labor and dream for the Ireland before your eyes, which you see as you look out of your own door in the morning, and on which you walk up and down through the day?

"What dream shall we dream or what labor shall we undertake?" you may ask, and it is right that those who exhort should be asked in what manner and how precisely they would have the listener act or think. I answer: the first thing to do is to create and realize the feeling for the community, and break up the evil and petty isolation of man from man. This can be done by every kind of co-operative effort where combined action is better than individual action. The parish cannot take care of the child as well as the parents, but you will find in most of the labors of life combined action is more fruitful than individual action. Some of you have found this out in many branches of agriculture, of which your dairying, agricultural, credit, poultry, and flax societies are witness. Some of you have combined to manufacture; some to buy in common, some to sell in common. Some of you have the common ownership of thousands of pounds' worth of expensive machinery. Some of you have carried the idea of co-operation for economic ends farther, and have used the power which combination gives you to erect village halls and to have libraries of books, the windows through which the life and wonder and power of humanity can be seen. Some of you have light-heartedly, in the growing sympathy of unity, revived the dances and songs and sports which are the right relaxation of labor. Some Irishwomen here and there have heard beyond the four walls in which so much of their lives are spent the music of a new day, and have started out to help and inspire the men and be good comrades to them; and calling themselves United Irish-women, they have joined, as men have joined, to help their sisters who are in economic servitude, or who suffer from the ignorance and indifference to their special needs in life which pervade the administration of local government. We cannot build up a rural civilization in Ireland without the aid of Irish women. It will help life little if we have methods of the twentieth century in the fields, and those of the fifth century in the home. A great writer said: "Woman is the last thing man will civilize." If a woman had written on that subject she would have said: "Woman is the last thing a man thinks about when he is building up his empires." It is true that the consciousness of woman has been always centered too close to the dark and obscure roots of the Tree of Life, while men have branched out more to the sun an wind, and today the starved soul of womanhood is crying out over the world for an intellectual life and for more chance of earning a living. If Ireland will not listen to this cry, its daughters will go on slipping silently away to other countries, as they have been doing--all the best of them, all the bravest, all those most mentally alive, all those who would have made the best wives and the best mothers--and they will leave at home the timid, the stupid and the dull to help in the deterioration of the race and to breed sons as sluggish as themselves. In the New World women have taken an important part in the work of the National Grange, the greatest agency in bettering the economic and social conditions of the agricultural population in the States. In Ireland the women must be welcomed into the work of building up a rural civilization, and be aided by men in the promotion of those industries with which women have been immemorially associated. We should not want to see women separated from the activities and ideals and inspirations of men. We should want to see them working together and in harmony. If the women carry on their work in connection with the associations by which men earn their living they will have a greater certainty of permanence. I have seen too many little industries and little associations of women workers spring up and perish in Ireland, which depended on the efforts of some one person who had not drunk of the elixir of immortal youth, and could not always continue the work she started; and I have come to the conclusion that the women's organizations must be connected with the men's organizations, must use their premises, village halls, and rooms for women's meetings. I do not believe women's work can be promoted so well in any other way. Men and women have been companions in the world from the dawn of time. I do not know where they are journeying to, but I believe they will never get to the Delectable City if they journey apart from each other, and do not share each other's burdens. Working so, we create the conditions in which the spirit of the community grows strong. We create the true communal idea, which the Socialists miss in their dream of a vast amalgamation of whole nationalities in one great commercial undertaking. The true idea of the clan or commune or tribe is to have in it as many people as will give it strength and importance, and so few people that a personal tie may be established between them. Humanity has always grouped itself instinctively in this way. It did so in the ancient clans and rural communes, and it does so in the parishes and co-operative associations. If they were larger they would lose the sense of unity. If they were smaller they would be too feeble for effectual work, and could not take over the affairs of their district. A rural commune or co-operative community ought to have, to a large extent, the character of a nation. It should manufacture for its members all things which it profitably can manufacture for them, employing its own workmen, carpenters, bootmakers, makers and menders of farming equipment, saddlery, harness, etc. It should aim at feeding its members and their families cheaply and well, as far as possible, out of the meat and grain produced in the district. It should have a mill to grind their grain, a creamery to manufacture their butter; or where certain enterprises like a bacon factory are too great for it, it should unite with other co-operative communities to furnish out such an enterprise. It should sell for the members their produce, and buy for them their requirements, and hold for them labor-saving machinery. It should put aside a certain portion of its profits every year for the creation of halls, libraries, places for recreation and games, and it should pursue this plan steadily with the purpose of giving its members every social and educational advantage which the civilization of their time affords. It should have its councils or village parliaments, where improvements and new ventures could be discussed. Such a community would soon generate a passionate devotion to its own ideals and interests among the members, who would feel how their fortunes rose with the fortunes of the associations of which they were all members. It would kindle and quicken the intellect of every person in the community. It would create the atmosphere in which national genius would emerge and find opportunities for its activity. The clan ought to be the antechamber of the nation and the training ground for its statesmen. What opportunity leadership in the councils of such a rural community would give to the best minds! The man of social genius at present finds an unorganized community, and he does not know how to affect his fellow-citizens. A man might easily despair of affecting the destinies of a nation of forty million people, but yet start with eagerness to build up a kingdom of the size of Sligo, and shape it nearer to the heart's desire. The organization of the rural population of Ireland in co-operative associations will provide the instrument ready to the hand of the social reformer.

Some associations will be more dowered with ability than others, but one will learn from another, and a vast network of living, progressive organizations will cover rural Ireland, democratic in constitution and governed by the aristocracy of intellect and character.

Such associations would have great economic advantages in that they would be self-reliant and self-contained, and would be less subject to fluctuation in their prosperity brought about by national disasters and commercial crises than the present unorganized rural communities are. They would have all their business under local control; and, aiming at feeding, clothing, and manufacturing locally from local resources as far as possible, the slumps in foreign trade, the shortage in supplies, the dislocations of commerce would affect them but little. They would make the community wealthier. Every step towards this organization already taken in Ireland has brought with it increased prosperity, and the towns benefit by increased purchasing power on the part of these rural associations. New arts and industries would spring up under the aegis of the local associations. Here we should find the weaving of rugs, there the manufacture of toys, elsewhere the women would be engaged in embroidery or lace-making, and, perhaps, everywhere we might get a revival of the old local industry of weaving homespuns. We are dreaming of nothing impossible, nothing which has not been done somewhere already, nothing which we could not do here in Ireland. True, it cannot be done all at once, but if we get the idea clearly in our minds of the building up of a rural civilization in Ireland, we can labor at it with the grand persistence of medieval burghers in their little towns, where one generation laid down the foundations of a great cathedral, and saw only in hope and faith the gorgeous glooms over altar and sanctuary, and the blaze and flame of stained glass, where apostles, prophets, and angelic presences were pictured in fire: and the next generation raised high the walls, and only the third generation saw the realization of what their grandsires had dreamed. We in Ireland should not live only from day to day, for the day only, like the beasts in the field, but should think of where all this long cavalcade of the Gael is tending, and how and in what manner their tents will be pitched in the evening of their generation. A national purpose is the most unconquerable and victorious of all things on earth. It can raise up Babylons from the sands of the desert, and make imperial civilizations spring from out a score of huts, and after it has wrought its will it can leave monuments that seem as everlasting a portion of nature as the rocks. The Pyramids and the Sphinx in the sands of Egypt have seemed to humanity for centuries as much a portion of nature as Erigal, or Benbulben, or Slieve Gullion have seemed a portion of nature to our eyes in Ireland.

We must have some purpose or plan in building up an Irish civilization. No artist takes up his paints and brushes and begins to work on his canvas without a clear idea burning in his brain of what he has to do, else were his work all smudges. Does anyone think that out of all these little cabins and farmhouses dotting the green of Ireland there will come harmonious effort to a common end without organization and set purpose? The idea and plan of a great rural civilization must shine like a burning lamp in the imagination of the youth of Ireland, or we shall only be at cross- purposes and end in little fatuities. We are very fond in Ireland of talking of Ireland a nation. The word "nation" has a kind of satisfying sound, but I am afraid it is an empty word with no rich significance to most who use it. The word "laboratory" has as fine a sound, but only the practical scientist has a true conception of what may take place there, what roar of strange forces, what mingling of subtle elements, what mystery and magnificence in atomic life. The word without the idea is like the purse without the coin, the skull without the soul, or any other sham or empty deceit. Nations are not built up by the repetition of words, but by the organizing of intellectual forces. If any of my readers would like to know what kind of thought goes to the building up of a great nation, let him read the life of Alexander Hamilton by Oliver. To that extraordinary man the United States owe their constitution, almost their existence. To him, far more than to Washington, the idea, plan, shape of all that marvelous dominion owes its origin and character. He seemed to hold in his brain, while America was yet a group of half-barbaric settlements, the idea of what it might become. He laid down the plans, the constitution, the foreign policy, the trade policy, the relation of State to State, and it is only within the last few years almost, that America has realized that she had in Hamilton a supreme political and social intelligence, the true fountain-head of what she has since become.

We have not half a continent to deal with, but size matters nothing. The Russian Empire, which covers half Europe, and stretches over the Ural Mountains to the Pacific, would weigh light as a feather in the balance if we compare its services to humanity with those of the little State of Attica, which was no larger than Tipperary. Every State which has come to command the admiration of the world has had clearly conceived ideals which it realized before it went the way which all empires, even the greatest, must go; becoming finally a legend, a fable, or a symbol. We have to lay down the foundations of a new social order in Ireland, and, if the possibilities of it are realized, our thousand years of sorrow and darkness may be followed by as long a cycle of happy effort and ever-growing prosperity. We shall want all these plans whether we are ruled from Westminster or College Green. Without an imaginative conception of what kind of civilization we wish to create, the best government from either quarter will never avail to lift us beyond national mediocrity. I write for those who have joined the ranks of the co-operators without perhaps realizing all that the movement meant, or all that it tended to. Because we hold in our hearts and keep holy there the vision of a great future, I have fought passionately for the entire freedom of our movement from external control, lest the meddling of politicians or official persons without any inspiration should deflect, for some petty purpose or official gratification, the strength of that current which was flowing and gathering strength unto the realization of great ideals. Every country has its proportion of little souls which could find ample room on a threepenny bit, and be majestically housed in a thimble, who follow out some little minute practice in an ecstasy of self-satisfaction, seeking some little job which is the El Dorado of their desires as if there were naught else, as if humanity were not going from the Great Deep to the Great Deep of Deity, with wind and water, fire and earth, stars and sun, lordly companions for it on its path to a divine destiny. We have our share of these in Ireland in high and low places, but I do not write for them. This essay is for those who are working at laying deep the foundations of a new social order, to hearten them with some thought of what their labor may bring to Ireland. I welcome to this work the United Irishwomen. As one of their poetesses has said in a beautiful song, the services of women to Ireland in the past have been the services of mourners to the stricken. But for today and tomorrow we need hope and courage and gaiety, and I repeat for them the last passionate words of her verse:

Rise to your feet, O daughters, rise,
Our mother still is young and fair.
Let the world look into your eyes
And see her beauty shining there.
Grant of that beauty but one ray,
Heroes shall leap from every hill;
Today shall be as yesterday,
The red blood burns in Ireland still.

THOUGHTS FOR A CONVENTION

1. There are moments in history when by the urgency of circumstance everyone in a country is drawn from normal pursuits to consider the affairs of the nation. The merchant is turned from his warehouse, the bookman from his books, the farmer from his fields, because they realize that the very foundations of the society, under whose shelter they were able to carry on their avocation, are being shaken, and they can no longer be voiceless, or leave it to deputies, unadvised by them, to arrange national destinies. We are all accustomed to endure the annoyances and irritations caused by legislation which is not agreeable to us, and solace ourselves by remembering that the things which really matter are not affected. But when the destiny of a nation, the principles by which life is to be guided are at stake, all are on a level, are equally affected and are bound to give expression to their opinions. Ireland is in one of these moments of history. Circumstances with which we are all familiar and the fever in which the world exists have infected it, and it is like molten metal the skilled political artificer might pour into a desirable mould. But if it is not handled rightly, if any factor is ignored, there may be an explosion which would bring on us a fate as tragic as anything in our past history. Irishmen can no longer afford to remain aloof from each other, or to address each other distantly and defiantly from press or platform, but must strive to understand each other truly, and to give due weight to each other's opinions, and, if possible, arrive at a compromise, a balancing of their diversities, which may save our country from anarchy and chaos for generations to come.

2. An agreement about Irish Government must be an agreement, not between two but three Irish parties first of all, and afterwards with Great Britain. The Premier of a Coalition Cabinet has declared that there is no measure of self government which Great Britain would not assent to being set up in Ireland, if Irishmen

themselves could but come to an agreement. Before such a compromise between Irish parties is possible there must be a clear understanding of the ideals of these parties, as they are understood by themselves, and not as they are presented in party controversy by special pleaders whose object too often is to pervert or discredit the principles and actions of opponents, a thing which is easy to do because all parties, even the noblest, have followers who do them disservice by ignorant advocacy or excited action. If we are to unite Ireland we can only do so by recognizing what truly are the principles each party stands for, and will not forsake, and for which, if necessary they will risk life. True understanding is to see ideas as they are held by men between themselves and Heaven; and in this mood I will try, first of all, to understand the position of Unionists, Sinn Feiners and Constitutional Nationalists as they have been explained to me by the best minds among them, those who have induced others of their countrymen to accept those ideals. When this is done we will see if compromise, a balancing of diversities be not possible in an Irish State where all that is essential in these varied ideals may be harmonized and retained.

3. I will take first of all the position of Unionists. They are, many of them, the descendants of settlers who by their entrance into Ireland broke up the Gaelic uniformity and introduced the speech, the thoughts, characteristic of another race. While they have grown to love their country as much as any of Gaelic origin, and their peculiarities have been modified by centuries of life in Ireland and by inter-marriage, so that they are much more akin to their fellow-countrymen in mind and manner than they are to any other people, they still retain habits, beliefs and traditions from which they will not part. They form a class economically powerful. They have openness and energy of character, great organizing power and a mastery over materials, all qualities invaluable in an Irish State. In North-East Ulster, where they are most homogeneous they conduct the affairs of their cities with great efficiency, carrying on an international trade not only with Great Britain but with the rest of the world. They have made these industries famous. They believe that their prosperity is in large measure due to their acceptance of the Union, that it would be lessened if they threw in their lot with the other Ireland and accepted its ideals, that business which now goes to their shipyards and factories would cease if they were absorbed in a self-governing Ireland whose spokesmen had an unfortunate habit of nagging their neighbors and of conveying the impression that they are in-

spired by race hatred. They believe that an Irish legislature would be controlled by a majority, representatives mainly of small farmers, men who had no knowledge of affairs, or of the peculiar needs of Ulster industry, or the intricacy of the problems involved in carrying on an international trade; that the religious ideas of the majority would be so favored in education and government that the favoritism would amount to religious oppression. They are also convinced that no small country in the present state of the world can really be independent, that such only exist by sufferance of their mighty neighbors, and must be subservient in trade policy and military policy to retain even a nominal freedom; and that an independent Ireland would by its position be a focus for the intrigues of powers hostile to Great Britain, and if it achieved independence Great Britain in self protection would be forced to conquer it again. They consider that security for industry and freedom for the individual can best be preserved in Ireland by the maintenance of the Union, and that the world spirit is with the great empires.

4. The second political group may be described as the spiritual inheritors of the more ancient race in Ireland. They regard the preservation of their nationality as a sacred charge, themselves as a conquered people owing no allegiance to the dominant race. They cannot be called traitors to it because neither they nor their predecessors have ever admitted the right of another people to govern them against their will. They are inspired by an ancient history, a literature stretching beyond the Christian era, a national culture and distinct national ideals which they desire to manifest in a civilization which shall not be an echo or imitation of any other. While they do not depreciate the worth of English culture or its political system they are as angry at its being imposed on them as a young man with a passion for art would be if his guardian insisted on his adopting another profession and denied him any chance of manifesting his own genius. Few hatreds equal those caused by the denial or obstruction of national aptitudes. Many of those who fought in the last Irish insurrection were fighters not merely for a political change but were rather desperate and despairing champions of a culture which they held was being stifled from infancy in Irish children in the schools of the nation. They believe that the national genius cannot manifest itself in a civilization and is not allowed to manifest itself while the Union persists. They wish Ireland to be as much itself as Japan, and as free to make its own choice of political principles, its culture and social or-

der, and to develop its industries unfettered by the trade policy of their neighbors. Their mood is unconquerable, and while often overcome it has emerged again and again in Irish history, and it has perhaps more adherents today than at any period since the Act of Union, and this has been helped on by the incarnation of the Gaelic spirit in the modem Anglo-Irish literature, and a host of brilliant poets, dramatists and prose writers who have won international recognition, and have increased the dignity of spirit and the self-respect of the followers of this tradition. They assert that the Union kills the soul of the people; that empires do not permit the intensive cultivation of human life: that they destroy the richness and variety of existence by the extinction of peculiar and unique gifts, and the substitution therefor of a culture which has its value mainly for the people who created it, but is as alien to our race as the mood of the scientist is to the artist or poet.

5. The third group occupies a middle position between those who desire the perfecting of the Union and those whose claim is for complete independence: and because they occupy a middle position, and have taken coloring from the extremes between which they exist they have been exposed to the charge of insincerity, which is unjust so far as the best minds among them are concerned. They have aimed at a middle course, not going far enough on one side or another to secure the confidence of the extremists. They have sought to maintain the connection with the empire, and at the same time to acquire an Irish control over administration and legislation. They have been more practical than ideal, and to their credit must be placed the organizing of the movements which secured most of the reforms in Ireland since the Union, such as religious equality, the acts securing to farmers fair rents and fixity of tenure, the wise and salutary measures making possible the transfer of land from landlord to tenant, facilities for education at popular universities, the laborers' acts and many others. They are a practical party taking what they could get, and because they could show ostensible results they have had a greater following in Ireland than any other party. This is natural because the average man in all countries is a realist. But this reliance on material results to secure support meant that they must always show results, or the minds of their countrymen veered to those ultimates and fundamentals which await settlement here as they do in all civilizations. As in the race with Atalanta the golden apples had to be thrown in order to win the race. The intellect of Ireland is now fixed on fundamentals, and the

compromise this middle party is able to offer does not make provision for the ideals of either of the extremists, and indeed meets little favor anywhere in a country excited by recent events in world history, where revolutionary changes are expected and a settlement far more in accord with fundamental principles.

6. It is possible that many of the rank and file of these parties will not at first agree with the portraits painted of their opponents, and that is because the special pleaders of the press, who in Ireland are, as a rule, allowed little freedom to state private convictions, have come to regard themselves as barristers paid to conduct a case, and have acquired the habit of isolating particular events, the hasty speech or violent action of individuals in localities, and of exhibiting these as indicating the whole character of the party attacked. They misrepresent Irishmen to each other. The Ulster advocates of the Union, for example, are accustomed to hear from their advisers that the favorite employment of Irish farmers in the three southern provinces is cattle driving, if not worse. They are told that Protestants in these provinces live in fear of their lives, whereas anybody who has knowledge of the true conditions knows that, so far from being riotous and unbusinesslike, the farmers in these provinces have developed a net-work of rural associations, dairies, bacon factories, agricultural and poultry societies, etc., doing their business efficiently, applying the teachings of science in their factories, competing in quality of output with the very best of the same class of society in Ulster and obtaining as good prices in the same market. As a matter of fact this method of organization now largely adopted by Ulster farmers was initiated in the South. With regard to the charge of intolerance I do not believe it. Here, as in all other countries, there are unfortunate souls obsessed by dark powers, whose human malignity takes the form of religious hatreds, but I believe, and the thousands of Irish Protestants in the Southern Counties will affirm it as true that they have nothing to complain of in this respect. I am sure that in this matter of religious tolerance these provinces can stand favorable comparison with any country in the world where there are varieties of religions, even with Great Britain. I would plead with my Ulster compatriots not to gaze too long or too credulously into that distorting mirror held up to them, nor be tempted to take individual action as representative of the mass. How would they like to have the depth or quality of spiritual life in their great city represented by the scrawlings and revilings about the head of the Catholic Church to be found occasionally on the

blank walls of Belfast. If the same method of distortion by selection of facts was carried out there is not a single city or nation which could not be made to appear baser than Sodom or Gomorrah and as deserving of their fate.

7. The Ulster character is better appreciated by Southern Ireland, and there is little reason to vindicate it against any charges except the slander that Ulster Unionists do not regard themselves as Irishmen, and that they have no love for their own country. Their position is that they are Unionists, not merely because it is for the good of Great Britain, but because they hold it to be for the good of Ireland, and it is the Irish argument weighs with them, and if they were convinced it would be better for Ireland to be self-governed they would throw in their lot with the rest of Ireland, which would accept them gladly and greet them as a prodigal son who had returned, having made, unlike most prodigal sons, a fortune, and well able to be the wisest adviser in family affairs. It is necessary to preface what I have to say by way of argument or remonstrance to Irish parties by words making it clear that I write without prejudice against any party, and that I do not in the least underestimate their good qualities or the weight to be attached to their opinions and ideals. It is the traditional Irish way, which we have too often forgotten, to notice the good in the opponent before battling with what is evil. So Maeve, the ancient Queen of Connacht, looking over the walls of her city of Cruachan at the Ulster foemen, said of them, "Noble and regal is their appearance," and her own followers said, "Noble and regal are those of whom you speak." When we lost the old Irish culture we lost the tradition of courtesy to each other which lessens the difficulties of life and makes it possible to conduct controversy without creating bitter memories.

8. I desire first to argue with Irish Unionists whether it is accurate to say of them, as it would appear to be from their spokesmen, that the principle of nationality cannot be recognized by them or allowed to take root in the commonwealth of dominions which form the Empire. Must one culture only exist? Must all citizens have their minds poured into the same mould, and varieties of gifts and cultural traditions be extinguished? What would India with its myriad races say to that theory? What would Canada enclosing in its dominion and cherishing a French Canadian nation say? Unionists have by every means in their power discouraged the study of the national literature of Ireland though it is one of the most ancient in Europe, though the scholars of France and Germany have founded journals for its

study, and its beauty is being recognized by all who have read it. It contains the race memory of Ireland, its imaginations and thoughts for two thousand years. Must that be obliterated? Must national character be sterilized of all taint of its peculiar beauty? Must Ireland have no character of its own but be servilely imitative of its neighbor in all things and be nothing of itself? It is objected that the study of Irish history, Irish literature and the national culture generates hostility to the Empire. Is that a true psychological analysis? Is it not true in all human happenings that if people are denied what is right and natural they will instantly assume an attitude of hostility to the power which denies? The hostility is not inherent in the subject but is evoked by the denial. I put it to my Unionist compatriots that the ideal is to aim at a diversity of culture, and the greatest freedom, richness and variety of thought. The more this richness and variety prevail in a nation the less likelihood is there of the tyranny of one culture over the rest. We should aim in Ireland at that freedom of the ancient Athenians, who, as Pericles said, listened gladly to the opinions of others and did not turn sour faces on those who disagreed with them. A culture which is allowed essential freedom to develop will soon perish if it does not in itself contain the elements of human worth which make for immortality. The world has to its sorrow many instances of freak religions which were persecuted and by natural opposition were perpetuated and hardened in belief. We should allow the greatest freedom in respect of cultural developments in Ireland so that the best may triumph by reason of superior beauty and not because the police are relied upon to maintain one culture in a dominant position.

9. I have also an argument to address to the extremists whose claim, uttered lately with more openness and vehemence, is for the complete independence of the whole of Ireland, who cry out against partition, who will not have a square mile of Irish soil subject to foreign rule. That implies they desire the inclusion of Ulster and the inhabitants of Ulster in their Irish State. I tell them frankly that if they expect Ulster to throw its lot in with a self-governing Ireland they must remain within the commonwealth of dominions which constitute the Empire, be prepared loyally, once Ireland has complete control over its internal affairs, to accept the status of a dominion and the responsibilities of that wider union. If they will not accept that status as the Boers did, they will never draw that important and powerful Irish party into an Irish State except by force, and do they think there is any possibility

of that? It is extremely doubtful whether if the world stood aloof, and allowed Irishmen to fight out their own quarrels among themselves, that the fighters for complete independence could conquer a community so numerous, so determined, so wealthy, so much more capable of providing for themselves the plentiful munitions by which alone one army can hope to conquer another. In South Africa men who had fiercer traditional hostilities than Irishmen of different parties here have had, who belonged to different races, who had a few years before been engaged in a racial war, were great enough to rise above these past antagonisms, to make an agreement and abide faithfully by it. Is the same magnanimity not possible in Ireland? I say to my countrymen who cry out for the complete separation of Ireland from the Empire, that they will not in this generation bring with them the most powerful and wealthy, if not the most numerous, party in their country. Complete control of Irish affairs is a possibility, and I suggest to the extremists that the status of a self-governing dominion inside a federation of dominions is a proposal which, if other safeguards for minority interests are incorporated, would attract Unionist attention. But if these men who depend so much in their economic enterprises upon a friendly relation with their largest customers are to be allured into self-governing Ireland there must be acceptance of the Empire as an essential condition. The Boers found it not impossible to accept this status for the sake of a United South Africa. Are our Irish Boers not prepared to make a compromise and abide by it loyally for the sake of a United Ireland?

10. A remonstrance must also be addressed to the middle party in that it has made no real effort to understand and conciliate the feelings of Irish Unionists. They have indeed made promises, no doubt sincerely, but they have undone the effect of all they said by encouraging of recent years the growth of sectarian organizations with political aims and have relied on these as on a party machine. It may be said that in Ulster a similar organization, sectarian with political objects, has long existed, and that this justified a counter organization. Both in my opinion are unjustifiable and evil, but the backing of such an organization was specially foolish in the case of the majority, whose main object ought to be to allure the minority into the same political fold. The baser elements in society, the intriguers, the job seekers, and all who would acquire by influence what they cannot attain by merit, flock into such bodies, and create a sinister impression as to their objects and de-

liberations. If we are to have national concord among Irishmen religion must be left to the Churches whose duty it is to promote it, and be dissevered from party politics, and it should be regarded as contrary to national idealism to organize men of one religion into secret societies with political or economic aims. So shall be left to Caesar the realm which is Caesar's, and it shall not appear part of the politics of eternity that Michael's sister's son obtains a particular post beginning at thirty shillings a week. I am not certain that it should not be an essential condition of any Irish settlement that all such sectarian organizations should be disbanded in so far as their objects are political, and remain solely as friendly societies. It is useless assuring a minority already suspicious, of the tolerance it may expect from the majority, if the party machine of the majority is sectarian and semi-secret, if no one of the religion of the minority can join it. I believe in spite of the recent growth of sectarian societies that it has affected but little the general tolerant spirit in Ireland, and where the evils have appeared they have speedily resulted in the break up of the organization in the locality. Irishmen individually as a rule are much nobler in spirit than the political organizations they belong to.

11. It is necessary to speak with the utmost frankness and not to slur over any real difficulty in the way of a settlement. Irish parties must rise above themselves if they are to bring about an Irish unity. They appear on the surface irreconcilable, but that, in my opinion, is because the spokesmen of parties are under the illusion that they should never indicate in public that they might possibly abate one jot of the claims of their party. A crowd or organization is often more extreme than its individual members. I have spoken to Unionists and Sinn Feiners and find them as reasonable in private as they are unreasonable in public. I am convinced that an immense relief would be felt by all Irishmen if a real settlement of the Irish question could be arrived at, a compromise which would reconcile them to living under one government, and would at the same time enable us to live at peace with our neighbors. The suggestions which follow were the result of discussions between a group of Unionists, Nationalists and Sinn Feiners, and as they found it possible to agree upon a compromise it is hoped that the policy which harmonized their diversities may help to bring about a similar result in Ireland.

12. I may now turn to consider the Anglo-Irish problem and to make specific suggestions for its solution and the character of the government to be established in

Ireland. The factors are triple. There is first the desire many centuries old of Irish nationalists for self-government and the political unity of the people: secondly, there is the problem of the Unionists who require that the self- governing Ireland they enter shall be friendly to the imperial connection, and that their religious and economic interests shall be safeguarded by real and not merely by verbal guarantees; and, thirdly, there is the position of Great Britain which requires, reasonably enough, that any self-governing dominion set up alongside it shall be friendly to the Empire. In this matter Great Britain has priority of claim to consideration, for it has first proposed a solution, the Home Rule Act which is on the Statute Book, though later variants of that have been outlined because of the attitude of Unionists in North-East Ulster, variants which suggest the partition of Ireland, the elimination of six counties from the area controlled by the Irish government. This Act, or the variants of it offered to Ireland, is the British contribution to the settlement of the Anglo-Irish problem.

13. If it is believed that this scheme, or any diminutive of it, will settle the Anglo-Irish problem, British statesmen and people who trust them are only preparing for themselves bitter disappointment. I believe that nothing less than complete self-government has ever been the object of Irish Nationalism. However ready certain sections have been to accept installments, no Irish political leader had authority to pledge his countrymen to ever accept a half measure as a final settlement of the Irish claim. The Home Rule Act, if put into operation tomorrow, even if Ulster were cajoled or coerced into accepting it, would not be regarded by Irish Nationalists as a final settlement, no matter what may be said at Westminster. Nowhere in Ireland has it been accepted as final. Received without enthusiasm at first, every year which has passed since the Bill was introduced has seen the system of self-government formulated there subjected to more acute and hostile criticism: and I believe it would be perfectly accurate to say that its passing tomorrow would only be the preliminary for another agitation, made fiercer by the unrest of the world, where revolutions and the upsetting of dynasties are in the air, and where the claims of nationalities no more ancient than the Irish, like the Poles, the Finns, and the Arabs, to political freedom are admitted by the spokesmen of the great powers, Great Britain included, or are already conceded. If any partition of Ireland is contemplated this will intensify the bitterness now existing. I believe it is to the

interest of Great Britain to settle the Anglo-Irish dispute. It has been countered in many of its policies in America and the Colonies by the vengeful feelings of Irish exiles. There may yet come a time when the refusal of the Irish mouse to gnaw at a net spread about the lion may bring about the downfall of the Empire. It cannot be to the interest of Great Britain to have on its flank some millions of people who, whenever Great Britain is engaged in a war which threatens its existence, feel a thrill running through them, as prisoners do hearing the guns sounding closer of an army which comes, as they think, to liberate them. Nations denied essential freedom ever feel like that when the power which dominates them is itself in peril. Who can doubt but for the creation of Dominion Government in South Africa that the present war would have found the Boers thirsty for revenge, and the Home Government incapable of dealing with a distant people who taxed its resources but a few years previously. I have no doubt that if Ireland was granted the essential freedom and wholeness in its political life it desires, its mood also would be turned. I have no feelings of race hatred, no exultation in thought of the downfall of any race; but as a close observer of the mood of millions in Ireland, I feel certain that if their claim is not met they will brood and scheme and Wait to strike a blow, though the dream may be handed on from them to their children and their children's children, yet they will hope, sometime, to give the last vengeful thrust of enmity at the stricken heart of the Empire.

14. Any measure which is not a settlement which leaves Ireland still actively discontented is a waste of effort, and the sooner English statesmen realize the futility of half measures the better. A man who claims a debt he believes is due to him, who is offered half of it in payment, is not going to be conciliated or to be one iota more friendly, if he knows that the other is able to pay the full amount and it could be yielded without detriment to the donor. Ireland will never be content with a system of self-government which lessens its representation in the Imperial Parliament, and still retains for that Parliament control over all-important matters like taxation and trade policy. Whoever controls these controls the character of an Irish civilization, and the demand of Ireland is not merely for administrative powers, but the power to fashion its own national policy, and to build up a civilization of its own with an economic character in keeping by self-devised and self- checked efforts. To misunderstand this is to suppose there is no such thing as national ideal-

ism, and that a people will accept substitutes for the principle of nationality, whereas the past history of the world and present circumstance in Europe are evidence that nothing is more unconquerable and immortal than national feeling, and that it emerges from centuries of alien government, and is ready at any time to flare out in insurrection. At no period in Irish history was that sentiment more self-conscious than it is today.

15. Nationalist Ireland requires that the Home Rule Act should be radically changed to give Ireland unfettered control over taxation, customs, excise and trade policy. These powers are at present denied, and if the Act were in operation, Irish people instead of trying to make the best of it, would begin at once to use whatever powers they had as a lever to gain the desired control, and this would lead to fresh antagonism and a prolonged struggle between the two countries, and in this last effort Irish Nationalists would have the support of that wealthy class now Unionist in the three southern provinces, and also in Ulster if it were included, for they would then desire as much as Nationalists that, while they live in a self- governing Ireland, the powers of the Irish government should be such as would enable it to build up Irish industries by an Irish trade policy, and to impose taxation in a way to suit Irish conditions. As the object of British consent to Irish self-government is to dispose of Irish antagonism nothing is to be gained by passing measures which will not dispose of it. The practically unanimous claim of Nationalists as exhibited in the press in Ireland is for the status and power of economic control possessed by the self- governing dominions. By this alone will the causes of friction between the two nations be removed, and a real solidarity of interest based on a federal union for joint defense of the freedom and well-being of the federated communities be possible and I have no doubt it would take place. I do not believe that hatreds remain for long among people when the causes which created them are removed. We have seen in Europe and in the dominions the continual reversals of feeling which have taken place when a sore has been removed. Antagonisms are replaced by alliances. It is mercifully true of human nature that it prefers to exercise goodwill to hatred when it can, and the common sense of the best in Ireland would operate once there was no longer interference in our internal affairs, to allay and keep in order these turbulent elements which exist in every country, but which only become a danger to society when real grievances based on the violation of true principles of govern-

ment are present.

16. The Union has failed absolutely to conciliate Ireland. Every generation there have been rebellions and shootings and agitations of a vehement and exhausting character carried continually to the point of lawlessness before Irish grievances could be redressed. A form of government which requires a succession of rebellions to secure reforms afterwards admitted to be reasonable cannot be a good form of government. These agitations have inflicted grave material and moral injury on Ireland. The instability of the political system has prejudiced natural economic development. Capital will not be invested in industries where no one is certain about the future. And because the will of the people was so passionately set on political freedom an atmosphere of suspicion gathered around public movements which in other countries would have been allowed to carry on their beneficent work unhindered by any party. Here they were continually being forced to declare themselves either for or against self-government. The long attack on the movement for the organization of Irish agriculture was an instance. Men are elected on public bodies not because they are efficient administrators, but because they can be trusted to pass resolutions favoring one party or another. This has led to corruption. Every conceivable rascality in Ireland has hid itself behind the great names of nation or empire. The least and the most harmless actions of men engaged in philanthropic or educational work or social reform are scrutinized and criticized so as to obstruct good work. If a phrase even suggests the possibility of a political partiality, or a tendency to anything which might be construed by the most suspicious scrutineer to indicate a remote desire to use the work done as an argument either for or against self-government the man or movement is never allowed to forget it. Public service becomes intolerable and often impossible under such conditions, and while the struggle continues this also will continue to the moral detriment of the people. There are only two forms of government possible. A people may either be governed by force or may govern themselves. The dual government of Ireland by two Parliaments, one sitting in Dublin and one in London, contemplated in the Home Rule Act, would be impossible and irritating. Whatever may be said for two bodies each with their spheres of influence clearly defined, there is nothing to be said for two legislatures with concurrent powers of legislation and taxation, and with members from Ireland retained at Westminster to provide some kind of democratic excuse

for the exercise of powers of Irish legislation and taxation by the Parliament at Westminster. The Irish demand is that Great Britain shall throw upon our shoulders the full weight of responsibility for the management of our own affairs, so that we can only blame ourselves and our political guides and not Great Britain if we err in our policies.

17. I have stated what I believe to be sound reasons for the recognition of the justice of the Irish demand by Great Britain and I now turn to Ulster, and ask it whether the unstable condition of things in Ireland does not affect it even more than Great Britain. If it persists in its present attitude, if it remains out of a self- governing Ireland, it will not thereby exempt itself from political, social and economic trouble. Ireland will regard the six Ulster counties as the French have regarded Alsace-Lorraine, whose hopes of reconquest turned Europe into an armed camp, with the endless suspicions, secret treaties, military and naval developments, the expense of maintaining huge armies, and finally the inevitable war. So sure as Ulster remains out, so surely will it become a focus for nationalist designs. I say nothing of the injury to the great wholesale business carried on from its capital city throughout the rest of Ireland where the inevitable and logical answer of merchants in the rest of Ireland to requests for orders will be: "You would die rather than live in the same political house with us. We will die rather than trade with you." There will be lamentably and inevitably a fiercer tone between North and South. Everything that happens in one quarter will be distorted in the other. Each will lie about the other. The materials will exist more than before for civil commotion, and this will be aided by the powerful minority of Nationalists in the excluded counties working in conjunction with their allies across the border. Nothing was ever gained in life by hatred; nothing good ever came of it or could come of it; and the first and most important of all the commandments of the spirit that there should be brotherhood between men will be deliberately broken to the ruin of the spiritual life of Ireland.

18. So far from Irish Nationalists wishing to oppress Ulster, I believe that there is hardly any demand which could be made, even involving democratic injustice to themselves, which would not willingly be granted if their Ulster compatriots would fling their lot in with the rest of Ireland and heal the eternal sore. I ask Ulster what is there that they could not do as efficiently in an Ireland with the status and economic power of a self-governing dominion as they do at present. Could they

not build their ships and sell them, manufacture and export their linens? What do they mean when they say Ulster industries would be taxed? I cannot imagine any Irish taxation which their wildest dreams imagined so heavy as the taxation which they will endure as part of the United Kingdom in future. They will be implicated in all the revolutionary legislation made inevitable in Great Britain by the recoil on society of the munition workers and disbanded conscripts. Ireland, which luckily for itself, has the majority of its population economically independent as workers on the land, and which, in the development of agriculture now made necessary as a result of changes in naval warfare, will be able to absorb without much trouble its returning workers. Ireland will be much quieter, less revolutionary and less expensive to govern. I ask what reason is there to suppose that taxation in a self-governing Ireland would be greater than in Great Britain after the war, or in what way Ulster industries could be singled out, or for what evil purpose by an Irish Parliament? It would be only too anxious rather to develop still further the one great industrial centre in Ireland; and would, it is my firm conviction, allow the representatives of Ulster practically to dictate the industrial policy of Ireland. Has there ever at any time been the slightest opposition by any Irish Nationalist to pro-posals made by Ulster industrialists which would lend color to such a suspicion? Personally, I think that Ulster without safeguards of any kind might trust its fellow-countrymen; the weight, the intelligence, the vigor of character of Ulster people in any case would enable them to dominate Ireland economically. But I do not for a moment say that Ulster is not justified in demanding safeguards. Its leader, speaking at Westminster during one of the debates on the Home Rule Bill, said scornfully, "We do not fear oppressive legislation. We know in fact there would be none. What we do fear is oppressive administration." That I translate to mean that Ulster feels that the policy of the spoils to the victors would be adopted, and that jobbery in Nationalist and Catholic interests would be rampant. There are as many honest Nationalists and Catholics who would object to this as there are Protestant Union-ists, and they would readily accept as part of any settlement the proposal that all posts which can rightly be filled by competitive examination shall only be filled af-ter examination by Irish Civil Service Commissioners, and that this should include all posts paid for out of public funds whether directly under the Irish Government or under County Councils, Urban Councils, Corporations, or Boards of Guardians.

Further, they would allow the Ulster Counties through their members a veto on any important administrative position where the area of the official's operation was largely confined to North-East Ulster, if such posts were of a character which could not rightly be filled after examination and-must needs be a government appointment. I have heard the suspicion expressed that Gaelic might be made a subject compulsory on all candidates, and that this would prejudice the chances of Ulster candidates desirous of entering the Civil Service. Nationalist opinion would readily agree that, if marks were given for Gaelic, an alternative language, such as French or German, should be allowed the candidate as a matter of choice and the marks given be of equal value. By such concession jobbery would be made impossible. The corruption and bribery now prevalent in local government would be a thing of the past. Nationalists and Unionists alike would be assured of honest administration and that merit and efficiency, not membership of some sectarian or political association, would lead to public service.

20. If that would not be regarded as adequate protection Nationalists are ready to consider with friendly minds any other safeguards proposed either by Ulster or Southern Unionists, though in my opinion the less there are formal and legal acknowledgments of differences the better, for it is desirable that Protestant and Catholic, Unionist and Nationalist should meet and redivide along other lines than those of religion or past party politics, and it is obvious that the raising of artificial barriers might perpetuate the present lines of division. A real settlement is impossible without the inclusion of the whole province in the Irish State, and apart from the passionate sentiment existing in Nationalist Ireland for the unity of the whole country there are strong economic bonds between Ulster and the three provinces. Further, the exclusion of all or a large part of Ulster would make the excluded part too predominantly industrial and the rest of Ireland too exclusively agricultural, tending to prevent that right balance between rural and urban industry which all nations should aim at and which makes for a varied intellectual life, social and political wisdom and a healthy national being. Though for the sake of obliteration of past differences I would prefer as little building by legislation of fences isolating one section of the community from another, still I am certain that if Ulster, as the price of coming into a self- governing Ireland, demanded some application of the Swiss Cantonal system to itself which would give it control over local administra-

tion it could have it; or, again, it could be conceded the powers of local control vested in the provincial governments in Canada, where the provincial assemblies have exclusive power to legislate for themselves in respect of local works, municipal institutions, licenses, and administration of justice in the province. Further, subject to certain provisions protecting the interests of different religious bodies, the provincial assemblies have the exclusive power to make laws upon education. Would not this give Ulster all the guarantees for civil and religious liberty it requires? What arguments of theirs, what fears have they expressed which would not be met by such control over local administration? I would prefer that the mind of Ulster should argue its points with the whole of Ireland and press its ideals upon it without reservation of its wisdom for itself. But doubtless if Ulster accepted this proposal it would benefit the rest of Ireland by the model it would set of efficient administration: and it would, I have no doubt, insert in its provincial constitution all the safeguards for minorities there which they would ask should be inserted in any Irish constitution to protect the interest of their co-religionists in that part of Ireland where they are in a minority.

21. I can deal only with fundamentals in this memorandum, because it is upon fundamentals there are differences of thinking. Once these are settled it would be comparatively easy to devise the necessary clauses in an Irish constitution, giving safeguards to England for the due payment of the advances under the Land Acts, and the principles upon which an Irish contribution should be made to the empire for naval and military purposes. It was suggested by Mr. Lionel Curtis in his "Problems of the Commonwealth," that assessors might be appointed by the dominions to fix the fair taxable capacity of each for this purpose. It will be observed that while I have claimed for Ireland the status of a dominion, I have referred solely hitherto to the powers of control over trade policy, customs, excise, taxation and legislation possessed by the dominions, and have not claimed for Ireland the right to have an army or a navy of its own. I recognize that the proximity of the two islands makes it desirable to consolidate the naval power under the control of the Admiralty. The regular army should remain in the same way under the War Office which would have the power of recruiting in Ireland. The Irish Parliament would, I have no doubt, be willing to raise at its own expense under an Irish Territorial Council a Territorial Force similar to that of England but not removable from Ireland. Mili-

tary conscription could never be permitted except by Act of the Irish Parliament. It would be a denial of the first principle of nationality if the power of conscripting the citizens of the country lay not in the hands of the National Parliament but was exercised by another nation.

22. While a self-governing Ireland would contribute money to the defense of the federated empire, it would not be content that that money should be spent on dockyards, arsenals, camps, harbors, naval stations, ship-building and supplies in Great Britain to the almost complete neglect of Ireland as at present. A large contribution for such purposes spent outside Ireland would be an economic drain if not balanced by counter expenditure here. This might be effected by the training of a portion of the navy and army and the Irish regiments of the regular army in Ireland, and their equipment, clothing, supplies, munitions and rations being obtained through an Irish department. Naval dockyards should be constructed here and a proportion of ships built in them. Just as surely as there must be a balance between the imports and exports of a country, so must there be a balance between the revenue raised in a nation and the public expenditure on that nation. Irish economic depression after the Act of Union was due in large measure to absentee landlordism and the expenditure of Irish revenue outside Ireland with no proportionate return. This must not be expected to continue against Irish interests. Ireland, granted the freedom it desires, would be willing to defend its freedom and the freedom of other dominions in the commonwealth of nations it belonged to, but it is not willing to allow millions to be raised in Ireland and spent outside Ireland. If three or five millions are raised in Ireland for imperial purposes and spent in Great Britain it simply means that the vast employment of labor necessitated takes place outside Ireland: whereas if spent here it would mean the employment of many thousands of men, the support of their families, and in the economic chain would follow the support of those who cater for them in food, clothing, housing, etc. Even with the best will in the world, to do its share towards its defense of the freedom it had attained, Ireland could not permit such an economic drain on its resources. No country could approve of a policy which in its application means the emigration of thousands of its people every year while it continued.

23. I believe even if there were no historical basis for Irish nationalism that such claims as I have stated would have become inevitable, because the tendency

of humanity as it develops intellectually and spiritually is to desire more and more freedom, and to substitute more and more an internal law for the external law or government, and that the solidarity of empires or nations will depend not so much upon the close texture of their political organization or the uniformity of mind so engendered as upon the freedom allowed and the delight people feel in that freedom. The more educated a man is the more it is hateful to him to be constrained and the more impossible does it become for central governments to provide by regulation for the infinite variety of desires and cultural developments which spring up everywhere and are in themselves laudable, and in no way endanger the State. A recognition of this has already led to much decentralization in Great Britain itself. And if the claim for more power in the administration of local affairs was so strongly felt in a homogeneous country like Great Britain that, through its county council system, people in districts like Kent or Essex have been permitted control over education and the purchase of land, and the distribution of it to small holders, how much more passionately must this desire for self-control be felt in Ireland where people have a different national character which has survived all the educational experiments to change them into the likeness of their neighbors. The battle which is going on in the world has been stated to be a spiritual conflict between those who desire greater freedom for the individual and think that the State exists to preserve that freedom, and those who believe in the predominance of the state and the complete subjection of the individual to it and the molding of the individual mind in its image. This has been stated, and if the first view is a declaration of ideals sincerely held by Great Britain it would mean the granting to Ireland, a country which has expressed its wishes by vaster majorities than were ever polled in any other country for political changes, the satisfaction of its desires.

24. The acceptance of the proposals here made would mean sacrifices for the two extremes in Ireland, and neither party has as yet made any real sacrifice to meet the other, but each has gone on its own way. I urge upon them that if the suggestions made here were accepted both would obtain substantially what they desire, the Ulster Unionists that safety for their interests and provision for Ireland's unity with the commonwealth of dominions inside the empire; the Nationalists that power they desire to create an Irish civilization by self-devised and self-checked efforts. The brotherhood of domimons of which they would form one would be

inspired as much by the fresh life and wide democratic outlook of Australia, New Zealand, South Africa and Canada, as by the hoarier political wisdom of Great Britain; and military, naval, foreign and colonial policy must in the future be devised by the representatives of those dominions sitting in council together with the representatives of Great Britain. Does not that indicate a different form of imperialism from that they hold in no friendly memory? It would not be imperialism in the ancient sense but a federal union of independent nations to protect national liberties, which might draw into its union other peoples hitherto unconnected with it, and so beget a league of nations to make a common international law prevail. The allegiance would be to common principles which mankind desire and would not permit the domination of any one race. We have not only to be good Irishmen but good citizens of the world, and one is as important as the other, for earth is more and more forcing on its children a recognition of their fundamental unity, and that all rise and fall and suffer together, and that none can escape the infection from their common humanity. If these ideas emerge from the world conflict and are accepted as world morality it will be some compensation for the anguish of learning the lesson. We in Ireland like the rest of the world must rise above ourselves and our differences if we are to manifest the genius which is in us, and play a noble part in world history.

THE NEW NATION

In that cycle of history which closed in 1914, but which seems now to the imagination as far sunken behind time as Babylon or Samarcand, it was customary at the festival of the Incarnation to forego our enmities for a little and allow freer play to the spiritual in our being. Since 1914 all things in the world and with us, too, in Ireland have existed in a welter of hate, but the rhythm of ancient habit cannot altogether have passed away, and now if at any time, it should be possible to blow the bugles of Heaven and recall men to that old allegiance. I do not think it would help now if I, or another, put forward arguments drawn from Irish history or economics to convince any party that they were wrong and their opponents right. I think absolute truth might be stated in respect of these things, and yet it would affect nothing in our present mood. It would not be recognized any more than Heaven, when It walked on earth in the guise of a Carpenter, was hailed by men whose minds were filled by other imaginations of that coming.

I will not argue about the past, but would ask Irishmen to consider how in future they may live together. Do they contemplate the continuance of these bitter hatreds in our own household? The war must have a finale. Many thousands of Irishmen will return to their country who have faced death for other ideals than those which inspire many more thousands now in Ireland and make them also fearless of death. How are these to co-exist in the same island if there is no change of heart? Each will receive passionate support from relatives, friends, and parties who uphold their action. This will be a most unhappy country if we cannot arrive at some moral agreement, as necessary as a political agreement. Partition is no settlement, because there is no geographical limitation of these passions. There is scarce a locality in Ireland where antagonisms do not gather about the thought of Ireland as in the caduceus of Mercury the twin serpents writhe about the sceptre of the god.

I ask our national extremists in what mood do they propose to meet those who return, men of temper as stern as their own? Will these endure being termed traitors to Ireland? Will their friends endure it? Will those who mourn their dead endure to hear scornful speech of those they loved? That way is for us a path to Hell. The unimaginative who see only a majority in their own locality, or, perhaps, in the nation, do not realize what a powerful factor in national life are those who differ from them, and how they are upheld by a neighboring nation which, for all its present travail, is more powerful by far than Ireland even if its people were united in purpose as the fingers of one hand. Nor can those who hold to, and are upheld by, the Empire hope to coerce to a uniformity of feeling with themselves the millions clinging to Irish nationality. Seven centuries of repression have left that spirit unshaken, nor can it be destroyed save by the destruction of the Irish people, because it springs from biological necessity. As well might a foolish gardener trust that his apple-tree would bring forth grapes as to dream that there could be uniformity of character and civilization between Irishmen and Englishmen. It would be a crime against life if it could be brought about and diversities of culture and civilization made impossible. We may live at peace with our neighbors when it is agreed that we must be different, and no peace is possible in the world between nations except on this understanding. But I am not now thinking of that, but of the more urgent problem how we are to live at peace with each other. I am convinced Irish enmities are perpetuated because we live by memory more than by hope, and that even now on the facts of character there is no justification for these enmities.

We have been told that there are two nations in Ireland. That may have been so in the past, but it is not true today. The union of Norman and Dane and Saxon and Celt which has been going on through the centuries is now completed, and there is but one powerful Irish character--not Celtic or Norman-Saxon, but a new race. We should recognize our moral identity. It was apparent before the war in the methods by which Ulstermen and Nationalists alike strove to defend or win their political objects. There is scarce an Ulsterman, whether he regards his ancestors as settlers or not, who is not allied through marriage by his forbears to the ancient race. There is in his veins the blood of the people who existed before Patrick, and he can look backward through time to the legends of the Red Branch, the Fianna and the gods as the legends of his people. It would be as difficult to find even on the Western Coast a family which has not lost in the same way its Celtic purity of race. The character of all is fed from many streams which have mingled in them and have given them a new distinctiveness. The invasions of Ireland and the Plantations, however morally unjustifiable, however cruel in method, are justified by biology. The invasion of one race by another was nature's ancient way of reinvigorating a people.

Mr. Flinders Petrie, in his "Revolutions of Civilization," has demonstrated that civilization comes in waves, that races rise to a pinnacle of power and culture, and decline from that, and fall into decadence, from which they do not emerge until there has been a crossing of races, a fresh intermingling of cultures. He showed in ancient Egypt eight such periods, and after every decline into decadence there was an invasion, the necessary precedent to a fresh ascent with reinvigorated energies. I prefer to dwell upon the final human results of this commingling of races than upon the tyrannies and conflicts which made it possible. The mixture of races has added to the elemental force of the Celtic character a more complex mentality, and has saved us from becoming, as in our island isolation we might easily have become, thin and weedy, like herds where there has been too much in-breeding. The modern Irish are a race built up from many races who have to prove themselves for the future. Their animosities, based on past history, have little justification in racial diversity today, for they are a new people with only superficial cultural and political differences, but with the same fundamental characteristics. It is hopeless, the dream held by some that the ancient Celtic character could absorb the new elements, become dominant once more, and be itself unchanged. It is equally hopeless to dream the Celtic element could be eliminated. We are a new people, and not the past, but the future, is to justify this new nationality.

I believe it was this powerful Irish character which stirred in Ulster before the war, leading it to adopt methods unlike the Anglo- Saxon tradition in politics. I believe that new character, far more than the spirit of the ancient race, was the ferment in the blood of those who brought about the astonishing enterprise of Easter Week. Pearse himself, for all his Gaelic culture, was sired by one of the race he fought against. He might stand in that respect as a symbol of the new race which is springing up. We are slowly realizing the vigor of the modern Irish character just becoming self-conscious of itself. I had met many men who were in the enterprise of Easter Week and listened to their spirit their speech, but they had to prove to myself and others by more than words. I listened with that half-cynical feeling which is customary with us when men advocate a cause with which we are temperamentally sympathetic, but about whose realization we are hopeless. I could not gauge the strength of the new spirit, for words do not by themselves convey the quality of power in men; and even when the reverberations from Easter Week were echoing everywhere in Ireland, for a time I, and many others, thought and felt about those who died as some pagan concourse in ancient Italy might have felt looking down upon an arena, seeing below a foam of glorious faces turned to them, the noble, undismayed, inflexible faces of martyrs, and, without understanding, have realized that this spirit was stronger than death. I believe that capacity for sacrifice, that devotion to ideals exists equally among the opponents of these men. It would have been proved in Ireland, in Ulster, if the need had arisen. It has been proved on many a battlefield of Europe. Whatever views we may hold about the relative value of national or Imperial ideals, we may recognize that there is moral equality where the sacrifice is equal. No one has more to give than life, and, when that is given, neither Nationalist nor Imperialist in Ireland can claim moral superiority for the dead champions of their causes.

And here I come to the purpose of my letter, which is to deprecate the scornful repudiation by Irishmen of other Irishmen, which is so common at present, and which helps to perpetuate our feuds. We are all one people. We are closer to each other in character than we are to any other race. The necessary preliminary to political adjustment is moral adjustment, forgiveness, and mutual understanding. I have been in council with others of my countrymen for several months, and I noticed what an obstacle it was to agreement how few, how very few, there were who had been on terms of friendly intimacy with men of all parties. There was hardly one who could have given an impartial account of the ideals and principles of his opponents. Our political differences have brought about social isolations, and there can be no understanding where there is no eagerness to meet those who differ from us, and hear the best they have to say for themselves. This letter is an appeal to Irishmen to seek out and understand their political opponents. If they come to know each other, they will come to trust each other, and will realize their kinship, and will set their faces to the future together, to build up a civilization which will justify their nationality.

I myself am Anglo-Irish, with the blood of both races in me, and when the rising of Easter Week took place all that was Irish in me was profoundly stirred, and out of that mood I wrote commemorating the dead. And then later there rose in memory the faces of others I knew who loved their country, but had died in other battles. They fought in those because they believed they would serve Ireland, and I felt these were no less my people. I could hold them also in my heart and pay tribute to them. Because it was possible for me to do so, I think it is possible for others; and in the hope that the deeds of all may in the future be a matter of pride to the new nation I append here these verses I have written:--

To the Memory of Some I knew Who are Dead and Who Loved Ireland.

> Their dream had left me numb and cold,
>   But yet my spirit rose in pride,
> Refashioning in burnished gold
>   The images of those who died,
> Or were shut in the penal cell.
>   Here's to you, Pearse, your dream not mine,
> But yet the thought, for this you fell,
>   Has turned life's water into wine.
>
> You who have died on Eastern hills
>   Or fields of France as undismayed,
> Who lit with interlinked wills
>   The long heroic barricade,
> You, too, in all the dreams you had,
>   Thought of some thing for Ireland done.
> Was it not so, Oh, shining lad,
>   What lured you, Alan Anderson?
>
> I listened to high talk from you,
>   Thomas McDonagh, and it seemed
> The words were idle, but they grew
>   To nobleness by death redeemed.

Life cannot utter words more great
    Than life may meet by sacrifice,
High words were equaled by high fate,
    You paid the price. You paid the price.

You who have fought on fields afar,
    That other Ireland did you wrong
Who said you shadowed Ireland's star,
    Nor gave you laurel wreath nor song.
You proved by death as true as they,
    In mightier conflicts played your part,
Equal your sacrifice may weigh,
    Dear Kettle, of the generous heart.

The hope lives on age after age,
    Earth with its beauty might be won
For labor as a heritage,
    For this has Ireland lost a son.
This hope unto a flame to fan
    Men have put life by with a smile,
Here's to you Connolly, my man,
    Who cast the last torch on the pile.

You too, had Ireland in your care,
    Who watched o'er pits of blood and mire,
From iron roots leap up in air
    Wild forests, magical, of fire;
Yet while the Nuts of Death were shed
    Your memory would ever stray
To your own isle. Oh, gallant dead--
    This wreath, Will Redmond, on your clay.

Here's to you, men I never met,
    Yet hope to meet behind the veil,
Thronged on some starry parapet,
    That looks down upon Innisfail,
And sees the confluence of dreams
    That clashed together in our night,
One river, born from many streams,
    Roll in one blaze of blinding light.

THE SPIRITUAL CONFLICT

Prophetic

I am told when a gun is fired it recoils with almost as much force as urges forward the projectile. It is the triumph of the military engineer that he anticipates and provides for this recoil when designing the weapon. Nations prepare for war, but do not, as the military engineer in his sphere does, provide for the recoil on society. It is difficult to foresee clearly what will happen. Possible changes in territory, economic results, the effect on a social order receive consideration while war is being waged. But how war may affect our intellectual and spiritual life is not always apparent. Material victories are often spiritual defeats. History has record of nationalities which were destroyed and causes whose followers were overborne, yet they left their ideas behind them as a glory in the air, and these incarnated anew in the minds of the conquerors. Ideas are things which can only be conquered by a greater beauty or intellectual power, and they are never more powerful than when they do not come threatening us in alliance with physical forces. I have no doubt there are many today who watch the cloud over Europe as we may imagine some Israelite of old gazing on that awful cloudy pillar wherein was the Lord, in hope or fear for some revelation of the spirit hidden in cloud and fire. What idea is hidden in the fiery pillar which moves over Europe? What form will it assume in its manifestation? How will it exercise dominion over the spirit? Whatever idea is most powerful in the world must draw to it the intellect and spirit of humanity, and it will be monarch over their minds either by reason of their love or hate for it. It is more true to say we must think of the most powerful than to say we must love the highest, because even the blind can feel power, while it is rare to have vision of high things.

A little over a century ago all the needles of being pointed to France. A peculiar manifestation of the democratic idea had become the most powerful thing in the world of moral forces. It went on multiplying images of itself in men's minds through after generations; and, because thought, like matter, is subject to the laws of action and reaction, which indeed is the only safe basis for prophecy, this idea inevitably found itself opposed by a contrary idea in the world. Today all the needles of being point to Germany, where the apparition of the organized State is manifest with every factor, force, and entity co-ordinated, so that the State might move myriads and yet have the swift freedom of the athletic individual. The idea that the State exists for the people is countered by the idea that the individual exists for the State. France in a violent reaction found itself dominated by a Caesar. Germany may find itself without a Caesar, but with a social democracy.

But, if it does, will the idea Europe is fighting be conquered? Was the French idea conquered either by the European confederation without or by Napoleon within? It invaded men's minds everywhere; and in few countries did the democratic ideas operate more powerfully than in these islands, where the State was a most determined antagonist of their material manifestations in France. The German idea has sufficient power to unite the free minds of half the world against it. But is it not already invading, and Will it not still more invade, the minds of rulers? All Governments are august kinsmen of each other, and discreetly imitate each other in policy where it may conduce to power or efficiency. The efficiency of the highly organized State as a vehicle for the manifestation of power must today be sinking into the minds of those who guide the destinies of races. The State in these islands, before a year of war has passed, has already assumed control over myriads of industrial enterprises. The back-wash of great wars, their reaction within the national being after prolonged effort, is social disturbance; and it seems that the State will be unable easily, after this war, to relax its autocratic power. There may come a time when it would be possible for it to do so; but the habit of overlordship will have grown, there will be many who will wish it to grow still more, and a thousand reasons can be found why the mastery over national organizations should be relaxed but little. The recoil on society after the war will be almost as powerful as the energy expended in conflict; and our political engineers will have to provide for the recoil. By the analogy of the French Revolution, by what we see taking place today, it seems safe to prophesy that the State will become more dominant over the lives of men than ever before.

In a quarter of a century there will hardly be anybody so obscure, so isolated in his employment, that he will not, by the development of the organized State, be turned round to face it and to recognize it as the most potent factor in his life. From that it follows of necessity that literature will be concerned more and more with the shaping of the character of this Great Being. In free democracies, where the State interferes little with the lives of men, the mood in literature tends to become personal and subjective; the poets sing a solitary song about nature, love, twilight, and the stars; the novelists deal with the lives of private persons, enlarging individual liberties of action and thought. Few concern themselves with the character of the State. But when it strides in, an omnipresent overlord, organizing and directing life and industry, then the individual imagination must be directed to that collective life and power. For one writer today concerned with high politics we may expect to find hundreds engaged in a passionate attempt to create the new god in their own image.

This may seem a far-fetched speculation, but not to those who see how through the centuries humanity has oscillated like a pendulum betwixt opposing ideals. The greatest reactions have been from solidarity to liberty and from liberty to solidarity. The religious solidarity of Europe in the Middle Ages was broken by a passionate desire in the heart of millions for liberty of thought. A reaction rarely, if ever, brings people back to a pole deserted centuries before. The coming solidarity is the domination of the State; and to speculate whether that again will be broken up by a new religious movement would be to speculate without utility. What we ought to realize is that these reactions take place within one being, humanity, and indicate eternal desires of the soul. They seem to urge on us the idea that there is a pleroma, or human fullness, in which the opposites may be reconciled, and that the divine event to which we are moving is a State in which there will be essential freedom combined with an organic unity. At the last analysis are not all empires, nationalities, and movements spiritual in their origin, beginning with desires of the soul and externalizing themselves in immense manifestations of energy in which the original will is often submerged and lost sight of? If in their inception national ideals are spiritual, their final object must also be spiritual, perhaps to make man a yet freer agent, but acting out of a continual consciousness of his unity with humanity. The discipline which the highly organized State imposes on its subjects connects them continuously in thought to something greater than themselves, and so ennobles the average man. The freedom which the policy of other nations permits quickens intelligence and will. Each policy has its own defects; with one a loss in individual initiative, with the other self-absorption and a lower standard of citizenship or interest in national affairs. The oscillations in society provide the corrective.

We are going to have our free individualism tempered by a more autocratic action by the State. There are signs that with our enemy the moral power which attracts the free to the source of their liberty is being appreciated, and the policy which retained for Britain its Colonies and secured their support in an hour of peril is contrasted with the policy of the iron hand in Poland. Neither Germany nor Britain can escape being impressed by the characteristics of the other in the shock of conflict. It may seem a paradoxical outcome of the spiritual conflict Mr. Asquith announced. But history is quick with such ironies. What we condemned in others is the measure which is meted out to us. Indeed it might almost be said that all war results in an exchange of characteristics, and if the element of hatred is strong in the conflict it will certainly bring a nation to every baseness of the foe it fights. Love and hate are alike in this, that they change us into the image we contemplate. We grow nobly like what we adore through love and ignobly like what we contemplate through hate. It will be well for us if we remember that all our political ideals are symbols of spiritual destinies. These clashings of solidarity and freedom will enrich our spiritual life if we understand of the first that our thirst for greatness, for the majesty of empire, is a symbol of our final unity with a greater majesty, and if we remember of the second that, as an old scripture said, "The universe exists for the purposes of soul."

1915

ON AN IRISH HILL

It has been my dream for many years that I might at some time dwell in a cabin on the hillside in this dear and living land of ours, and there I would lay my head in the lap of a serene nature, and be on friendly terms with the winds and mountains who hold enough of unexplored mystery and infinitude to engage me at present. I would not dwell too far from men, for above an enchanted valley, only a morning's walk from the city, is the mountain of my dream. Here, between heaven and earth and my brothers, there might come on me some foretaste of the destiny which the great powers are shaping for us in this isle, the mingling of God and nature and man in a being, one, yet infinite in number. Old tradition has it that there was in our mysterious past such a union, a sympathy between man and the elements so complete, that at every great deed of hero or king the three swelling waves of Fohla responded: the wave of Toth, the wave of Rury, and the long, slow, white, foaming wave of Cleena. O mysterious kinsmen, would that today some deed great enough could call forth the thunder of your response once again! But perhaps he is now rocked in his cradle who will hereafter rock you into joyous foam.

The mountain which I praise has not hitherto been considered one of the sacred places in Eire, no glittering tradition hangs about it as a lure and indeed I would not have it considered as one in any special sense apart from its companions, but I take it here as a type of what any high place in nature may become for us if well loved; a haunt of deep peace, a spot where the Mother lays aside veil after veil, until at last the great Spirit seems in brooding gentleness to be in the boundless fields alone. I am not inspired by that brotherhood which does not overflow with love into the being of the elements, not hail in them the same spirit as that which calls us with so many pathetic and loving voices from the lives of men. So I build my dream cabin in hope of its wider intimacy:

> A cabin on the mountain side hid in a grassy nook,
> With door and windows open wide, where friendly stars may look;
> The rabbit shy can patter in; the winds may enter free
> Who throng around the mountain throne in living ecstasy.
> And when the sun sets dimmed in eve and purple fills the air,
> I think the sacred Hazel Tree is dropping berries there
> From starry fruitage waved aloft where Connla's well o'er-flows:
> For sure the immortal waters pour through every wind that blows.
> I think when night towers up aloft and shakes the trembling dew,
> How every high and lonely thought that thrills my being through
> Is but a shining berry dropped down through the purple air,
> And from the magic tree of life the fruit falls everywhere.

The Sacred Hazel was the Celtic branch of the Tree of Life; its scarlet nuts gave wisdom and inspiration; and fed on this ethereal fruit, the ancient Gael grew to greatness. Though today none eat of the fruit or drink the purple flood welling from Connla's fountain, I think that the fire which still kindles the Celtic races was flashed into their blood in that magical time, and is our heritage from the Druidic past. It is still here, the magic and mystery: it lingers in the heart of a people to whom their neighbors of another world are frequent visitors in the spirit and over-shadowers of reverie and imagination.

The earth here remembers her past, and to bring about its renewal she whispers with honeyed entreaty and lures with bewitching glamour. At this mountain I speak of it was that our greatest poet, the last and most beautiful voice of Eire, first found freedom in song, so he tells me: and it was the pleading for a return to herself that this mysterious nature first fluted through his lips:

> Come away, O human child,
> To the Woods and waters wild

With a faery hand in hand:

For the world's more full of weeping than you can understand.

Away! yes, yes; to wander on and on under star-rich skies, ever getting deeper into the net, the love that will not let us rest, the peace above the desire of love. The village lights in heaven and earth, each with their own peculiar hint of home, draw us hither and thither, where it matters not, so the voice calls and the heart-light burns.

Some it leads to the crowded ways; some it draws apart: and the Light knows, and not any other, the need and the way.

If you ask me what has the mountain to do with these inspirations, and whether the singer would not anywhere out of his own soul have made an equal song, I answer to the latter, I think not. In these lofty places the barrier between the sphere of light and the sphere of darkness are fragile, and the continual ecstasy of the high air communicates itself, and I have also heard from others many tales of things seen and heard here which show that the races of the Sidhe are often present. Some have seen below the mountain a blazing heart of light, others have heard the Musical beating of a heart, of faery bells, or aerial clashings, and the heart-beings have also spoken; so it has gathered around itself its own traditions of spiritual romance and adventures of the soul.

Let no one call us dreamers when the mind is awake. If we grew forgetful and felt no more the bitter human struggle--yes. But if we bring to it the hope and courage of those who are assured of the nearby presence and encircling love of the great powers? I would bring to my mountain the weary spirits who are obscured in the fetid city where life decays into rottenness; and call thither those who are in doubt, the pitiful and trembling hearts who are skeptic of any hope, and place them where the dusky vapors of their thought might dissolve in the inner light, and their doubts vanish on the mountain top where the earthbreath streams away to the vast, when the night glows like a seraph, and the spirit is beset by the evidence of a million of suns to the grandeur of the nature wherein it lives and whose destiny must be its also.

After all, is not this longing but a search for ourselves, and where shall we find ourselves at last? Not in this land nor wrapped in these garments of an hour, but wearing the robes of space whither these voices out of the illimitable allure us, now with love, and anon with beauty or power. In our past the mighty ones came glittering across the foam of the mystic waters and brought their warriors away.

Perhaps, and this also is my hope, they may again return; Manannan, on his ocean-sweeping boat, a living creature, diamond-winged, or Lu, bright as the dawn, on his fiery steed, manned with tumultuous flame, or some hitherto unknown divinity may stand suddenly by me on the hill, and hold out the Silver Branch with white blossoms from the Land of Youth, and stay me ere I depart with the sung call as of old:

> Tarry thou yet, late lingerer in the twilight's glory
> Gay are the hills with song: earth's faery children leave
> More dim abodes to roam the primrose-hearted eve,
> Opening their glimmering lips to breathe some wondrous story.
> Hush, not a whisper! Let your heart alone go dreaming.
> Dream unto dream may pass: deep in the heart alone
> Murmurs the Mighty One his solemn undertone.
> Canst thou not see adown the silver cloudland streaming
> Rivers of faery light, dewdrop on dewdrop falling,
> Starfire of silver flames, lighting the dark beneath?
> And what enraptured hosts burn on the dusky heath!
> Come thou away with them for Heaven to Earth is calling.
> These are Earth's voice--her answer--spirits thronging.
> Come to the Land of Youth: the trees grown heavy there
> Drop on the purple wave the starry fruit they bear.
> Drink! the immortal waters quench the spirit's longing.
> Art thou not now, bright one, all sorrow past, in elation,
> Filled with wild joy, grown brother-hearted with the vast,
> Whither thy spirit wending flits the dim stars past
> Unto the Light of Lights in burning adoration.

1896

RELIGION AND LOVE

I have often wondered whether there is not something wrong in our religious systems in that the same ritual, the same doctrines, the same aspirations are held to be sufficient both for men and women. The tendency everywhere is to obliterate distinctions, and if a woman be herself she is looked upon unkindly. She rarely understands our metaphysics, and she gazes on the expounder of the mystery of the Logos with enigmatic eyes which reveal the enchantment of another divinity. The ancients were wiser than we in this, for they had Aphrodite and Hera and many another form of the Mighty Mother who bestowed on women their peculiar graces and powers. Surely no girl in ancient Greece ever sent up to all- pervading Zeus a prayer that her natural longings might be fulfilled; but we may be sure that to Aphrodite came many such prayers. The deities we worship today are too austere for women to approach with their peculiar desires, and indeed in Ireland the largest number of our people do not see any necessity for love-making at all, or what connection spiritual powers have with the affections. A girl, without repining, will follow her four-legged dowry to the house of a man she may never have spoken twenty words to before her marriage. We praise our women for their virtue, but the general acceptance of the marriage as arranged shows so unemotional, so undesirable a temperament, that it is not to be wondered at. One wonders was there temptation.

What the loss to the race may be it is impossible to say, but it is true that beautiful civilizations are built up by the desire of man to give his beloved all her desires. Where there is no beloved, but only a housekeeper, there are no beautiful fancies to create the beautiful arts, no spiritual protest against the mean dwelling, no hunger build the world anew for her sake. Aphrodite is outcast and with her many of the other immortals have also departed. The home life in Ireland is probably more squalid than with any other people equally prosperous in Europe. The children begotten without love fill more and more the teeming asylums. We are without art; literature is despised; we have few of those industries which spring up in other countries in response to the desire of woman to make gracious influences pervade the home of her partner, a desire to which man readily yields, and toils to satisfy if he loves truly. The desire for beauty has come almost to be regarded as dangerous, if not sinful; and the woman who is still the natural child of the Great Mother and priestess of the mysteries, if she betray the desire to exercise her divinely-given powers, if there be enchantment in her eyes and her laugh, and if she bewilder too many men, is in our latest code of morals distinctly an evil influence. The spirit, melted and tortured with love, which does not achieve its earthly desire, is held to have wasted its strength, and the judgment which declares the life to be wrecked is equally severe on that which caused this wild conflagration in the heart. But the end of life is not comfort but divine being. We do not regard the life which closed in the martyr's fire as ended ignobly. The spiritual philosophy which separates human emotions and ideas, and declares some to be secular and others spiritual, is to blame. There is no meditation which if prolonged will not bring us to the same world where religion would carry us, and if a flower in the wall will lead us to all knowledge, so the understanding of the peculiar nature of one half of humanity will bring us far on our journey to the sacred deep. I believe it was this wise understanding which in the ancient world declared the embodied spirit in man to be influenced more by the Divine Mind and in woman by the Mighty Mother, by which nature in its spiritual aspect was understood. In this philosophy, Boundless Being, when manifested, revealed itself in two forms of life, spirit and substance; and the endless evolution of its divided rays had as its root impulse the desire to return to that boundless being. By many ways blindly or half consciously the individual life strives to regain its old fullness. The spirit seeks union with nature to pass from the life of vision into Pure being; and nature, conscious that its grosser forms are impermanent, is for ever dissolving and leading its votary to a more distant shrine. "Nature is timid like a woman," declares an Indian scripture. "She reveals herself shyly and withdraws again." All this metaphysic will not appear out of place if we regard women as influenced beyond herself and her conscious life for spiritual ends. I do not enter a defense of the loveless coquette, but the woman who has a natural delight in awakening love in men is priestess of a divinity than which there is none mightier among the rulers of the heavens. Through her eyes, her laugh, in all her motions, there is expressed more than she is conscious of herself. The Mighty Mother through the woman is kindling a symbol of herself in the spirit, and through that symbol she breathes her secret life into the heart, so that it is fed from within and is drawn to herself. We remember that with Dante, the image of a woman became at last the purified vesture of his spirit through which the mysteries were revealed. We are for ever making our souls with effort and pain, and shaping them into images which reveal or are voiceless according to their degree; and the man whose spirit has been obsessed by a beauty so long brooded upon that he has almost become that which he contemplated, owes much to the woman who may never be his; and if he or the world understood aright, he has no cause of complaint. It is the essentially irreligious spirit of Ireland which has come to regard love as an unnecessary emotion and the mingling of the sexes as dangerous. For it is a curious thing that while we commonly regard ourselves as the most religious people in Europe, the reverse is probably true. The country which has never produced spiritual thinkers or religious teachers of whom men have heard if we except Berkeley and perhaps the remote Johannes Scotus Erigena, cannot pride itself on its spiritual achievement; and it might seem even more paradoxical, but I think it would be almost equally true, to say that the first spiritual note in our literature was struck when a poet generally regarded as pagan wrote it as the aim of his art to reveal--

In all poor foolish things that live a day
Eternal beauty wandering on her way.

The heavens do not declare the glory of God any more than do shining eyes, nor the firmament show His handiwork more than the woven wind of hair, for these were wrought with no lesser love than set the young stars swimming in seas of joyous and primeval air. If we drink in the beauty of the night or the mountains, it is deemed to be praise of the Maker, but if we show an equal adoration of the beauty of man or woman, it is dangerous, it is almost wicked. Of course it is dangerous; and without danger there is no passage to eternal things. There is the valley of the shadow beside the pathway of light, and it always will be there, and the heavens will never be entered by those who shrink from it. Spirituality is the power of apprehending formless spiritual essences, of seeing the eternal in the transitory, and in the things which are seen the unseen things of which they are the shadow. I call Mr. Yeats' poetry spiritual when it declares, as in the lines I quoted, that there is no beauty so trivial that it is not the shadow of the Eternal Beauty. A country is religious where it is common belief that all things are instinct with divinity, and where the love between man and woman is seen as a symbol, the highest we have, of the union of spirit and nature, and their final blending in the boundless being. For this reason the lightest desires even, the lightest graces of women have a philosophical value for what suggestions they bring us of the divinity behind them.

As men and women feel themselves more and more to be sharers of universal aims, they will contemplate in each other and in themselves that aspect of the boundless being under whose influence they are cast, and will appeal to it for understanding and power. Time, which is for ever bringing back the old and renewing it, may yet bring back to us some counterpart of Aphrodite or Hera as they were understood by the most profound thinkers of the ancient world; and women may again have her temples and her mysteries, and renew again her radiant life at its fountain, and feel that in seeking for beauty she is growing more into her own ancestral being, and that in its shining forth she is giving to man, as he may give to her, something of that completeness of spirit of which it is written, "neither is the man without the woman nor the woman without the man in the Highest."

It may seem strange that what is so clear should require statement, but it is only with a kind of despair the man or woman of religious mind can contemplate the materialism of our thought about life. It is not our natural heritage from the past, for the bardic poetry shows that a heaven lay about us in the mystical childhood of our race, and a supernatural original was often divined for the great hero, or the beautiful woman. All this perception has withered away, for religion has become observance of rule and adherence to doctrine. The first steps to the goal have been made sufficient in themselves; but religion is useless unless it has a transforming power, unless it is able "to turn fishermen into divines," and make the blind see and the deaf hear. They are no true teachers who cannot rise beyond the world of sense and darkness and awaken the links within us from earth to heaven, who cannot see within the heart what are its needs, and who have not the power to open the poor blind eyes and touch the ears that have heard no sound of the heavenly harmonies. Our clergymen do their best to deliver us from what they think is evil, but do not lead us into the Kingdom. They forget that the faculties cannot be spiritualized by restraint but in use, and that the greatest evil of all is not to be able to see the divine everywhere, in life and love no less than in the solemn architecture of the spheres. In the free play of the beautiful and natural human relations lie the greatest possibilities of spiritual development, for heaven is not prayer nor praise but the fullness of life, which is only divined through the richness and variety of life on earth. There is a certain infinitude in the emotions of love, tenderness, pity, joy, and all that is begotten in love, and this limitless character of the emotions has never received the philosophical consideration which is due to it, for even laughter may be considered solemnly, and gaiety and joy in us are the shadowy echoes of that joy spoken of the radiant Morning Stars, and there is not an emotion in man or woman which has not, however perverted and muddied in its coming, in some way flowed from the first fountain. We are no more divided from supernature than we are from our own bodies, and where the life of man or woman is naturally most intense it most naturally overflows and mingles with the subtler and more lovely world within. If religion has no word to say upon this it is incomplete, and we wander in the narrow circle of prayers and praise, wondering all the while what is it we are praising God for, because we feel so melancholy and lifeless. Dante had a place in his Inferno for the joyless souls, and if his conception be true the population of that circle will be largely modern Irish. A reaction against this conventional restraint is setting in, and the needs of life will perhaps in the future no longer be violated as they are today; and since it is the pent-up flood of the joy which ought to be in life which is causing this reaction, and since there is a divine root in it, it is difficult to say where it might not carry us; I hope into some renewal of ancient conceptions of the fundamental purpose of womanhood and its relations to Divine Nature, and that from the temples where woman may be instructed she will come forth, with strength in her to resist all pleading until the lover worship in her a divine womanhood, and that through their love the divided portions of the immortal nature may come together and be one as before the beginning of worlds.

1904

THE RENEWAL OF YOUTH

I am a part of all that I have met;
Yet all experience is an arch wherethro'
Gleams that untravel'd world .....
Come, my friends,
'Tis not too late to seek a newer world.
                                        --Ulysses

I.

Humanity is no longer the child it was at the beginning of the world. The spirit which prompted by some divine intent, flung itself long ago into a vague, nebulous, drifting nature, though it has endured through many periods of youth, maturity, and age, has yet had its own transformations. Its gay, wonderful childhood gave way, as cycle after cycle coiled itself into slumber, to more definite purposes, and now it is old and burdened with experiences. It is not an age that quenches its fire, but it will not renew again the activities which gave it wisdom. And so it comes that men pause with a feeling which they translate into weariness of life before the accustomed joys and purposes of their race. They wonder at the spell which induced their fathers to plot and execute deeds which seem to them to have no more meaning than a whirl of dust. But their fathers had this weariness also and concealed it from each other in fear, for it meant the laying aside of the sceptre, the toppling over of empires, the chilling of the household warmth, and all for a voice whose inner significance revealed itself but to one or two among myriads.

The spirit has hardly emerged from the childhood with which nature clothes it afresh at every new birth, when the disparity between the garment and the wearer becomes manifest: the little tissue of joys and dreams woven about it is found inadequate for shelter: it trembles exposed to the winds blowing out of the unknown. We linger at twilight with some companion, still glad, contented, and in tune with the nature which fills the orchards with blossom and sprays the hedges with dewy blooms. The laughing lips give utterance to wishes--ours until that moment. Then the spirit, without warning, suddenly falls into immeasurable age: a sphinx- like face looks at us: our lips answer, but far from the region of elemental being we inhabit, they syllable in shadowy sound, out of old usage, the response, speaking of a love and a hope which we know have vanished from us for evermore. So hour by hour the scourge of the infinite drives us out of every nook and corner of life we find pleasant. And this always takes place when all is fashioned to our liking: then into our dream strides the wielder of the lightning: we get glimpses of a world beyond us thronged with mighty, exultant beings: our own deeds become infinitesimal to us: the colors of our imagination, once so shining, grow pale as the living lights of God glow upon them. We find a little honey in the heart which we make sweeter for some one, and then another Lover, whose forms are legion, sighs to us out of its multitudinous being: we know that the old love is gone. There is a sweetness in song or in the cunning re-imaging of the beauty we see; but the Magician of the Beautiful whispers to us of his art, how we were with him when he laid the foundations of the world, and the song is unfinished, the fingers grow listless. As we receive these intimations of age our very sins become negative: we are still pleased if a voice praises us, but we grow lethargic in enterprises where the spur to activity is fame or the acclamation of men. At some point in the past we may have struggled mightily for the sweet incense which men offer to a towering personality; but the infinite is for ever within man: we sighed for other worlds and found that to be saluted as victor by men did not mean acceptance by the gods.

But the placing of an invisible finger upon our lips when we would speak, the heart-throb of warning where we would love, that we grow contemptuous of the prizes of life, does not mean that the spirit has ceased from its labors, that the high-built beauty of the spheres is to topple mistily into chaos, as a mighty temple in the desert sinks into the sand, watched only by a few barbarians too feeble to renew its ancient pomp and the ritual of its once shining congregations. Before we, who were the bright children of the dawn, may return as the twilight race into the silence, our purpose must be achieved, we have to assume mastery over that nature which now overwhelms us, driving into the Fire-fold the flocks of stars and wandering fires. Does it seem very vast and far away? Do you sigh at the long, long time? Or does it appear hopeless to you who perhaps return with trembling feet evening after evening from a little labor? But it is behind all these things that the renewal takes place, when love and grief are dead; when they loosen their hold on the spirit and it sinks back into itself, looking out on the pitiful plight of those who, like it, are the weary inheritors of so great destinies: then a tenderness which is the most profound quality of its being springs up like the outraying of the dawn, and if in that mood it would plan or execute it knows no weariness, for it is nourished from the First Fountain. As for these feeble children of the once glorious spirits of the dawn, only a vast hope can arouse them from so vast a despair, for the fire will not invigorate them for the repetition of petty deeds but only for the eternal enterprise, the war in heaven, that conflict between Titan and Zeus which is part of the never-ending struggle of the human spirit to assert its supremacy over nature. We, who he crushed by this mountain nature piled above us, must arise again, unite to storm the heavens and sit on the seats of the mighty.

II.

We speak out of too petty a spirit to each other; the true poems, said Whitman:
Bring none to his or to her terminus or to be content and full,
Whom they take they take into space to behold the birth of stars,
to learn one of the meanings,
To launch off with absolute faith, to sweep through the ceaseless
rings and never be quiet again.

Here is inspiration--the voice of the soul. Every word which really inspires is spoken as if the Golden Age had never passed. The great teachers ignore the personal identity and speak to the eternal pilgrim. Too often the form or surface far removed from beauty makes us falter, and we speak to that form and the soul is not stirred. But an equal temper arouses it. To whoever hails in it the lover, the hero, the magician, it will respond, but not to him who accosts it in the name and style of its outer self. How often do we not long to break through the veils which divide us from some one, but custom, convention, or a fear of being misunderstood prevent us, and so the moment passes whose heat might have burned through every barrier. Out with it--out with it, the hidden heart, the love that is voiceless, the secret tender germ of an infinite forgiveness. That speaks to the heart. That pierces through many a vesture of the Soul. Our companion struggles in some labyrinth of passion. We help him, we, think, with ethic and moralities.

Ah, very well they are; well to know and to keep, but wherefore? For their own sake? No, but that the King may arise in his beauty. We write that in letters, in books, but to the face of the fallen who brings back remembrance? Who calls him by his secret name? Let a man but feel for what high cause is his battle, for what is his cyclic labor, and a warrior who is invincible fights for him and he draws upon divine powers. Our attitude to man and to nature, expressed or not, has something of the effect of ritual, of evocation. As our aspiration so is our inspiration. We believe in life universal, in a brotherhood which links the elements to man, and makes the glow- worm feel far off something of the rapture of the seraph hosts. Then we go out into the living world, and what influences pour through us! We are "at league with the stones of the field." The winds of the world blow radiantly upon us as in the early time. We feel wrapt about with love, with an infinite tenderness that caresses us. Alone in our rooms as we ponder, what sudden abysses of light open within us! The Gods are so much nearer than we dreamed. We rise up intoxicated with the thought, and reel out seeking an equal companionship under the great night and the stars.

Let us get near to realities. We read too much. We think of that which is "the goal, the Comforter, the Lord, the Witness, the resting- place, the asylum, and the Friend." Is it by any of these dear and familiar names? The soul of the modern mystic is becoming a mere hoarding-place for uncomely theories. He creates an uncouth symbolism, and blinds his soul within with names drawn from the Kabala or ancient Sanskrit, and makes alien to himself the intimate powers of his spirit, things which in truth are more his than the beatings of his heart. Could we not speak of them in our own tongue, and the language of today will be as sacred as any of the past. From the Golden One, the child of the divine, comes a voice to its shadow. It is stranger to our world, aloof from our ambitions, with a destiny not here to be fulfilled. It says: "You are of dust while I am robed in opalescent airs. You dwell in houses of clay, I in a temple not made by hands. I will not go with thee, but thou must come with me." And not alone is the form of the divine aloof but the spirit behind the form. It is called the Goal truly, but it has no ending. It is the Comforter, but it waves away our joys and hopes like the angel with the flaming sword. Though it is the Resting-place, it stirs to all heroic strife, to outgoing, to conquest. It is the Friend indeed, but it will not yield to our desires. Is it this strange, unfathomable self we think to know, and awaken to, by what is written, or by study of it as so many planes of consciousness? But in vain we store the upper chambers of the mind with such quaint furniture of thought. No archangel makes his abode therein. They abide only in the shining. No wonder that the Gods do not incarnate. We cannot say we do pay reverence to these awful powers. We repulse the living truth by our doubts and reasonings. We would compel the Gods to fall in with our petty philosophy rather than trust in the heavenly guidance. Ah, to think of it, those dread deities, the divine Fires, to be so enslaved! We have not comprehended the meaning of the voice which cried "Prepare ye the way of the Lord," or this, "Lift up your heads, O ye gates. Be ye lifted up, ye everlasting doors, and the King of Glory shall come in." Nothing that we read is useful unless it calls up living things in the soul. To read a mystic book truly is to invoke the powers. If they do not rise up plumed and radiant, the apparitions of spiritual things, then is our labor barren. We only encumber the mind with useless symbols. They knew better ways long ago. "Master of the Green- waving Planisphere, . . . Lord of the Azure Expanse, . . . it is thus we invoke," cried the magicians of old.

And us, let us invoke them with joy, let us call upon them with love, the Light we hail, or the Divine Darkness we worship with silent breath. That silence cries aloud to the Gods. Then they will approach us. Then we may learn that speech of many colors, for they will not speak in our mortal tongue; they will not answer to the names of men. Their names are rainbow glories. Yet these are mysteries, and they cannot be reasoned out or argued over. We cannot speak truly of them from report, or description, or from what another has written. A relation to the thing in itself alone is our warrant, and this means we must set aside our intellectual self-sufficiency and await guidance. It will surely come to those who wait in trust, a glow, a heat in the heart announcing the awakening of the Fire. And, as it blows with its mystic breath into the brain, there is a hurtling of visions, a brilliance of lights, a sound as of great waters vibrant and musical in their flowing, and murmurs from a single yet multitudinous being. In such a mood, when the far becomes near, the strange familiar, and the infinite possible, he wrote from whose words we get the inspiration:

> To launch off with absolute faith, to sweep through the
> ceaseless rings
> and never be quiet again.

Such a faith and such an unrest be ours: faith which is mistrust of the visible; unrest which is full of a hidden surety and reliance. We, when we fall into pleasant places, rest and dream our strength away. Before every enterprise and adventure of the soul we calculate in fear our power to do. But remember, "Oh, disciple, in thy work for thy brother thou hast many allies; in the winds, in the air, in all the voices of the silent shore." These are the far-wandered powers of our own nature, and they turn again home at our need. We came out of the Great Mother-Life for the purposes of soul. Are her darlings forgotten where they darkly wander and strive? Never. Are not the lives of all her heroes proof? Though they seem to stand alone the eternal Mother keeps watch on them, and voices far away and unknown to them before arise in passionate defense, and hearts beat warm to help them. Aye, if we could look within we would see vast nature stirred on their behalf, and institutions shaken, until the truth they fight for triumphs, and they pass, and a wake of glory ever widening behind them trails down the ocean of the years.

Thus the warrior within us works, or, if we choose to phrase it so, it is the action of the spiritual will. Shall we not, then, trust in it and face the unknown, defiant and fearless of its dangers. Though we seem to go alone to the high, the lonely, the pure, we need not despair. Let no one bring to this task the mood of the martyr or of one who thinks he sacrifices something. Yet let all who will come. Let them enter the path, facing all things in life and death with a mood at once gay and reverent, as beseems those who are immortal--who are children today, but whose hands tomorrow may grasp the sceptre, sitting down with the Gods as equals and companions. "What a man thinks, that he is: that is the old secret." In this self-conception lies the secret of life, the way of escape and return. We have imagined ourselves into littleness, darkness, and feebleness. We must imagine ourselves into greatness. "If thou wilt not equal thyself to God thou canst not understand God. The like is only intelligible by the like." In some moment of more complete imagination the thought-born may go forth and look on the ancient Beauty. So it was in the mysteries long ago, and may well be today. The poor dead shadow was laid to sleep, forgotten in its darkness, as the fiery power, mounting from heart to head, went forth in radiance. Not then did it rest, nor ought we. The dim worlds dropped behind it, the lights of earth disappeared as it neared the heights of the immortals. There was One seated on a throne, One dark and bright with ethereal glory. It arose in greeting. The radiant figure laid its head against the breast which grew suddenly golden, and Father and Son vanished in that which has no place or name.

III.

Who are exiles? as for me
Where beneath the diamond dome
Lies the light on hills or tree
There my palace is and home.

We are outcasts from Deity, therefore we defame the place of our exile. But who is there may set apart his destiny from the earth which bore him? I am one of those who would bring back the old reverence for the Mother, the magic, the love. I think, metaphysician, you have gone astray. You would seek within yourself for the fountain of life. Yes, there is the true, the only light. But do not dream it will lead you farther away from the earth, but rather deeper into its' heart. By it you are nourished with those living waters you would drink. You are yet in the womb and unborn, and the Mother breathes for you the diviner airs. Dart out your farthest ray of thought to the original, and yet you have not found a new path of your own. Your ray is still enclosed in the parent ray, and only on the sidereal streams are you borne to the freedom of the deep, to the sacred stars whose distance maddens, and to the lonely Light of Lights. Let us, therefore, accept the conditions and address ourselves with wonder, with awe, with love, as we well may, to that being in whom we move. I abate no jot of those vaster hopes, yet I would pursue that ardent aspiration, content as to here and today. I do not believe in a nature red with tooth and claw. If indeed she appears so terrible to any it is because they themselves have armed her. Again, behind the anger of the Gods there is a love. Are the rocks barren? Lay your brow against them and learn what memories they keep. Is the brown earth unbeautiful? Yet lie on the breast of the Mother and you shall be aureoled with the dews of faery. The earth is the entrance to the Halls of Twilight. What emanations are those that make radiant the dark woods of pine! Round every leaf and tree and over all the mountains wave the fiery tresses of that hidden sun which is the soul of the earth and parent of your soul. But we think of these things no longer. Like the prodigal we have wandered far from our home, but no more return. We idly pass or wait as strangers in the halls our spirit built.

> Sad or fain no more to live?
> I have pressed the lips of pain
> With the kisses lovers give
> Ransomed ancient powers again.

I would raise this shrinking soul to a universal acceptance. What! does it aspire to the All, and yet deny by its revolt and inner test the justice of Law? From sorrow we take no less and no more than from our joys. If the one reveals to the soul the mode by which the power overflows and fills it here, the other indicates to it the unalterable will which checks excess and leads it on to true proportion and its own ancestral ideal. Yet men seem for ever to fly from their destiny of inevitable beauty; because of delay the power invites and lures no longer but goes out into the highways with a hand of iron. We look back cheerfully enough upon those old trials out of which we have passed; but we have gloaned only an aftermath of wisdom, and missed the full harvest if the will has not risen royally at the moment in unison with the will of the Immortal, even though it comes rolled round with terror and suffering and strikes at the heart of clay.

Through all these things, in doubt, despair, poverty, sick, feeble, or baffled, we have yet to learn reliance. "I will not leave thee or forsake thee" are the words of the most ancient spirit to the spark wandering in the immensity of its own being. This high courage brings with it a vision. It sees the true intent in all circumstance out of which its own emerges to meet it. Before it the blackness melts into forms of beauty, and back of all illusions is seen the old enchanter tenderly smiling, the dark, hidden Father enveloping his children. All things have their compensations. For what is absent here there is always, if we seek, a nobler presence about us.

> Captive, see what stars give light
>   In the hidden heart of clay:
> At their radiance dark and bright
>   Fades the dreamy King of Day.

We complain of conditions, but this very imperfection it is which urges us to arise and seek for the Isles of the Immortals. What we lack recalls the fullness. The soul has seen a brighter day than this and a sun which never sets. Hence the retrospect: "Thou hast been in Eden the garden of God; every precious stone was thy covering, the sardius, topaz, and the diamond, the beryl, the onyx, the jasper, the sapphire, emerald. . . . Thou wast upon the holy mountain of God; thou hast walked up and down in the midst of the stones of fire." We would point out these radiant avenues of return; but sometimes we feel in our hearts that we sound but cockney voices as guides amid the ancient temples, the cyclopean crypts sanctified by the mysteries. To be intelligible we replace the opalescent shining by the terms of the scientist, and we prate of occult physiology in the same breath with the Most High. Yet when the soul has the divine vision it knows not it has a body. Let it remember, and the breath of glory kindles it no more; it is once again a captive. After all it does not make the mysteries clearer to speak in physical terms and do violence to our intuitions. If we ever use these centres, as fires we shall see them, or they shall well up within us as fountains of potent sound. We may satisfy people's mind with a sense correspondence, and their souls may yet hold aloof. We shall only inspire by the magic of a superior beauty. Yet this too has its dangers. "Thou hast corrupted thy wisdom by reason of thy brightness," continues the seer. If we follow too much the elusive beauty of form we will miss the spirit. The last secrets are for those who translate vision into being. Does the glory fade away before you? Say truly in your heart, "I care not. I will wear the robes I am endowed with today." You are already become beautiful, being beyond desire and free.

> Night and day no more eclipse
>   Friendly eyes that on us shine,
> Speech from old familiar lips.
>   Playmates of a youth divine.

To childhood once again. We must regain the lost state. But it is to the giant and spiritual childhood of the young immortals we must return, when into their dear and translucent souls first fell the rays of the father-beings. The men of old were intimates of wind and wave and playmates of many a brightness long since forgotten. The rapture of the fire was their rest; their out-going was still consciously through universal being. By darkened images we may figure something vaguely akin, as when in rare moments under the stars the big dreamy heart of childhood is pervaded with quiet and brimmed full with love. Dear children of the world, so tired today-- so weary seeking after the light. Would you recover strength and immortal vigor? Not one star alone, your star, shall shed its happy light upon you, but the All you must adore. Something intimate, secret, unspeakable, akin to thee, will emerge silently, insensibly, and ally itself with thee as thou gatherest thyself from the four quarters of the earth. We shall go back to the world of the dawn, but to a brighter light than that which opened up this wondrous story of the cycles. The forms of elder years will reappear in our vision, the father-beings once again. So we shall grow at home amid these grandeurs, and with that All-Presence about us may cry in our hearts, "At last is our meeting, Immortal. O starry one, now is our rest!"

> Come away, oh, come away;
>   We will quench the heart's desire
> Past the gateways of the day
>   In the rapture of the fire.

1896

THE HERO IN MAN

I.

There sometimes comes on us a mood of strange reverence for people and things which in less contemplative hours we hold to be unworthy; and in such moments we may set side by side the head of the Christ and the head of an outcast, and there is an equal radiance around each, which makes of the darker face a shadow and is itself a shadow around the head of light. We feel a fundamental unity of purpose in their presence here, and would as willingly pay homage to the one who has fallen as to him who has become a master of life. I know that immemorial order decrees that the laurel crown be given only to the victor, but in these moments I speak of a profound intuition changes the decree and sets the aureole on both alike.

We feel such deep pity for the fallen that there must needs be a justice in it, for these diviner feelings are wiser in themselves and do not vaguely arise. They are lights from the Father. A justice lies in uttermost pity and forgiveness, even when we seem to ourselves to be most deeply wronged, or why is it that the awakening of resentment or hate brings such swift contrition? We are ever self-condemned, and the dark thought which went forth in us brooding revenge, when suddenly smitten by the light, withdraws and hides within itself in awful penitence. In asking myself why is it that the meanest are safe from our condemnation when we sit on the true seat of judgment in the heart, it seemed to me that their shield was the sense we have of a nobility hidden in them under the cover of ignoble things; that their present darkness was the result of some too weighty heroic labor undertaken long ago by the human spirit, that it was the consecration of past purpose which played with such a tender light about their ruined lives, and it was more pathetic because this nobleness was all unknown to the fallen, and the heroic cause of so much pain was forgotten in life's prison-house.

While feeling the service to us of the great ethical ideal which have been formulated by men I think that the idea of justice intellectually conceived tends to beget a certain hardness of heart. It is true that men have done wrong--hence their pain; but back of all this there is something infinitely soothing, a light that does not wound, which says no harsh thing, even although the darkest of the spirits turns to it in its agony, for the darkest of human spirits has still around him this first glory which shines from a deeper being within, whose history may be told as the legend of the Hero in Man.

Among the many immortals with whom ancient myth peopled the spiritual spheres of humanity are some figures which draw to themselves a more profound tenderness than the rest. Not Aphrodite rising in beauty from the faery foam of the first seas, not Apollo with sweetest singing, laughter, and youth, not the wielder of the lightning could exact the reverence accorded to the lonely Titan chained on the mountain, or to that bowed figure heavy with the burden of the sins of the world; for the brighter divinities had no part in the labor of man, no such intimate relation with the wherefore of his own existence so full of struggle. The more radiant figures are prophecies to him of his destiny, but the Titan and the Christ are a revelation of his more immediate state; their giant sorrows companion his own, and in contemplating them he awakens what is noblest in his own nature; or, in other words, in understanding their divine heroism he understands himself. For this in truth it seems to me to mean: all knowledge is a revelation of the self to the self, and our deepest comprehension of the seemingly apart divine is also our farthest inroad to self-knowledge; Prometheus, Christ, are in every heart; the story of one is the story of all; the Titan and the Crucified are humanity.

If, then, we consider them as representing the human spirit and disentangle from the myths their meaning, we shall find that whatever reverence is due to that heroic love, which descended from heaven for the redeeming of a lower nature, must be paid to every human being. Christ is incarnate in all humanity. Prometheus is bound for ever within us. They are the same. They are a host, and the divine incarnation was not spoken of one, but of all those who, descending into the lower world, tried to change it into the divine image, and to wrest out of chaos a kingdom for the empire of light. The angels saw below them in chaos a senseless rout blind with elemental passion, for ever warring with discordant cries which broke in upon the world of divine beauty; and that the pain might depart, they grew rebellious in the Master's peace, and descending to earth the angelic lights were crucified in men. They left so radiant worlds, such a light of beauty, for earth's gray twilight filled with tears, that through this elemental life might breathe the starry music brought from Him. If the "Fore-seer" be a true name for the Titan, it follows that in the host which he represents was a light which well foreknew all the dark paths of its journey; foreseeing the bitter struggle with a hostile nature, but foreseeing perhaps a gain, a distant glory o'er the hills of sorrow, and that chaos, divine and transformed, with only gentle breathing, lit up by the Christ-soul of the universe. There is a transforming power in the thought itself: we can no longer condemn the fallen, they who laid aside their thrones of ancient power, their spirit ecstasy and beauty on such a mission. Perhaps those who sank lowest did so to raise a greater burden, and of these most fallen it may in the hour of their resurrection be said, "The last shall be first."

So, placing side by side the head of the outcast with the head of Christ, it has this equal beauty--with as bright a glory it sped from the Father in ages past on its redeeming labor. Of his present darkness what shall we say? "He is altogether dead in sin?" Nay, rather with tenderness forbear, and think the foreseeing spirit has taken its own dread path to mastery; that that which foresaw the sorrow foresaw also beyond it a greater joy and a mightier existence, when it would rise again in a new robe, woven out of the treasure hidden in the deep of its submergence, and shine at last like the stars of the morning, and live among the Sons of God.

II.

Our deepest life is when we are alone. We think most truly, love best, when isolated from the outer world in that mystic abyss we call soul. Nothing external can equal the fullness of these moments. We may sit in the blue twilight with a friend, or bend together by the hearth, half whispering or in a silence populous with loving thoughts mutually understood; then we may feel happy and at peace, but it is only because we are lulled by a semblance to deeper intimacies. When we think of a friend and the loved one draws nigh, we sometimes feel half-pained, for we touched something in our solitude which the living presence shut out; we seem more apart, and would fain wave them away and cry, "Call me not forth from this; I am no more a spirit if I leave my throne." But these moods, though lit up by intuitions of the true, are too partial, they belong too much to the twilight of the heart, they have too dreamy a temper to serve us well in life. We would wish rather for our thoughts a directness such as belongs to the messengers of the gods, swift, beautiful, flashing presences bent on purposes well understood.

What we need is that this interior tenderness shall be elevated into seership, that what in most is only yearning or blind love shall see clearly its way and hope. To this end we have to observe more intently the nature of the interior life. We find, indeed, that it is not a solitude at all, but dense with multitudinous being: instead of being alone we are in the thronged highways of existence. For our guidance when entering here many words of warning have been uttered, laws have been outlined, and beings full of wonder, terror, and beauty described. Yet there is a spirit in us deeper than our intellectual being which I think of as the Hero in man, who feels the nobility of its place in the midst of all this, and who would fain equal the greatness of perception with deeds as great. The weariness and sense of futility which often falls upon the mystic after much thought is due to this, that he has not recognized that he must be worker as well as seer, that here he has duties demanding a more sustained endurance, just as the inner life is so much vaster and more intense than the life he has left behind.

Now the duties which can be taken up by the soul are exactly those which it feels most inadequate to perform when acting as an embodied being. What shall be done to quiet the heart-cry of the world: how answer the dumb appeal for help we so often divine below eyes that laugh? It is the saddest of all sorrows to think that pity with no hands to heal, that love without a voice to speak should helplessly heap their pain upon pain while earth shall endure. But there is a truth about sorrow which I think may make it seem not so hopeless. There are fewer barriers than we think: there is, in truth, an inner alliance between the soul who would fain give and the soul who is in need. Nature has well provided that not one golden ray of all our thoughts is sped ineffective through the dark; not one drop of the magical elixirs love distils is wasted. Let us consider how this may be. There is a habit we nearly all have indulged in. We weave little stories in our minds, expending love and pity upon the imaginary beings we have created, and I have been led to think that many of these are not imaginary, that somewhere in the world beings are living just in that way, and we merely reform and live over again in our life the story of another life. Sometimes these far-away intimates assume so vivid a shape, they come so near with their appeal for sympathy that the pictures are unforgettable; and the more I ponder over them the more it seems to me that they often convey the actual need of some soul whose cry for comfort has gone out into the vast, perhaps to meet with an answer, perhaps to hear only silence. I will supply an instance. I see a child, a curious, delicate little thing, seated on the doorstep of a house. It is an alley in some great city, and there is a gloom of evening and vapor over the sky. I see the child is bending over the path; he is picking cinders and arranging them, and as I ponder I become aware that he is laying down in gritty lines the walls of a house, the mansion of his dream. Here spread along the pavement are large rooms, these for his friends, and a tiny room in the centre, that is his own. So his thought plays. Just then I catch a glimpse of the corduroy trousers of a passing workman, and a heavy boot crushes through the cinders. I feel the pain in the child's heart as he shrinks back, his little lovelit house of dreams all rudely shattered. Ah, poor child, building the City Beautiful out of a few cinders, yet nigher, truer in intent than many a stately, gold-rich palace reared by princes, thou wert not forgotten by that mighty spirit who lives through the falling of empires, whose home has been in many a ruined heart. Surely it was to bring comfort to hearts like thine that that most noble of all meditations was ordained by the Buddha. "He lets his mind pervade one quarter of the world with thoughts of Love, and so the second, and so the third, and so the fourth. And thus the whole wide world, above, below, around, and everywhere does he continue to pervade with heart of Love far-reaching, grown great and beyond measure."

That love, though the very faery breath of life, should by itself, and so imparted have a sustaining power some may question, not those who have felt the sunlight fall from distant friends who think of them; but, to make clearer how it seems to me to act, I say that love, Eros, is a being. It is more than a power of the soul, though it is that also; it has a universal life of its own, and just as the dark heaving waters do not know what jewel lights they reflect with blinding radiance, so the soul, partially absorbing and feeling the ray of Eros within it, does not know that often a part of its nature nearer to the sun of love shines with a brilliant light to other eyes than its own. Many people move unconscious of their own charm, unknowing of the beauty and power they seem to others to impart. It is some past attainment of the soul, a jewel won in some old battle which it may have forgotten, but none the less this gleams on its tiara, and the star-flame inspires others to hope and victory.

If it is true here that many exert a spiritual influence they are unconscious of, it is still truer of the spheres within. Once the soul has attained to any possession like love, or persistent will, or faith, or a power of thought, it comes into spiritual contact with others who are struggling for these very powers. The attainment of any of these means that the soul is able to absorb and radiate some of the diviner elements of being. The soul may or may nor be aware of the position it is placed in or its new duties, but yet that Living Light, having found a way into the being of any one person, does not rest there, but sends its rays and extends its influence on and on to illume the darkness of another nature. So it comes that there are ties which bind us to people other than those whom we meet in our everyday life. I think they are most real ties, most important to understand, for if we let our lamp go out some far away who had reached out in the dark and felt a steady will, a persistent hope, a compassionate love, may reach out once again in an hour of need, and finding no support may give way and fold the hands in despair. Often we allow gloom to overcome us and so hinder the bright rays in their passage; but would we do it so often if we thought that perhaps a sadness which besets us, we do not know why, was caused by some one drawing nigh to us for comfort, whom our lethargy might make feel still more his helplessnes, while our courage, our faith might cause "our light to shine in some other heart which as yet has no light of its own"?

III.

The night was wet, and as I was moving down the streets my mind was also journeying on a way of its own, and the things which were bodily present before

me were no less with me in my unseen traveling. Every now and then a transfer would take place, and some of the moving shadows in the street would begin
walking about in the clear interior light. The children of the city, crouched in the
doorways or racing through the hurrying multitude and flashing lights, began their
elfin play again in my heart; and that was because I had heard these tiny outcasts
shouting with glee. I wondered if the glitter and shadow of such sordid things were
thronged with magnificence and mystery for those who were unaware of a greater
light and deeper shade which made up the romance and fascination of my own
life. In imagination I narrowed myself to their ignorance, littleness, and youth, and
seemed for a moment to flit amid great uncomprehended beings and a dim wonderful city of palaces.

Then another transfer took place, and I was pondering anew, for a face I had
seen flickering through the warm wet mist haunted me; it entered into the realm
of the interpreter, and I was made aware by the pale cheeks and by the close-shut
lips of pain, and by some inward knowledge, that there the Tree of Life was beginning to grow, and I wondered why it is that it always springs up through a heart in
ashes; I wondered also if that which springs up, which in itself is an immortal joy,
has knowledge that its shoots are piercing through such anguish; or, again, if it was
the piercing of the shoots which caused the pain, and if every throb of the beautiful
flame darting upward to blossom meant the perishing of some more earthly growth
which had kept the heart in shadow.

Seeing, too, how many thoughts spring up from such a simple thing, I questioned whether that which started the impulse had any share in the outcome, and
if these musings of mine in any way affected their subject. I then began thinking
about those secret ties on which I have speculated before, and in the darkness my
heart grew suddenly warm and glowing, for I had chanced upon one of these shining imaginations which are the wealth of those who travel upon the hidden ways.
In describing that which comes to us all at once, there is a difficulty in choosing
between what is first and what is last to say; but, interpreting as best I can, I seemed
to behold the onward movement of a Light, one among many lights, all living,
throbbing, now dim with perturbations and now again clear, and all subtly woven
together, outwardly in some more shadowy shining, and inwardly in a greater fire,
which, though it was invisible, I knew to be the Lamp of the World. This Light

which I beheld I felt to be a human soul, and these perturbations which dimmed it were its struggles and passionate longings for something, and that was for a more brilliant shining of the light within itself. It was in love with its own beauty, enraptured by its own lucidity; and I saw that as these things were more beloved they grew paler, for this light is the light which the Mighty Mother has in her heart for her children, and she means that it shall go through each one unto all, and whoever restrains it in himself is himself shut out; not that the great heart has ceased in its love for that soul, but that the soul has shut itself off from influx, for every imagination of man is the opening or the closing of a door to the divine world; now he is solitary, cut off, and, seemingly to himself, on the desert and distant verge of things; and then his thought throws open the shut portals, he hears the chant of the seraphs in his heart, and he is made luminous by the lighting of a sudden aureole. This soul which I watched seemed to have learned at last the secret love; for, in the anguish begotten by its loss, it followed the departing glory in penitence to the inmost shrine, where it ceased altogether; and because it seemed utterly lost and hopeless of attainment and capriciously denied to the seeker, a profound pity arose in the soul for those who, like it, were seeking, but still in hope, for they had not come to the vain end of their endeavors. I understood that such pity is the last of the precious essences which make up the elixir of immortality, and when it is poured into the cup it is ready for drinking. And so it was with this soul which grew brilliant with the passage of the eternal light through its new purity of self-oblivion, and joyful in the comprehension of the mystery of the secret love, which, though it has been declared many times by the greatest of teachers among men, is yet never known truly unless the Mighty Mother has herself breathed it in the heart.

And now that the soul has divined this secret, the shadowy shining which was woven in bonds of union between it and its fellow lights grew clearer; and a multitude of these strands were, so it seemed, strengthened and placed in its keeping: along these it was to send the message of the wisdom and the love which were the secret sweetness of its own being. Then a spiritual tragedy began, infinitely more pathetic than the old desolation, because it was brought about by the very nobility of the spirit. This soul, shedding its love like rays of glory, seemed itself the centre of a ring of wounding spears: it sent forth love, and the arrowy response came hate-impelled: it whispered peace, and was answered by the clash of rebellion: and to all this for defense it could only bare more openly its heart that a profounder love from the Mother Nature might pass through upon the rest. I knew this was what a teacher, who wrote long ago, meant when he said: "Put on the whole armor of God," which is love and endurance, for the truly divine children of the Flame are not armed otherwise: and of those protests set up in ignorance or rebellion against the whisper of the wisdom, I saw that some melted in the fierce and tender heat of the heart, and there came in their stead a golden response, which made closer the ties, and drew these souls upward to an understanding and to share in the overshadowing nature. And this is part of the plan of the Great Alchemist, whereby the red ruby of the heart is transmuted into the tender light of the opal; for the beholding of love made bare acts like the flame of the furnace: and the dissolving passions, through an anguish of remorse, the lightnings of pain, and through an adoring pity are changed into the image they contemplate, and melt in the ecstasy of self-forgetful love, the spirit which lit the thorn-crowned brows which perceived only in its last agony the retribution due to its tormentors, and cried out, "Father, forgive them, for they know not what they do."

Now, although the love of the few may alleviate the hurt due to the ignorance of the mass, it is not in the power of any one to withstand for ever this warfare; for by the perpetual wounding of the inner nature it is so wearied that the spirit must withdraw from a tabernacle grown too frail to support the increase of light within and the jarring of the demoniac nature without; and at length comes the call which means, for a while, release and a deep rest in regions beyond the paradise of lesser souls. So, withdrawn into the divine darkness, vanished the light of my dream. And now it seemed as if this wonderful weft of souls intertwining as one being must come to naught; and all those who through the gloom had nourished a longing for the light would stretch out hands in vain for guidance; but that I did not understand the love of the Mother, and that, although few, there is no decaying of her heroic brood; for, as the seer of old caught at the mantle of him who went up in the fiery chariot, so another took up the burden and gathered the shining strands together: and of this sequence of spiritual guides there is no ending.

Here I may say that the love of the Mother, which, acting through the burnished will of the hero, is wrought to its highest uses, is in reality everywhere, and pervades with profoundest tenderness the homeliest circumstance of daily life, and there is not lacking, even among the humblest, an understanding of the spiritual tragedy which follows upon every effort of the divine nature, bowing itself down in pity to our shadowy sphere, an understanding where the nature of the love is gauged through the extent of the sacrifice and the pain which is overcome. I recall the instance of an old Irish peasant, who, as he lay in hospital wakeful from a grinding pain in the leg, forgot himself in making drawings, rude, yet reverently done, of incidents in the life of the Galilean Teacher. One of these which he showed me was a crucifixion, where, amidst much grotesque symbolism, were some tracings which indicated a purely beautiful intuition; the heart of this crucified figure, no less than the brow, was wreathed about with thorns and radiant with light: "For that," said he, "was where he really suffered." When I think of this old man, bringing forgetfulness of his own bodily pain through contemplation of the spiritual suffering of his Master, my memory of him shines with something of the transcendent light he himself perceived, for I feel that some suffering of his own, nobly undergone, had given him understanding, and he had laid his heart in love against the Heart of Many Sorrows, seeing it wounded by unnumbered spears, yet burning with undying love.

Though much may be learned by observance of the superficial life and actions of a spiritual teacher, it is only in the deeper life of meditation and imagination that it can be truly realized; for the soul is a midnight blossom which opens its leaves in dream, and its perfect bloom is unfolded only where another sun shines in another heaven; there it feels what celestial dews descend on it and what influences draw it up to its divine archetype. Here in the shadow of earth root intercoils with root, and the finer distinctions of the blossom are not perceived. If we knew also who they really are, who sometimes in silence and sometimes with the eyes of the world at gaze take upon them the mantle of teacher, an unutterable awe would prevail, for underneath a bodily presence not in any sense beautiful may burn the glory of some ancient divinity, some hero who has laid aside his sceptre in the enchanted land, to rescue old-time comrades fallen into oblivion; or, again, if we had the insight of the simple old peasant into the nature of his enduring love, out of the exquisite and poignant emotions kindled would arise the flame of a passionate love, which would endure long aeons of anguish that it might shield, though but for a little, the kingly hearts who may not shield themselves.

But I, too, who write, have launched the rebellious spear, or in lethargy have oft times gone down the great drift numbering myself among those who, not being with must needs be against. Therefore I make no appeal: they only may call who stand upon the lofty mountains; but I reveal the thought which arose like a star in my soul with such bright and pathetic meaning, leaving it to you who read to approve and apply it.

1897

THE MEDITATION OF ANANDA

Ananda rose from his seat under the banyan tree. He passed his hand unsteadily over his brow. Throughout the day the young ascetic had been plunged in profound meditation; and now, returning from heaven to earth, he was bewildered like one who awakens in darkness and knows not where he is. All day long before his inner eye burned the light of the Lokas, until he was wearied and exhausted with their splendors; space glowed like a diamond with intolerable lustre, and there was no end to the dazzling procession of figures. He had seen the fiery dreams of the dead in heaven. He had been tormented by the music of celestial singers, whose choral song reflected in its ripples the rhythmic pulse of being. He saw how these orbs were held within luminous orbs of wider circuit; and vaste and vaster grew the vistas, until at last, a mere speck of life, he bore the burden of innumerable worlds. Seeking for Brahma, he found only the great illusion as infinite as Brahma's being.

If these things were shadows, the earth and the forests he returned to, viewed at evening, seemed still more unreal, the mere dusky flutter of a moth's wings in space, so filmy and evanescent that if he had sunk as through transparent aether into the void, it would not have been wonderful.

Ananda, still half entranced, turned homeward. As he threaded the dim alleys he noticed not the flaming eyes which regarded him from the gloom; the serpents rustling amid the undergrowth; the lizards, fireflies, insects, and the innumerable lives of which the Indian forest was rumorous; they also were but shadows. He paused near the village hearing the sound of human voices, of children at play. He felt a pity for these tiny beings, who struggled and shouted, rolling over each other in ecstasies of joy. The great illusion had indeed devoured them, before whose spirits the Devas themselves once were worshippers. Then, close beside him, he heard a voice, whose low tone of reverence soothed him; it was akin to his own nature, and it awakened him fully. A little crowd of five or six people were listening silently to an old man who read from a palm- leaf manuscript. Ananda knew, by the orange-colored robes of the old man that here was a brother of the new faith, and he paused with the others. What was his illusion? The old man lifted his head for a moment as the ascetic came closer, and then continued as before. He was reading "The Legend of the Great King of Glory," and Ananda listened while the story was told of the Wonderful Wheel, the Elephant Treasure, the Lake and Palace of Righteousness, and of the meditation, how the Great King of Glory entered the golden chamber, and set himself down on the silver couch, and he let his mind pervade one quarter of the world with thoughts of love; and so the second quarter, and so the third, and so the fourth. And thus the whole wide world, above, below, around, and everywhere, did he continue to pervade with heart of Love, far reaching, grown great, and beyond measure.

When the old man had ended Ananda went back into the forest. He had found the secret of the true, how the Vision could be left behind and the Being entered. Another legend rose in his mind, a faery legend of righteousness expanding and filling the universe, a vision beautiful and full of old enchantment, and his heart sang within him. He seated himself again under the banyan tree. He rose up in soul. He saw before him images long forgotten of those who suffer in the sorrowful earth. He saw the desolation and loneliness of old age, the insults of the captive, the misery of the leper and outcast, the chill horror and darkness of life in a dungeon. He drank in all their sorrow. From his heart he went out to them. Love, a fierce and tender flame, arose; pity, a breath from the vast; sympathy, born of unity. This triple fire sent forth its rays; they surrounded those dark souls; they pervaded them; they beat down oppression. -------------

While Ananda, with spiritual magic, sent forth the healing powers through the four quarters of the world, far away at that moment a king sat enthroned in his hall. A captive was bound before him-- bound, but proud, defiant, unconquerable of soul. There was silence in the hall until the king spake the doom and torture for this ancient enemy.

The king spake: "I had thought to do some fierce thing to thee and so end thy days, my enemy. But I remember now, with sorrow, the great wrongs we have done to each other, and the hearts made sore by our hatred. I shall do no more wrong to thee; thou art free to depart. Do what thou wilt. I will make restitution to thee as far as may be for thy ruined state."

Then the soul which no might could conquer was conquered utterly-- the knees of the captive were bowed and his pride was overcome. "My brother," he said, and could say no more. -------------

To watch for years a little narrow slit high up in a dark cell, so high that he could not reach up and look out, and there to see daily the change from blue to dark in the sky, had withered a prisoner's soul. The bitter tears came no more, hardly even sorrow, only a dull, dead feeling. But that day a great groan burst from him. He heard outside the laugh of a child who was playing and gathering flowers under the high, gray walls. Then it all came over him--the divine things missed, the light, the glory, and the beauty that the earth puts forth for her children. The arrow slit was darkened, and half of a little bronze face appeared.

"Who are you down there in the darkness who sigh so? Are you all alone there? For so many years! Ah, poor man! I would come down to you if I could, but I will sit here and talk to you for a while. Here are flowers for you," and a little arm showered them in by handfuls until the room was full of the intoxicating fragrance of summer. Day after day the child came, and the dull heart entered once more into the great human love. --------------

At twilight, by a deep and wide river, an old woman sat alone, dreamy and full of memories. The lights of the swift passing boats and the light of the stars were just as in childhood and the old love-time. Old, feeble, it was time for her to hurry away from the place which changed not with her sorrow.

"Do you see our old neighbor there?" said Ayesha to her lover. "They say she was once as beautiful as you would make me think I now am. How lonely she must be! Let us come near and speak to her," and the lover went gladly. Though they spoke to each other rather than to her, yet something of the past, which never dies when love, the immortal, has pervaded it, rose up again as she heard their voices. She smiled, thinking of years of burning beauty. --------------

A teacher, accompanied by his disciples, was passing by the wayside where a leper sat.

The teacher said: "Here is our brother, whom we may not touch, but he need not be shut out from truth. We may sit down where he can listen."

He sat on the wayside near the leper, and his disciples stood around him. He spoke words full of love, kindliness, and pity--the eternal truths which make the soul grow full of sweetness and youth. A small, old spot began to glow in the heart of the leper, and the tears ran down his blighted face. --------------

All these were the deeds of Ananda the ascetic, and the Watcher who was over him from all eternity made a great stride towards that soul.

1893

THE MIDNIGHT BLOSSOM

"Arhans are born at midnight hour, together with the holy flower that opes and blossoms in darkness."
            --From an Eastern Scripture.

We stood together at the door of our hut. We could see through the gathering gloom where our sheep and goats were cropping the sweet grass on the side of the hill. We were full of drowsy content as they were. We had naught to mar our happiness, neither memory nor unrest for the future. We lingered on while the vast twilight encircled us; we were one with its dewy stillness. The lustre of the early stars first broke in upon our dreaming: we looked up and around. The yellow constellations began to sing their choral hymn together. As the night deepened they came out swiftly from their hiding-places in depths of still and unfathomable blue--they hung in burning clusters, they advanced in multitudes that dazzled. The shadowy shining of night was strewn all over with nebulous dust of silver, with long mists of gold, with jewels of glittering green. We felt how fit a place the earth was to live on with these nightly glories over us, with silence and coolness upon our lawns and lakes after the consuming day. Valmika, Kedar, Ananda, and I watched together. Through the rich gloom we could see far distant forests and lights, the lights of village and city in King Suddhodana's realm.

"Brothers," said Valmika, "how good it is to be here and not yonder in the city, where they know not peace, even in sleep."

"Yonder and yonder," said Kedar I saw the inner air full of a red glow where they were busy in toiling and strife. It seemed to reach up to me. I could not breathe. I climbed the hill at dawn to laugh where the snows were, and the sun is as white as they are white."

"But, brothers, if we went down among them and told them how happy we were, and how the flower's grow on the hillside, they would surely come up and leave all sorrow. They cannot know or they would come." Ananda was a mere child, though so tall for his years.

"They would not come," said Kedar; "all their joy is to haggle and hoard. When Siva blows upon them with angry breath they will lament, or when the demons in fierce hunger devour them."

"It is good to be here," repeated Valmika, drowsily, "to mind the flocks and be at rest, and to hear the wise Varunna speak when he comes among us."

I was silent. I knew better than they that busy city which glowed beyond the dark forests. I had lived there until, grown sick and weary, I had gone back to my brothers on the hillside. I wondered, would life, indeed, go on ceaselessly until it ended in the pain of the world. I said within myself: "O mighty Brahma, on the outermost verges of thy dream are our lives. Thou old invisible, how faintly through our hearts comes the sound of thy song, the light of thy glory!" Full of yearning to rise and return, I strove to hear in my heart the music Anahata, spoken of in our sacred scrolls. There was silence and then I thought I heard sounds, not glad, a myriad murmur. As I listened they deepened--they grew into passionate prayer and appeal and tears, as if the cry of the long- forgotten souls of men went echoing through empty chambers. My eyes filled with tears, for it seemed world-wide and to sigh from out many ages, long agone, to be and yet to be.

"Ananda! Ananda! Where is the boy running to?" cried Valmika. Ananda had vanished in the gloom. We heard his glad laugh below, and then another voice speaking. The tall figure of Varunna loomed up presently. Ananda held his hand, and danced beside him. We knew the Yogi, and bowed reverently before him. We could see by the starlight his simple robe of white. I could trace clearly every feature of the grave and beautiful face and radiant eyes. I saw not by the starlight, but by a silvery radiance which rayed a little way into the blackness around the dark hair and face. Valmika, as elder, first spoke:

"Holy sir, be welcome. Will you come in and rest?"

"I cannot stay now. I must pass over the mountains ere dawn; but you may come a little way with me--such of you as will."

We assented gladly, Kedar and I, Valmika remained. Then Ananda prayed to go. We bade him stay, fearing for him the labor of climbing and the chill of the snows. But Varunna said: "Let the child come. He is hardy, and will not tire if he holds my hand."

So we set out together, and faced the highlands that rose and rose above us. We knew the way well, even at night. We waited in silence for Varunna to speak; but for nigh an hour we mounted without words, save for Ananda's shouts of delight and wonder at the heavens spread above valleys that lay behind us. Then I grew hungry for an answer to my thoughts, and I spake:

"Master, Valmika was saying, ere you came, how good it was to be here rather than in the city, where they are full of strife. And Kedar thought their lives would flow on into fiery pain, and no speech would avail. Ananda, speaking as a child, indeed, said if one went down among they would listen to his story of the happy life. But, Master, do not many speak and interpret the sacred writings, and how few are they who lay to heart the words of the gods! They seem, indeed, to go on through desire into pain, and even here upon the hills we are not free, for Kedar felt the hot glow of their passion, and I heard in my heart their sobs of despair. Master, it was terrible, for they seemed to come from the wide earth over, and out of ages far away.

"In the child's words is the truth," said Varunna, "for it is better to aid even in sorrow than to withdraw from pain to a happy solitude. Yet only the knowers of Brahma can interpret the sacred writings truly, and it is well to be free ere we speak of freedom. Then we have power and many hearken."

"But who would leave joy for sorrow? And who, being one with Brahma, would return to give counsel?"

"Brother," said Varunna, "here is the hope of the world. Though many seek only for the eternal joy, yet the cry you heard has been heard by great ones who have turned backwards, called by these beseeching voices. The small old path stretching far away leads through many wonderful beings to the place of Brahma. There is the first fountain, the world of beautiful silence, the light which has been undimmed since the beginning of time. But turning backwards from the gate the small old path winds away into the world of men, and it enters every sorrowful heart. This is the way the great ones go. They turn with the path from the door of Brahma. They move along its myriad ways, and overcome pain with compassion.

After many conquered worlds, after many races of purified and uplifted men, they go to a greater than Brahma. In these, though few, is the hope of the world. These are the heroes for whose returning the earth puts forth her signal fires, and the Devas sing their hymns of welcome."

We paused where the plateau widened out. There was scarce a ripple in the chill air. In quietness the snows glistened, a light reflected from the crores of stars that swung with glittering motion above us. We could hear the immense heart-beat of the world in the stillness. We had thoughts that went ranging through the heavens, not sad, but full of solemn hope.

"Brothers! Master! look! The wonderful thing! And another, and yet another!" we heard Ananda calling. We looked and saw the holy blossom, the midnight flower. Oh, may the earth again put forth such beauty. It grew up from the snows with leaves of delicate crystal. A nimbus encircled each radiant bloom, a halo pale yet lustrous. I bowed over it in awe; and I heard Varunna say, "The earth indeed puts forth her signal fires, and the Devas sing their hymn. Listen!" We heard a music as of beautiful thoughts moving along the high places of the earth, full of infinite love and hope and yearning.

"Be glad now, for one is born who has chosen the greater way. Kedar, Narayan, Ananda, farewell! Nay, no farther. It is a long way to return, and the child will tire."

He went on and passed from our sight. But we did not return. We remained long, long in silence, looking at the sacred flower. -------------

Vow, taken long ago, be strong in our hearts today. Here, where the pain is fiercer, to rest is more sweet. Here, where beauty dies away, it is more joy to be lulled in dream. Here, the good, the true, our hope seem but a madness born of ancient pain. Out of rest, dream, or despair may we arise, and go the way the great ones go.

1894

THE CHILDHOOD OF APOLLO

It was long ago, so long that only the spirit of earth remembers truly. The old shepherd Admetus sat before the door of his hut waiting for his grandson to return. He watched with drowsy eyes the eve gather, and the woods and mountains grow dark over the isles--the isles of ancient Greece. It was Greece before its day of beauty, and day was never lovelier. The cloudy blossoms of smoke, curling upward from the valley, sparkled a while high up in the sunlit air, a vague memorial of the world of men below. From that, too, the color vanished, and those other lights began to shine which to some are the only lights of day. The skies dropped close upon the mountains and the silver seas like a vast face brooding with intentness. There was enchantment, mystery, and a living motion in its depths, the presence of all-pervading Zeus enfolding his starry children with the dark radiance of aether.

"Ah!" murmured the old man, looking upward, "once it was living; once it spoke to me. It speaks not now; but it speaks to others I know--to the child who looks and longs and trembles in the dewy night. Why does he linger now? He is beyond his hour. Ah, there now are his footsteps!"

A boy came up the valley driving the gray flocks which tumbled before him in the darkness. He lifted his young face for the shepherd to kiss. It was alight with ecstasy. Admetus looked at him with wonder. A golden and silvery light rayed all about the child, so that his delicate ethereal beauty seemed set in a star which followed his dancing footsteps.

"How bright your eyes!" the old man said, faltering with sudden awe. "Why do your limbs shine with moonfire light?"

"Oh, father," said the boy Apollo, "I am glad, for everything is living tonight. The evening is all a voice and many voices. While the flocks were browsing night gathered about me. I saw within it and it was everywhere living.

"The wind with dim-blown tresses, odor, incense, and secret falling dew, mingled in one warm breath. They whispered to me and called me 'Child of the Stars,' 'Dew Heart,' and 'Soul of Light.' Oh, father, as I came up the valley the voices followed me with song. Everything murmured love. Even the daffodils, nodding in the olive gloom, grew golden at my feet, and a flower within my heart knew of the still sweet secret of the flowers. Listen, listen!"

There were voices in the night, voices as of star-rays descending.

> Now the roof-tree of the midnight spreading
>   Buds in citron, green, and blue:
> From afar its mystic odors shedding,
>   Child, on you.

Then other sweet speakers from beneath the earth, and from the distant waters and air, followed in benediction, and a last voice like a murmur from universal nature:

> Now the buried stars beneath the mountains
>   And the vales their life renew,
> Jetting rainbow blooms from tiny fountains,
>   Child, for you.

> As within our quiet waters passing
>   Sun and moon and stars we view,
> So the loveliness of life is glassing,
>   Child, in you.

> In the diamond air the sun-star glowing
>   Up its feathered radiance threw;
> All the jewel glory there was flowing,
>   Child, for you.

And the fire divine in all things burning
    Yearns for home and rest anew,
From its wanderings far again returning,
    Child, to you.

"Oh, voices, voices," cried the child, "what you say I know not, but I give back love for love. Father, what is it they tell me? They enfold me in light, and I am far away even though I hold your hand."

"The gods are about us. Heaven mingles with the earth," said Admetus, trembling. "Let us go to Diotima. She has grown wise brooding for many a year where the great caves lead to the underworld. She sees the bright ones as they pass by, though she sits with shut eyes, her drowsy lips murmuring as nature's self."

That night the island seemed no more earth set in sea, but a music encircled by the silence. The trees, long rooted in antique slumber, were throbbing with rich life; through glimmering bark and drooping leaf a light fell on the old man and boy as they passed, and vague figures nodded at them. These were the hamadryad souls of the wood. They were bathed in tender colors and shimmering lights draping them from root to leaf. A murmur came from the heart of every one, a low enchantment breathing joy and peace. It grew and swelled until at last it seemed as if through a myriad pipes Pan the earth spirit was fluting his magical creative song.

They found the cave of Diotima covered by vines and tangled trailers at the end of the island where the dark-green woodland rose up from the waters. Admetus paused, for he dreaded this mystic prophetess; but a voice from within called them:

"Come, child of light: come in, old shepherd, I know why you seek me!"

They entered, Admetus trembling with more fear than before. A fire was blazing in a recess of the cavern, and by it sat a majestic figure robed in purple. She was bent forward, her hand supporting her face, her burning eyes turned on the intruders.

"Come hither, child," she said, taking the boy by the hands and gazing into his face. "So this pale form is to be the home of the god. The gods Choose wisely. They take no wild warrior, no mighty hero to be their messenger, but crown this gentle head. Tell me, have you ever seen a light from the sun falling on you in your slumber? No, but look now. Look upward."

As she spoke she waved her hands over him, and the cavern with its dusky roof seemed to melt away, and beyond the heavens the heaven of heavens lay dark in pure tranquility, in a quiet which was the very hush of being. In an instant it vanished, and over the zenith broke a wonderful light.

"See now," cried Diotima, "the Ancient Beauty! Look how its petals expand, and what comes forth from its heart!" A vast and glowing breath, mutable and opalescent, spread itself between heaven and earth, and out of it slowly descended a radiant form like a god's. It drew nigh, radiating lights, pure, beautiful, and star-like. It stood for a moment by the child and placed its hand on his head, and then it was gone. The old shepherd fell upon his face in awe, while the boy stood breathless and entranced.

"Go now," said the Sybil, "I can teach thee naught. Nature herself will adore you, and sing through you her loveliest song. But, ah, the light you hail in joy you shall impart in tears. So from age to age the eternal Beauty bows itself down amid sorrows, that the children of men may not forget it, that their anguish may be transformed, smitten through by its fire."

THE MASK OF APOLLO

A tradition rises within me of quiet, unarmored years, ages before the demigods and heroes toiled at the making of Greece, long ages before the building of the temples and sparkling palaces of her day of glory. The land was pastoral, and over all the woods hung a stillness as of dawn and of unawakened beauty deep breathing in rest. Here and there little villages sent up their smoke and a dreamy people moved about. They grew up, toiled a little at their fields, followed their sheep and goats, wedded, and gray age overtook them, but they never ceased to be children. They worshipped the gods in little wooden temples, with ancient rites forgotten in later years.

Near one of these shrines lived a priest--an old man--who was held in reverence by all for his simple and kindly nature. To him, sitting one summer evening before his hut, came a stranger whom he invited to share his meal. The stranger seated himself and began to tell the priest many wonderful things--stories of the magic of the sun and of the bright beings who move at the gateways of the day. The old man grew drowsy in the warm sunlight and fell asleep. Then the stranger, who was Apollo, arose, and in the guise of the priest entered the little temple, and the people came in unto him one after the other.

First came Agathon, the husbandman, who said: "Father, as I bend over the fields or fasten up the vines I sometimes remember that you said the gods can be worshipped by doing these things as by sacrifice. How is it, father, that the pouring of cold water over roots or training up the vines can nourish Zeus? How can the sacrifice appear before his throne when it is not carried up in the fire and vapor?"

To him Apollo, in the guise of the old man, replied: "Agathon, the father omnipotent does not live only in the aether. He runs invisibly within the sun and stars, and as they whirl round and round they break out into streams and woods and flowers, and the clouds are shaken away from them as the leaves from off the roses. Great, strange, and bright, he busies himself within, and at the end of time his light shall shine, through, and men shall see it moving in a world of flame. Think then, as you bend over your fields, of what you nourish and what rises up within them. Know that every flower as it droops in the quiet of the woodland feels within and far away the approach of an unutterable life and is glad. They reflect that life as the little pools the light of the stars. Agathon, Agathon, Zeus is no greater in the aether than he is in the leaf of grass, and the hymns of men are no sweeter to him than a little water poured over one of his flowers."

Agathon, the husbandman, went away, and he bent tenderly in dreams over his fruit and his vines, and he loved them more than before, and he grew wise as he watched them and was happy working for the gods.

Then spake Damon, the shepherd Father, "while the flocks are browsing dreams rise up within me. They make the heart sick with longing. The forests vanish, and I hear no more the lambs' bleat or the rustling of the fleeces. Voices from a thousand depths call me; they whisper, they beseech me. Shadows more lovely than earth's children utter music, not for me though I faint while I listen. Father, why do I hear the things others hear not--voices calling to unknown hunters of wide fields, or to herdsmen, shepherds of the starry flocks?"

Apollo answered the shepherd: "Damon, a song stole from the silence while the gods were not yet, and a thousand ages passed ere they came, called forth by the music; and a thousand ages they listened, and then joined in the song. Then began the worlds to glimmer shadowy about them, and bright beings to bow before them. These, their children, began in their turn to sing the song that calls forth and awakens life. He is master of all things who has learned their music. Damon, heed not the shadows, but the voices. The voices have a message to thee from beyond the gods. Learn their song and sing it over again to the people until their hearts, too, grow sick with longing, and they can hear the song within themselves. Oh, my son, I see far off how the nations shall join in it as in a chorus, and, hearing it, the rushing planets shall cease from their speed and be steadfast. Men shall hold starry sway."

The face of the god shone through the face of the old man, and it was so full of secretness that, filled with awe, Damon, the herdsman, passed from the presence, and a strange fire was kindled in his heart. The songs that he sang thereafter caused childhood and peace to pass from the dwellers in the woods.

Then the two lovers, Dion and Nemra, came in and stood before Apollo, and Dion spake: "Father, you who are so wise can tell us what love is, so that we shall never miss it. Old Tithonus nods his gray head at us as we pass. He says only with the changeless gods has love endurance, and for men the loving time is short, and its sweetness is soon over."

Neaera added: "But it is not true, father, for his drowsy eyes light when he remembers the old days, when he was happy and proud in love as we are."

Apollo answered: "My children, I will tell you the legend how love came into the world, and how it may endure. On high Olympus the gods held council at the making of man, and each had brought a gift, and each gave to man something of their own nature. Aphrodite, the loveliest and sweetest, paused, and was about to add a new grace to his person; but Eros cried: 'Let them not be so lovely without; let them be lovelier within. Put your own soul in, O mother.' The mighty mother smiled, and so it was. And now, whenever love is like hers, which asks not return, but shines on all because it must, within that love Aphrodite dwells, and it becomes immortal by her presence."

Then Dion and Neaera went out, and as they walked home through the forest, purple and vaporous in the evening light, they drew closer together. Dion, looking into the eyes of Neaera, saw there a new gleam, violet, magical, shining--there was the presence of Aphrodite; there was her shrine.

After came in unto Apollo the two grand-children of old Tithonus, and they cried: "See the flowers we have brought you! We gathered them for you in the valley where they grow best!" Apollo said: "What wisdom shall we give to children that they may remember? Our most beautiful for them!" And as he stood and looked at them the mask of age and secretness vanished. He appeared radiant in light. They laughed in joy at his beauty. Bending down he kissed each upon the forehead, then faded away into the light which is his home.

As the sun sank down amid the blue hills, the old priest awoke with a sigh, and cried out: "Oh, that we could talk wisely as we do in our dreams!"

1893

THE CAVE OF LILITH

Out of her cave came the ancient Lilith; Lilith the wise; Lilith the enchantress. There ran a little path outside her dwelling; it wound away among the mountains and glittering peaks, and before the door one of the Wise Ones walked to and fro. Out of her cave came Lilith, scornful of his solitude, exultant in her wisdom, flaunting her shining and magical beauty.

"Still alone, star gazer! Is thy wisdom of no avail? Thou hast yet to learn that I am more powerful, knowing the ways of error, than you who know the ways of truth."

The Wise One heeded her not, but walked to and fro. His eyes were turned to the distant peaks, the abode of his brothers. The starlight fell about him; a sweet air came down the mountain path, fluttering his white robe; he did not cease from his steady musing. Lilith wavered in her cave like a mist rising between rocks. Her raiment was violet, with silvery gleams. Her face was dim, and over her head rayed a shadowy diadem, like that which a man imagines over the head of his beloved: and one looking closer at her face would have seen that this was the crown he reached out to; that the eyes burnt with his own longing; that the lips were parted to yield to the secret wishes of his heart.

"Tell me, for I would know, why do you wait so long? I, here in my cave between the valley and the height, blind the eyes of all who would pass. Those who by chance go forth to you, come back to me again, and but one in ten thousand passes on. My illusions are sweeter to them than truth. I offer every soul its own shadow. I pay them their own price. I have grown rich, though the simple shepards of old gave me birth. Men have made me; the mortals have made me immortal. I rose up like a vapor from their first dreams, and every sigh since then and every laugh remains with me. I am made up of hopes and fears. The subtle princes lay out their plans of conquest in my cave, and there the hero dreams, and there the lovers of all time write in flame their history. I am wise, holding all experience, to tempt, to blind, to terrify. None shall pass by. Why, therefore, dost thou wait?"

The Wise One looked at her, and she shrank back a little, and a little her silver and violet faded, but out of her cave her voice still sounded:

"The stars and the starry crown are not yours alone to offer, and every promise you make I make also. I offer the good and the bad indifferently. The lover, the poet, the mystic, and all who would drink of the first fountain, I delude with my mirage. I was the Beatrice who led Dante upwards: the gloom was in me, and the glory was mine also, and he went not out of my cave. The stars and the shining of heaven were illusions of the infinite I wove about him. I captured his soul with the shadow of space; a nutshell would have contained the film. I smote on the dim heart-chords the manifold music of being. God is sweeter in the human than the human in God. Therefore he rested in me."

She paused a little, and then went on: "There is that fantastic fellow who slipped by me. Could your wisdom not retain him? He returned to me full of anguish, and I wound my arms round him like a fair melancholy; and now his sadness is as sweet to him as hope was before his fall. Listen to his song!" She paused again. A voice came up from the depths chanting a sad knowledge:

> What of all the will to do?
>   It has vanished long ago,
> For a dream-shaft pierced it through
>   From the Unknown Archer's bow.
>
> What of all the soul to think?
>   Some one offered it a cup
> Filled with a diviner drink,
>   And the flame has burned it up.
>
> What of all the hope to climb?
>   Only in the self we grope
> To the misty end of time,

Truth has put an end to hope.

What of all the heart to love?
  Sadder than for will or soul,
No light lured it on above:
  Love has found itself the whole.

"Is it not pitiful? I pity only those who pity themselves. Yet he is mine more surely than ever. This is the end of human wisdom. How shall he now escape? What shall draw him up?"

"His will shall awaken," said the Wise One. "I do not sorrow over him, for long is the darkness before the spirit is born. He learns in your caves not to see, not to hear, not to think, for very anguish flying your illusions."

"Sorrow is a great bond," Lilith said.

It is a bond to the object of sorrow. He weeps what thou canst never give him, a life never breathed in thee. He shall come forth, and thou shalt not see him at the time of passing. When desire dies the swift and invisible will awakens. He shall go forth; and one by one the dwellers in your caves will awaken and pass onward. This small old path will be trodden by generation after generation. Thou, too, O shining Lilith, shalt follow, not as mistress, but as handmaiden."

"I will weave spells," Lilith cried. "They shall never pass me. I will drug them with the sweetest poison. They shall rest drowsily and content as of old. Were they not giants long ago, mighty men and heroes? I overcame them with young enchantment. Shall they pass by feeble and longing for bygone joys, for the sins of their exultant youth, while I have grown into a myriad wisdom?"

The Wise One walked to and fro as before, and there was silence: and I saw that with steady will he pierced the tumultuous gloom of the cave, and a spirit awoke here and there from its dream. And I though I saw that Sad Singer become filled with a new longing for true being, and that the illusions of good and evil fell from him, and that he came at last to the knees of the Wise One to learn the supreme truth. In the misty midnight I hear these three voices-- the Sad Singer, the Enchantress Lilith, and the Wise One. From the Sad Singer I learned that thought of itself leads nowhere, but blows the perfume from every flower, and cuts the flower from every tree, and hews down every tree from the valley, and in the end goes to and fro in waste places--gnawing itself in a last hunger. I learned from Lilith that we weave our own enchantment, and bind ourselves with out own imagination. To think of the true as beyond us or to love the symbol of being is to darken the path to wisdom, and to debar us from eternal beauty. From the Wise One I learned that the truest wisdom is to wait, to work, and to will in secret. Those who are voiceless today, tomorrow shall be eloquent, and the earth shall hear them and her children salute them. Of these three truths the hardest to learn is the silent will. Let us seek for the highest truth.

1894

THE STORY OF A STAR

The emotions that haunted me in that little cathedral town would be most difficult to describe. After the hurry, rattle, and fever of the city, the rare weeks spent here were infinitely peaceful. They were full of a quaint sense of childhood, with sometimes a deeper chord touched--the giant and spiritual things childhood has dreams of. The little room I slept in had opposite its window the great gray cathedral wall; it was only in the evening that the sunlight crept round it and appeared in the room strained through the faded green blind. It must have been this silvery quietness of color which in some subtle way affected me with the feeling of a continual Sabbath; and this was strengthened by the bells chiming hour after hour. The pathos, penitence, and hope expressed by the flying notes colored the intervals with faint and delicate memories. They haunted my dreams, and I heard with unutterable longing the dreamy chimes pealing from some dim and vast cathedral of the cosmic memory, until the peace they tolled became almost a nightmare, and I longed for utter oblivion or forgetfulness of their reverberations.

More remarkable were the strange lapses into other worlds and times. Almost as frequent as the changing of the bells were the changes from state to state. I realized what is meant by the Indian philosophy of Maya. Truly my days were full of Mayas, and my work-a-day city life was no more real to me than one of those bright, brief glimpses of things long past. I talk of the past, and yet these moments taught me how false our ideas of time are. In the Ever- living yesterday, today, and tomorrow are words of no meaning. I know I fell into what we call the past and the things I counted as dead for ever were the things I had yet to endure. Out of the old age of earth I stepped into its childhood, and received once more the primal blessing of youth, ecstasy, and beauty. But these things are too vast and vague to speak of, the words we use today cannot tell their story. Nearer to our time is the legend that follows.

I was, I thought, one of the Magi of old Persia, inheritor of its unforgotten lore, and using some of its powers. I tried to pierce through the great veil of nature, and feel the life that quickened it within. I tried to comprehend the birth and growth of planets, and to do this I rose spiritually and passed beyond earth's confines into that seeming void which is the Matrix where they germinate. On one of these journeys I was struck by the phantasm, so it seemed, of a planet I had not observed before. I could not then observe closer, and coming again on another occasion it had disappeared. After the lapse of many months I saw it once more, brilliant with fiery beauty. Its motion was slow, revolving around some invisible centre. I pondered over it, and seemed to know that the invisible centre was its primordial spiritual state, from which it emerged a little while and into which it then withdrew. Short was its day; its shining faded into a glimmer, and then into darkness in a few months. I learned its time and cycles; I made preparations and determined to await its coming.

The Birth of a Planet

At first silence and then an inner music, and then the sounds of song throughout the vastness of its orbit grew as many in number as there were stars at gaze. Avenues and vistas of sound! They reeled to and fro. They poured from a universal stillness quick with unheard things. They rushed forth and broke into a myriad voices gay with childhood. From age and the eternal they rushed forth into youth. They filled the void with reveling and exultation. In rebellion they then returned and entered the dreadful Fountain. Again they came forth, and the sounds faded into whispers; they rejoiced once again, and again died into silence.

And now all around glowed a vast twilight; it filled the cradle of the planet with colorless fire. I felt a rippling motion which impelled me away from the centre to the circumference. At that began to curdle, a milky and nebulous substance rocked to and fro. At every motion the pulsation of its rhythm carried it farther and farther away from the centre; it grew darker, and a great purple shadow covered it so that I could see it no longer. I was now on the outer verge, where the twilight still continued to encircle the planet with zones of clear transparent light.

As night after night I rose up to visit it they grew many-colored and brighter. I saw the imagination of nature visibly at work. I wandered through shadowy immaterial forests, a titanic vegetation built up of light and color; I saw it growing denser, hung with festoons and trailers of fire, and spotted with the light of myriad flowers such as earth never knew. Coincident with the appearance of these things I felt within myself, as if in harmonious movement, a sense of joyousness, an increase of self-consciousness: I felt full of gladness, youth, and the mystery of the new. I felt that greater powers were about to appear, those who had thrown outwards this world and erected it as a place in space.

I could not tell half the wonder of this strange race. I could not myself comprehend more than a little of the mystery of their being. They recognized my presence there, and communicated with me in such a way that I can only describe it by saying that they seemed to enter into my soul, breathing a fiery life; yet I knew that the highest I could reach to was but the outer verge of their spiritual nature, and to tell you but a little I have many times to translate it; for in the first unity with their thought I touched on an almost universal sphere of life, I peered into the ancient heart that beats throughout time; and this knowledge became change in me, first into a vast and nebulous symbology, and so down through many degrees of human thought into words which hold not at all the pristine and magical beauty.

I stood before one of this race, and I thought, "What is the meaning and end of life here?" Within me I felt the answering ecstasy that illuminated with vistas of dawn and rest: It seemed to say:

"Our spring and our summer are unfolding into light and form, and our autumn and winter are a fading into the infinite soul."

I questioned in my heart, "To what end is this life poured forth and withdrawn?"

He came nearer and touched me; once more I felt the thrill of being that changed itself into vision.

"The end is creation, and creation is joy. The One awakens out of quiescence as we come forth, and knows itself in us; as we return we enter it in gladness, knowing ourselves. After long cycles the world you live in will become like ours; it will be poured forth and withdrawn; a mystic breath, a mirror to glass your being."

He disappeared while I wondered what cyclic changes would transmute our ball of mud into the subtle substance of thought.

In that world I dared not stay during its period of withdrawal; having entered a little into its life, I became subject to its laws; the Powers on its return would have dissolved my being utterly. I felt with a wild terror its clutch upon me, and I withdrew from the departing glory, from the greatness that was my destiny--but not yet.

From such dreams I would be aroused, perhaps, by a gentle knock at my door, and my little cousin Margaret's quaint face would peep in with a "Cousin Robert, are you not coming down to supper?"

Of these visions in the light of after thought I would speak a little. All this was but symbol, requiring to be thrice sublimed in interpretation ere its true meaning can be grasped. I do not know whether worlds are heralded by such glad songs, or whether any have such a fleeting existence, for the mind that reflects truth is deluded with strange phantasies of time and place in which seconds are rolled out into centuries and long cycles are reflected in an instant of time. There is within us a little space through which all the threads of the universe are drawn; and, surrounding that incomprehensible centre, the mind of man sometimes catches glimpses of things which are true only in those glimpses; when we record them the true has vanished, and a shadowy story-- such as this--alone remains. Yet, perhaps, the time is not altogether wasted in considering legends like these, for they reveal, though but in phantasy and symbol, a greatness we are heirs to, a destiny which is ours though it be yet far away.

1894

A DREAM OF ANGUS OGE

The day had been wet and wild, and the woods looked dim and drenched from the window where Con sat. All the day long his ever restless feet were running to the door in a vain hope of sunshine. His sister, Norah, to quiet him had told him over and over again the tales which delighted him, the delight of hearing which was second only to the delight of living them over himself, when as Cuculain he kept the ford which led to Ulla, his sole hero heart matching the hosts of Meave; or as Fergus he wielded the sword of light the Druids made and gave to the champion, which in its sweep shore away the crests of the mountains; or as Brian, the ill-fated child of Turann, he went with his brothers in the ocean-sweeping boat farther than ever Columbus traveled, winning one by one in dire conflict with kings and enchanters the treasures which would appease the implacable heart of Lu.

He had just died in a corner of the room from his many wounds when Norah came in declaring that all these famous heroes must go to bed. He protested in vain, but indeed he was sleepy, and before he had been carried half-way to the room the little soft face drooped with half-closed eyes, while he drowsily rubbed his nose upon her shoulder in an effort to keep awake. For a while she flitted about him, looking, with her dark, shadowy hair flickering in the dim, silver light like one of the beautiful heroines of Gaelic romance, or one of the twilight, race of the Sidhe. Before going she sat by his bed and sang to him some verses of a song, set to an old Celtic air whose low intonations were full of a half-soundless mystery:

> Over the hill-tops the gay lights are peeping;
>   Down in the vale where the dim fleeces stray
> Ceases the smoke from the hamlet upcreeping:

Come, thou, my shepherd, and lead me away.

"Who's the shepherd?" said the boy, suddenly sitting up.

"Hush, alannah, I will tell you another time." She continued
still more softly:

> Lord of the Wand, draw forth from the darkness,
>   Warp of the silver, and woof of the gold:
> Leave the poor shade there bereft in its starkness:
>   Wrapped in the fleece we will enter the Fold.

> There from the many-orbed heart where the Mother
>   Breathes forth the love on her darlings who roam,
> We will send dreams to their land of another
>   Land of the Shining, their birthplace and home.

He would have asked a hundred questions, but she bent over him, enveloping
him with a sudden nightfall of hair, to give him his good-night kiss, and departed.
Immediately the boy sat up again; all his sleepiness gone. The pure, gay, delicate
spirit of childhood was darting at ideas dimly perceived in the delicious moonlight
of romance which silvered his brain, where may airy and beautiful figures were
moving: The Fianna with floating locks chasing the flying deer; shapes more solemn, vast, and misty, guarding the avenues to unspeakable secrets; but he steadily
pursued his idea.

"I guess he's one of the people who take you away to faeryland. Wonder if he'd
come to me? Think it's easy going away," with an intuitive perception of the frailty
of the link binding childhood to earth in its dreams. (As a man Con will strive with
passionate intensity to regain that free, gay motion in the upper airs.) "Think I'll try
if he'll come," and he sang, with as near an approach as he could make to the glimmering cadences of his sister's voice:

Come, thou, my shepherd, and lead me away.

He then lay back quite still and waited. He could not say whether hours or minutes had passed, or whether he had slept or not, until he was aware of a tall golden-bearded man standing by his bed. Wonderfully light was this figure, as if the sunlight ran through his limbs; a spiritual beauty was on the face, and those strange eyes of bronze and gold with their subtle intense gaze made Con aware for the first time of the difference between inner and out in himself.

"Come, Con, come away!" the child seemed to hear uttered silently.

"You're the Shepherd!" said Con, "I'll go." Then suddenly, "I won't come back and be old when they're all dead?" a vivid remembrance of Ossian's fate flashing upon him.

A most beautiful laughter, which again to Con seemed half soundless, came in reply. His fears vanished; the golden-bearded man stretched a hand over him for a moment, and he found himself out in the night, now clear and starlit. Together they moved on as if borne by the wind, past many woods and silver-gleaming lakes, and mountains which shone like a range of opals below the purple skies. The Shepherd stood still for a moment by one of these hills, and there flew out, riverlike, a melody mingled with a tinkling as of innumerable elfin hammers, and there, was a sound of many gay voices where an unseen people were holding festival, or enraptured hosts who were let loose for the awakening, the new day which was to dawn, for the delighted child felt that faeryland was come over again with its heroes and battles.

"Our brothers rejoice," said the Shepherd to Con.

"Who are they?" asked the boy.

"They are the thoughts of our Father."

"May we go in?" Con asked, for he was fascinated by the melody, mystery, and flashing lights.

"Not now. We are going to my home where I lived in the days past when there came to me many kings and queens of ancient Eire, many heroes and beautiful women, who longed for the Druid wisdom we taught."

"And did you fight like Finn, and carry spears as tall as trees, and chase the deer through the Woods, and have feastings and singing?"

"No, we, the Dananns, did none of those things--but those who were weary of battle, and to whom feast and song brought no pleasure, came to us and passed hence to a more wonderful land, a more immortal land than this."

As he spoke he paused before a great mound, grown over with trees, and around it silver clear in the moonlight were immense stones piled, the remains of an original circle, and there was a dark, low, narrow entrance leading within. He took Con by the hand, and in an instant they were standing in a lofty, cross-shaped cave, built roughly of huge stones.

"This was my palace. In days past many a one plucked here the purple flower of magic and the fruit of the tree of life."

"It is very dark," said the child disconsolately. He had expected something different.

"Nay, but look: you will see it is the palace of a god." And even as he spoke a light began to glow and to pervade the cave and to obliterate the stone walls and the antique hieroglyphs engraved thereon, and to melt the earthen floor into itself like a fiery sun suddenly uprisen within the world, and there was everywhere a wandering ecstasy of sound: light and sound were one; light had a voice, and the music hung glittering in the air.

"Look, how the sun is dawning for us, ever dawning; in the earth, in our hearts, with ever youthful and triumphant voices. Your sun is but a smoky shadow, ours the ruddy and eternal glow; yours is far way, ours is heart and hearth and home; yours is a light without, ours a fire within, in rock, in river, in plain, everywhere living, everywhere dawning, whence also it cometh that the mountains emit their wondrous rays."

As he spoke he seemed to breathe the brilliance of that mystical sunlight and to dilate and tower, so that the child looked up to a giant pillar of light, having in his heart a sun of ruddy gold which shed its blinding rays about him, and over his head there was a waving of fiery plumage and on his face an ecstasy of beauty and immortal youth.

"I am Angus," Con heard; "men call me the Young. I am the sunlight in the heart, the moonlight in the mind; I am the light at the end of every dream, the voice for ever calling to come away; I am the desire beyond you or tears. Come with me, come with me, I will make you immortal; for my palace opens into the Gardens of the Sun, and there are the fire-fountains which quench the heart's desire in rapture." And in the child's dream he was in a palace high as the stars, with dazzling pillars jeweled like the dawn, and all fashioned out of living and trembling opal. And upon their thrones sat the Danann gods with their sceptres and diadems of rainbow light, and upon their faces infinite wisdom and imperishable youth. In the turmoil and growing chaos of his dream he heard a voice crying out, "You remember, Con, Con, Conaire Mor, you remember!" and in an instant he was torn from himself and had grown vaster, and was with the Immortals, seated upon their thrones, they looking upon him as a brother, and he was flying away with them into the heart of the gold when he awoke, the spirit of childhood dazzled with the vision which is too lofty for princes.

1897

DEIRDRE

A LEGEND IN THREE ACTS

Dramatis Personae:

CONCOBAR .... Ardrie of Ulla.
NAISI
AINLE, ARDAN .... Brothers of Naisi.
FERGUS
BUINNE, ILANN .... Sons of Fergus
CATHVAH .... A Druid
DEIRDRE
LAVARCAN .... A Druidess
Herdsman, Messenger ....

ACT I.

SCENE.--The dun of DEIRDRE'S captivity. LAVARCAM, a Druidess, sits
before the door in the open air. DEIRDRE comes out of the dun.

DEIRDRE--Dear fostermother, how the spring is beginning! The music
of the Father's harp is awakening the flowers. Now the winter's

sleep is over, and the spring flows from the lips of the harp. Do
you not feel the thrill in the wind--a joy answering the trembling
strings? Dear fostermother, the spring and the music are in my heart!

LAVARCAM--The harp has but three notes; and, after sleep and laughter,
the last sound is of weeping.

DEIRDRE--Why should there be any sorrow while I am with you? I am
happy here. Last night in a dream I saw the blessed Sidhe upon
the mountains, and they looked on me with eyes of love.

(An old HERDSMAN enters, who bows before LAVARCAM.)

HERDSMAN--Lady, the High King is coming through the woods.

LAVARCAM--Deirdre, go to the grianan for a little. You shall tell
me your dream again, my child.

DEIRDRE--Why am I always hidden from the King's sight.

LAVARCAM--It is the King's will you should see no one except these
aged servants.

DEIRDRE--Am I indeed fearful to look upon, foster-mother? I do not
think so, or you would not love me.

LAVARCAM--It is the King's will.

DEIRDRE--Yet why must it be so, fostermother? Why must I hide away?
Why must I never leave the valley?

LAVARCAM--It is the king's will.

While she is speaking CONCOBAR enters. He stands still and looks on DEIRDRE. DEIRDRE gazes on the KING for a moment, and then covering her face with her hands, she hurries into the dun. The HERDSMAN goes out. LAVARCAM sees and bows before the KING.

CONCOBAR--Lady, is all well with you and your charge?

LAVARCAM--All is well.

CONCOBAR--Is there peace in Deirdre's heart?

LAVARCAM--She is happy, not knowing a greater happiness than to roam the woods or to dream of the immortal ones can bring her.

CONCOBAR--Fate has not found her yet hidden in this valley.

LAVARCAM--Her happiness is to be here. But she asks why must she never leave the glen. Her heart quickens within her. Like a bird she listens to the spring, and soon the valley will be narrow as a cage.

CONCOBAR--I cannot open the cage. Less ominous the Red Swineherd at a feast than this beautiful child in Ulla. You know the word of the Druids at her birth.

LAVARCAM--Aye, through her would come the destruction of the Red Branch. But sad is my heart, thinking of her lonely youth.

CONCOBAR--The gods did not guide us how the ruin might be averted. The Druids would have slain her, but I set myself against the wise ones, thinking in my heart that the chivalry of the Red Branch would be already gone if this child were slain. If we are to perish it shall be nobly, and without any departure from the laws of our order. So I have hidden her away from men, hoping to stay the coming of fate.

LAVARCAM--King, your mercy will return to you, and if any of the
Red Branch fall, you will not fall.

CONCOBAR--If her thoughts turned only to the Sidhe her heart would
grow cold to the light love that warriors give. The birds of Angus
cannot breathe or sing their maddening song in the chill air that
enfolds the wise. For this, Druidess, I made thee her fosterer.
Has she learned to know the beauty of the ever-living ones, after
which the earth fades and no voice can call us back?

LAVARCAM--The immortals have appeared to her in vision and looked
on her with eyes of love.

CONCOBAR--Her beauty is so great it would madden whole hosts, and
turn them from remembrance of their duty. We must guard well the
safety of the Red Branch. Druidess, you have seen with subtle eyes
the shining life beyond this. But through the ancient traditions
of Ulla, which the bards have kept and woven into song, I have seen
the shining law enter men's minds, and subdue the lawless into love
of justice. A great tradition is shaping a heroic race; and the
gods who fought at Moytura are descending and dwelling in the heart
of the Red Branch. Deeds will be done in our time as mighty as
those wrought by the giants who battled at the dawn; and through
the memory of our days and deeds the gods will build themselves an
eternal empire in the mind of the Gael. Wise woman, guard well
this beauty which fills my heart with terror. I go now, and will
doubly warn the spearmen at the passes, but will come hither again
and speak with thee of these things, and with Deirdre I would speak also.

LAVARCAM--King of Ulla, be at peace. It is not I who will break
through the design of the gods. (CONCOBAR goes through the woods,
after looking for a time at the door of the dun.) But Deirdre is
also one of the immortals. What the gods desire will utter itself

through her heart. I will seek counsel from the gods.

[DEIRDRE comes slowly through the door.]

DEIRDRE--Is he gone? I fear this stony king with his implacable eyes.

LAVARVAM--He is implacable only in his desire for justice.

DEIRDRE--No! No! There is a hunger in his eyes for I know not what.

LAVARCAM--He is the wisest king who ever sat on the chair of Macha.

DEIRDRE--He has placed a burden on my heart. Oh! fostermother, the harp of life is already trembling into sorrow!

LAVARCAM--Do not think of him. Tell me your dream, my child.

[DEIRDRE comes from the door of the dun and sits on a deerskin at LAVARCAM's feet.]

DEIRDRE--Tell me, do happy dreams bring happiness, and do our dreams of the Sidhe ever grow real to us as you are real to me? Do their eyes draw nigh to ours, and can the heart we dream of ever be a refuge for our hearts.

LAVARCAM--Tell me your dream.

DEIRDRE--Nay; but answer first of all, dear fostermother--you who are wise, and who have talked with the Sidhe.

LAVARCAM--Would it make you happy to have your dream real, my darling?

DEIRDRE--Oh, it would make me happy!

[She hides her face on LAVARCAM's knees.]

LAVARCAM--If I can make your dream real, I will, my beautiful fawn.

DEIRDRE--Dear fostermother, I think my dream is coming near to me. It is coming to me now.

LAVARCAM--Deirdre, tell me what hope has entered your heart?

DEIRDRE--In the night I saw in a dream the top of the mountain yonder, beyond the woods, and three hunters stood there in the dawn. The sun sent its breath upon their faces, but there was a light about them never kindled at the sun. They were surely hunters from some heavenly field, or the three gods whom Lu condemned to wander in mortal form, and they are come again to the world to seek some greater treasure.

LAVARCAM--Describe to me these immortal hunters. In Eire we know no gods who take such shape appearing unto men.

DEIRDRE--I cannot now make clear to thee my remembrance of two of the hunters, but the tallest of the three--oh, he stood like a flame against the flameless sky, and the whole sapphire of the heavens seemed to live in his fearless eyes! His hair was darker than the raven's wing, his face dazzling in its fairness. He pointed with his great flame-bright spear to the valley. His companions seemed in doubt, and pointed east and west. Then in my dream I came nigh him and whispered in his ear, and pointed the way through the valley to our dun. I looked into his eyes, and he started like one who sees a vision; and I know, dear fostermother, he will come here, and he will love me. Oh, I would die if he did not love me!

LAVARCAM--Make haste, my child, and tell me was there aught else memorable about this hero and his companions?

DEIRDRE--Yes, I remember each had the likeness of a torch shedding rays of gold embroidered on the breast.

LAVARCAM--Deirdre, Deirdre, these are no phantoms, but living heroes! O wise king, the eyes of the spirit thou wouldst open have seen farther than the eyes of the body thou wouldst blind! The Druid vision has only revealed to this child her destiny.

DEIRDRE--Why do you talk so strangely, fostermother?

LAVARCAM--Concobar, I will not fight against the will of the immortals. I am not thy servant, but theirs. Let the Red Branch fall! If the gods scatter it they have chosen to guide the people of Ulla in another I path.

DEIRDRE--What has disturbed your mind, dear foster-mother? What have I to do with the Red Branch? And why should the people of Ulla fall because of me?

LAVARCAM--O Deirdre, there were no warriors created could overcome the Red Branch. The gods have but smiled on this proud chivalry through thine eyes, and they are already melted. The waving of thy hand is more powerful to subdue than the silver rod of the king to sustain. Thy golden hair shall be the flame to burn up Ulla.

DEIDRE--Oh, what do you mean by these fateful prophecies? You fill me with terror. Why should a dream so gentle and sweet portend sorrow?

LAVARCAM--Dear golden head, cast sorrow aside for a time. The Father has not yet struck the last chords on the harp of life.

The chords of joy have but begun for thee.

DEIRDRE--You confuse my mind, dear fostermother, with your speech of joy and sorrow. It is not your wont. Indeed, I think my dream portends joy.

LAVARCAM--It is love, Deirdre, which is coming to thee. Love, which thou hast never known.

DEIRDRE--But I love thee, dearest and kindest of guardians.

LAVARCAM--Oh, in this love heaven and earth will be forgotten, and your own self unremembered, or dim and far off as a home the spirit fives in no longer.

DEIRDRE--Tell me, will the hunter from the hills come to us? I think I could forget all for him.

LAVARCAM--He is not one of the Sidhe, but the proudest and bravest of the Red Branch, Naisi, son of Usna. Three lights of valor among the Ultonians are Naisi and his brothers.

DEIRDRE--Will he love me, fostermother, as you love me, and will he live with us here?

LAVARCAM--Nay, where he goes you must go, and he must fly afar to live with you. But I will leave you now for a little, child, I would divine the future.

[LAVARCAM kisses DEIRDRE and goes within the dun. DEIRDRE walks to and fro before the door. NAISI enters. He sees DEIRDRE, who turns and looks at him, pressing her hands to her breast. Naisi bows before DEIRDRE.]

NAISI--Goddess, or enchantress, thy face shone on me at dawn on the mountain. Thy lips called me hither, and I have come.

DEIRDRE--I called thee, dear Naisi.

NAISI--Oh, knowing my name, never before having spoken to me, thou must know my heart also.

DEIRDRE--Nay, I know not. Tell me what is in thy heart.

NAISI--O enchantress, thou art there. The image of thine eyes is there and thy smiling lips, and the beating of my heart is muffled in a cloud of thy golden tresses.

DEIRDRE--Say on, dear Naisi.

NAISI--I have told thee all. Thou only art in my heart.

DEIRDRE--But I have never ere this spoken to any man. Tell me more.

NAISI--If thou hast never before spoken to any man, then indeed art thou one of the immortals, and my hope is vain. Hast thou only called me to thy world to extinguish my life hereafter in memories of thee?

DEIRDRE--What wouldst thou with me, dear Naisi?

NAISI--I would carry thee to my dun by the sea of Moyle, O beautiful woman, and set thee there on an ivory throne. The winter would not chill thee there, nor the summer burn thee, for I would enfold thee with my love, enchantress, if thou camest--to my world. Many warriors are there of the clan Usna, and two brothers I have who are strong above any hosts, and they would all die with me for thy sake.

DEIRDRE (taking the hands of NAISI)--I will go with thee where thou
goest. (Leaning her head on NAISI's shoulder.) Oh, fostermother,
too truly hast thou spoken! I know myself not. My spirit has gone
from me to this other heart for ever.

NAISI--Dost thou forego thy shining world for me?

LAVARCAM--(coming out of the dun). Naisi, this is the Deirdre of
the prophecies.

NAISI--Deirdre! Deirdre! I remember in some old tale of my childhood
that name. (Fiercely.) It was a lying prophecy. What has this girl
to do with the downfall of Ulla?

LAVARCAM--Thou art the light of the Ultonian's, Naisi, but thou art
not the star of knowledge. The Druids spake truly. Through her,
but not through her sin, will come the destruction of the Red Branch.

NAISI--I have counted death as nothing battling for the Red Branch;
and I would not, even for Deirdre, war upon my comrades. But Deirdre
I will not leave nor forget for a thousand prophecies made by the
Druids in their dotage. If the Red Branch must fall, it will fall
through treachery; but Deirdre I will love, and in my love is no
dishonor, nor any broken pledge.

LAVARCAM--Remember, Naisi, the law of the king. It is death to
thee to be here. Concobar is even now in the woods, and will come
hither again.

DEIRDRE--Is it death to thee to love me, Naisi? Oh, fly quickly,
and forget me. But first, before thou goest, bend down thy head--
low--rest it on my bosom. Listen to the beating of my heart. That
passionate tumult is for thee! There, I have kissed thee. I have

sweet memories for ever-lasting. Go now, my beloved, quickly. I
fear--I fear for thee this stony king.

NAISI--I do not fear the king, nor will I fly hence. It is due to
the chief of the Red Branch that I should stay and face him, having
set my mill against his.

LAVARCAM--You cannot remain now.

NAISI--It is due to the king.

LAVARCAM--You must go; both must go. Do not cloud your heart with
dreams of a false honor. It is not your death only, but Deirdre's
which will follow. Do you think the Red Branch would spare her,
after your death, to extinguish another light of valor, and another
who may wander here?

NAISI--I will go with Deirdre to Alba.

DEIRDRE--Through life or to death I will go with thee, Naisi.

[Voices of AINLE and ARDAN are heard in the wood.]

ARDAN--I think Naisi went this way.

AINLE--He has been wrapt in a dream since the dawn. See! This
is his footstep in the clay!

ARDAN--I heard voices.

AINLE--(entering with ARDAN) Here is our dream-led brother.

NAISI--Ainle and Ardan, this is Deirdre, your sister. I have

broken through the command of the king, and fly with her to Alba
to avoid warfare with the Red Branch.

ARDAN--Our love to thee, beautiful sister.

AINLE--Dear maiden, thou art already in my heart with Naisi.

LAVARCAM--You cannot linger here. With Concobar the deed follows
swiftly the counsel; tonight his spearmen will be on your track.

NAISI--Listen, Ainle and Ardan. Go you to Emain Macha. It may be
the Red Branch will make peace between the king and myself. You
are guiltless in this flight.

AINLE--Having seen Deirdre, my heart is with you, brother, and I
also am guilty.

ARDAN--I think, being here, we, too, have broken the command of
the king. We will go with thee to Alba, dear brother and sister.

LAVARCAM--Oh, tarry not, tarry not! Make haste while there is yet
time. The thoughts of the king are circling around Deirdre as
wolves around the fold. Try not the passes of the valley, but
over the hills. The passes are all filled with the spearmen of
the king.

NAISI--We will carry thee over the mountains, Deirdre, and tomorrow
will see us nigh to the isles of Alba.

DEIRDRE--Farewell, dear fostermother. I have passed the faery sea
since dawn, and have found the Island of Joy. Oh, see! what bright
birds are around us, with dazzling wings! Can you not hear their
singing? Oh, bright birds, make music for ever around my love and me!

LAVARCAM--They are the birds of Angus. Their singing brings love--
and death.

DEIRDRE--Nay, death has come before love, dear fostermother, and
all I was has vanished like a dewdrop in the sun. Oh, beloved,
let us go. We are leaving death behind us in the valley.

[DEIRDRE and the brothers go through the wood. LAVARCAM watches,
and when they are out of sight sits by the door of the dun with
her head bowed to her knees. After a little CONCOBAR enters.]

CONCOBAR--Where is Deirdre?

LAVARCAM--(not lifting her head). Deirdre has left death behind her,
and has entered into the Kingdom of her Youth.

CONCOBAR--Do not speak to me in portents. Lift up your head,
Druidess. Where is Deirdre?

LAVARCAM--(looking up). Deirdre is gone!

CONCOBAR--By the high gods, tell me whither, and who has dared to
take her hence?

LAVARCAM--She has fled with Naisi, son of Usna, and is beyond your
vengeance, king.

CONCOBAR--Woman, I swear by Balor, Tethra, and all the brood of
demons, I will have such a vengeance a thousand years hereafter
shall be frightened at the tale. If the Red Branch is to fall,
it will sink at least in the seas of the blood of the clan Usna.

LAVARCAM--O king, the doom of the Red Branch had already gone forth when you suffered love for Deirdre to enter your heart.

[Scene closes.]

ACT II.

SCENE.--In a dun by Loch Etive. Through the open door can be seen lakes and wooded islands in a silver twilight. DEIRDRE stands at the door looking over the lake. NAISI is within binding a spearhead to the shaft.

DEIRDRE--How still is the twihght! It is the sunset, not of one, but of many days--so still, so still, so living! The enchantment of Dana is upon the lakes and islands and woods, and the Great Father looks down through the deepening heavens.

NAISI--Thou art half of their world, beautiful woman, and it seems fair to me, gazing on thine eyes. But when thou art not beside me the flashing of spears is more to be admired than a whole heaven-full of stars.

DEIRDRE--O Naisi! still dost thou long, for the Red Branch and the peril of battles and death.

NAISI--Not for the Red Branch, nor the peril of battles, nor death, do I long. But--

DEIRDRE--But what, Naisi? What memory of Eri hast thou hoarded in thy heart?

NAISI--(bending over his spear) It is nothing, Deirdre.

DEIRDRE--It is a night of many days, Naisi. See, all the bright
day had hidden is revealed! Look, there! A star! and another star!
They could not see each other through the day, for the hot mists
of the sun were about them. Three years of the sun have we passed
in Alba, Naisi, and now, O star of my heart, truly do I see you,
this night of many days.

NAISI--Though my breast lay clear as a crystal before thee, thou
couldst see no change in my heart.

DEIRDRE--There is no change, beloved; but I see there one memory
warring on thy peace.

NAISI--What is it then, wise woman?

DEIRDRE--O Naisi, I have looked within thy heart, and thou hast
there imagined a king with scornful eyes thinking of thy flight.

NAISI--By the gods, but it is true! I would give this kingdom I
have won in Alba to tell the proud monarch I fear him not.

DEIRDRE--O Naisi, that thought will draw thee back to Eri, and to
I know not what peril and death beyond the seas.

NAISI--I will not war on the Red Branch. They were ever faithful
comrades. Be at peace, Deirdre.

DEIRDRE--Oh, how vain it is to say to the heart, "Be at peace,"
when the heart will not rest! Sorrow is on me, beloved, and I
know not wherefore. It has taken the strong and fast place of my
heart, and sighs there hidden in my love for thee.

NAISI--Dear one, the songs of Ainle and the pleasant tales of Ardan will drive away thy sorrow.

DEIRDRE--Ainle and Ardan! Where are they? They linger long.

NAISI--They are watching a sail that set hitherward from the south.

DEIRDRE--A sail!

NAISI--A sail! What is there to startle thee in that? Have not a thousand galleys lain in Loch Etive since I built this dun by the sea.

DEIRDRE--I do not know, but my spirit died down in my heart as you spake. I think the wind that brings it blows from Eri, and it is it has brought sorrow to me.

NAISI--My beautiful one, it is but a fancy. It is some merchant comes hither to barter Tyrian cloths for the cunning work of our smiths. But glad would I be if he came from Eri, and I would feast him here for a night, and sit round a fire of turves and hear of the deeds of the Red Branch.

DEIRDRE--Your heart for ever goes out to the Red Branch, Naisi. Were there any like unto thee, or Ainle, or Ardan?

NAISI--We were accounted most skilful, but no one was held to be braver than another. If there were one it was great Fergus who laid aside the silver rod which he held as Ardrie of Ulla, but he is in himself greater than any king.

DEIRDRE--And does one hero draw your heart back to Eri?

NAISI--A river of love, indeed, flows from my heart unto Fergus,

for there is no one more noble. But there were many others, Conal,
and the boy we called Cuculain, a dark, sad child, who was the
darling of the Red Branch, and truly he seemed like one who would be
a world-famous warrior. There were many held him to be a god in exile.

DEIRDRE--I think we, too, are in exile in this world. But tell me
who else among the Red Branch do you think of with love?

NAISI--There was the Ardrie, Concobar, whom ho man knows, indeed,
for he is unfathomable. But he is a wise king, though moody and
passionate at times, for he was cursed in his youth for a sin
against one of the Sidhe.

DEIRDRE--Oh, do not speak of him! My heart falls at the thought
of him as into a grave, and I know I will die when we meet.

NAISI--I know one who will die before that, my fawn.

DEIRDRE--Naisi! You remember when we fled that night; as I lay
by thy side--thou wert yet strange to me--I heard voices speaking
out of the air. The great ones were invisible, yet their voices
sounded solemnly. "Our brother and our sister do not remember,"
one said; and another spake: "They will serve the purpose all
the same," and there was more which I could not understand, but I
knew we were to bring some great gift to the Gael. Yesternight,
in a dream, I heard the voices again, and I cannot recall what they
said; but as I woke from sleep my pillow was wet with tears falling
softly, as out of another world, and I saw before me thy face, pale
and still, Naisi, and the king, with his implacable eyes. Oh,
pulse of my heart, I know the gift we shall give to the Gael will
be a memory to pity and sigh over, and I shall be the priestess of
tears. Naisi, promise me you will never go back to Ulla--swear
to me, Naisi.

NAISI--I will, if--

[Here AINLE and ARDAN enter.]

AINLE--Oh, great tidings, brother!

DEIRDRE--I feel fate is stealing on us with the footsteps of those we love. Before they speak, promise me, Naisi.

AINLE--What is it, dear sister? Naisi will promise thee anything, and if he does not we will make him do it all the same.

DEIDRE--Oh, let me speak! Both Death and the Heart's Desire are speeding to win the race. Promise me, Naisi, you will never return to Ulla.

ARDAN--Naisi, it were well to hear what tale may come from Emain Macha. One of the Red Branch displays our banner on a galley from the South. I have sent a boat to bring this warrior to our dun. It may be Concobar is dead.

DEIRDRE--Why should we return? Is not the Clan Usna greater here than ever in Eri.

AINLE--Dear sister, it is the land which gave us birth, which ever like a mother whispered to us, and its whisper is sweeter than the promise of beloved lips. Though we are kings here in Alba we are exiles, and the heart is afar from its home. [A distant shout is heard.]

NAISI--I hear a call like the voice of a man of Eri.

DEIRDRE--It is only a herdsman calling home his cattle. (She puts

her arms round NAISI's neck.) Beloved, am I become so little to
you that your heart is empty, and sighs for Eri?

NAISI--Deirdre, in my flight I have brought with me many whose
desire is afar, while you are set as a star by my side. They have
left their own land and many a maiden sighs for the clansmen who
never return. There is also the shadow of fear on my name, because
I fled and did not face the king. Shall I swear to keep my comrades
in exile, and let the shame of fear rest on the chieftain of their clan?

DEIRDRE--Can they not go? Are we not enough for each other, for
surely to me thou art hearth and home, and where thou art there
the dream ends, and beyond it. There is no other dream. [A voice
is heard without, more clearly calling.]

AINLE--It is a familiar voice that calls! And I thought I heard
thy name, Naisi.

ARDAN--It is the honey-sweet speech of a man of Eri.

DEIRDRE--It is one of our own clansmen. Naisi, will you not speak?
The hour is passing, and soon there will be naught but a destiny.

FERGUS--(without) Naisi! Naisi!

NAISI--A deep voice, like the roar of a storm god! It is Fergus
who comes from Eri.

ARDAN--He comes as a friend. There is no treachery in the Red Branch.

AINLE.--Let us meet him, and give him welcome! [The brothers go
to the door of the dun. DEIRDRE leans against the wall with terror
in her eyes.]

DEIRDRE--(in a low broken voice). Naisi! (NAISI returns to her side. AINLE and ARDAN go out. DEIRDRE rests one hand on NAISI's shoulders and with the other points upwards.) Do you not see them? The bright birds which sang at our flight! Look, how they wheel about us as they sing! What a heart-rending music! And their plumage, Naisi! It is all dabbled with crimson; and they shake a ruddy dew from their wings upon us! Your brow is stained with the drops. Let me clear away the stains. They pour over your face and hands. Oh! [She hides her face on NAISI's breast.]

NAISI--Poor, frightened one, there are no birds! See, how clear are my hands! Look again on my face.

DEIRDRE--(looking up for an instant). Oh! blind, staring eyes.

NAISI--Nay, they are filled with love, light of my heart. What has troubled your mind? Am I not beside you, and a thousand clansmen around our dun?

DEIRDRE--They go, and the music dies out. What was it Lavarcam said? Their singing brings love and death.

NAISI--What matters death, for love will find us among the Ever Living Ones. We are immortals and it does not become us to grieve.

DEIRDRE--Naisi, there is some treachery in the coming of Fergus.

NAISI--I say to you, Deirdre, that treachery is not to be spoken of with Fergus. He was my fosterer, who taught me all a chieftain should feel, and I shall not now accuse him on the foolish fancy of a woman. (He turns from DEIRDRE, and as he nears the door FERGUS enters with hands laid affectionately on a shoulder of each of the brothers; BUINNE and ILANN follow.) Welcome, Fergus! Glad is my heart at your coming, whether you bring good tidings or ill!

FERGUS--I would not have crossed the sea of Moyle to bring thee
ill tidings, Naisi. (He sees DEIRDRE.) My coming has affrighted
thy lady, who shakes like the white wave trembling before its fall.
I swear to thee, Deirdre, that the sons of Usna are dear to me as
children to a father.

DEIRDRE--The Birds of Angus showed all fiery and crimson as you came!

BUINNE--If we are not welcome in this dun let us return!

FERGUS--Be still, hasty boy.

ILANN--The lady Deirdre has received some omen or warning on our
account. When the Sidhe declare their will, we should with due
awe consider it.

ARDAN--Her mind has been troubled by a dream of some ill to Naisi.

NAISI--It was not by dreaming evils that the sons of Usna grew to
be champions in Ulla. And I took thee to my heart, Deirdre, though
the Druids trembled to murmur thy name.

FERGUS--If we listened to dreamers and foretellers the sword would
never flash from its sheath. In truth, I have never found the Sidhe
send omens to warriors; they rather bid them fly to herald our coming.

DEIRDRE--And what doom comes with thee now that such omens fled
before thee? I fear thy coming, warrior. I fear the Lights of
Valor will be soon extinguished.

FERGUS--Thou shalt smile again, pale princess, when thou hast heard my tale. It is not to the sons of Usna I would bring sorrow. Naisi, thou art free to return to Ulla.

NAISI--Does the king then forego his vengeance?

DEIRDRE--The king will never forego his vengeance. I have looked on his face--the face of one who never changes his purpose.

FERGUS--He sends forgiveness and greetings.

DEIRDRE--O Naisi, he sends honied words by the mouth of Fergus, but the pent-up death broods in his own heart.

BUINNE--We were tempest-beaten, indeed, on the sea of Moyle, but the storm of this girl's speech is more fearful to face.

FERGUS--Your tongue is too swift, Buinne. I say to you, Deirdre, that if all the kings of Eri brooded ill to Naisi, they dare not break through my protection.

NAISI--It is true, indeed, Fergus, though I have never asked any protection save my own sword. It is a chill welcome you give to Fergus and his sons, Deirdre. Ainle, tell them within to make ready the feasting hall. [AINLE goes into an inner room.]

DEIRDRE--I pray thy pardon, warrior. Thy love for Naisi I do not doubt. But in this holy place there is peace, and the doom that Cathvah the Druid cried cannot fall. And oh, I feel, too, there, is One here among us who pushes us silently from the place of life, and we are drifting away--away from the world, on a tide which goes down into the darkness!

ARDAN--The darkness is in your mind alone, poor sister. Great is our joy to hear the message of Fergus.

NAISI--It is not like the king to change his will. Fergus, what
has wrought upon his mind?

FERGUS--He took counsel with the Druids and Lavarcam, and thereafter
spake at Emain Macha, that for no woman in the world should the sons
of Usna be apart from the Red Branch. And so we all spake joyfully;
and I have come with the king's message of peace, for he knew that
for none else wouldst thou return.

NAISI--Surely, I will go with thee, Fergus. I long for the shining
eyes of friends and the fellowship of the Red Branch, and to see
my own country by the sea of Moyle. I weary of this barbarous
people in Alba.

DEIRDRE--O children of Usna, there is death in your going! Naisi,
will you not stay the storm bird of sorrow? I forehear the falling
of tears that cease not, and in generations unborn the sorrow of
it all that will never be stilled!

NAISI--Deirdre! Deirdre! It is not right for you, beautiful woman,
to come with tears between a thousand exiles and their own land!
Many battles have I fought, knowing well there would be death and
weeping after. If I feared to trust to the word of great kings
and warriors, it is not with tears I would be remembered. What
would the bards sing of Naisi--without trust! afraid of the
outstretched hand!--freighted by a woman's fears! By the gods,
before the clan Usna were so shamed I would shed my blood here
with my own hand.

DEIRDRE--O stay, stay your anger! Have pity on me, Naisi! Your
words, like lightnings, sear my heart. Never again will I seek

to stay thee. But speak to me with love once more, Naisi. Do not
bend your brows on me with anger; for, oh! but a little time
remains for us to love!

FERGUS--Nay, Deirdre, there are many years. Thou shalt yet
smile back on this hour in thy old years thinking of the love
and laughter between.

AINLE--(entering) The feast is ready for our guests.

ARDAN--The bards shall sing of Eri tonight. Let the harpers sound
their gayest music. Oh, to be back once more in royal Emain!

NAISI--Come, Deirdre, forget thy fears. Come, Fergus, I long to
hear from thy lips of the Red Branch and Ulla.

FERGUS--It is geasa with me not to refuse a feast offered by one
of the Red Branch.

[FERGUS, BUINNE, ILANN, and the sons of Usna go into the inner room.
DEIRDRE remains silently standing for a time, as if stunned. The
sound of laughter and music floats in. She goes to the door of
the dun, looking out again over the lakes and islands.]

DEIRDRE--Farewell O home of happy memories. Though thou art bleak
to Naisi, to me thou art bright. I shall never see thee more, save
as shadows we wander here, weeping over what is gone. Farewell, O
gentle people, who made music for me on the hills. The Father has
struck the last chord on the Harp of Life, and the music I shall
hear hereafter will be only sorrow. O Mother Dana, who breathed
up love through the dim earth to my heart, be with me where I am
going. Soon shall I lie close to thee for comfort, where many a
broken heart has lain and many a weeping head. [Music of harps

and laughter again floats in.]

VOICES--Deirdre! Deirdre! Deirdre!

[DEIRDRE leaves the door of the dun, and the scene closes as she flings herself on a couch, burying her face in her arms.]

ACT III.

SCENE.--The House of the Red Branch at Emain Macha. There is a door covered with curtains, through which the blue light of evening can be seen. CONCOBAR sits at a table on which is a chessboard, with figures arranged. LAVARCAM stands before the table.

CONCOBAR--The air is dense with omens, but all is uncertain. Cathvah, for all his Druid art, is uncertain, and cannot foresee the future; and in my dreams, too, I again see Macha, who died at my feet, and she passes by me with a secret exultant smile. O Druidess, is the sin of my boyhood to be avenged by this woman who comes back to Eri in a cloud of prophecy?

LAVARCAM--The great beauty has passed from Deirdre in her wanderings from place to place and from island to island. Many a time has she slept on the bare earth ere Naisi won a kingdom for himself in Alba. Surely the prophecy has already been fulfilled, for blood has been shed for Deirdre, and the Red Branch divided on her account. To Naisi the Red Branch are as brothers. Thou hast naught to fear.

CONCOBAR--Well, I have put aside my fears and taken thy counsel,

Druidess. For the sake of the Red Branch I have forgiven the sons
of Usna. Now, I will call together the Red Branch, for it is my
purpose to bring the five provinces under our sway, and there shall
be but one kingdom in Eri between the seas. [A distant shouting of
many voices is heard. LAVARCAM starts, clasping her hands.]

Why dost thou start, Druidess? Was it not foretold from of old,
that the gods would rule over one people in Eri? I sometimes think
the warrior soul of Lu shines through the boy Cuculain, who, after
me, shall guide the Red Branch; aye, and with him are many of the
old company who fought at Moytura, come back to renew the everlasting
battle. Is not this the Isle of Destiny, and the hour at hand? [The
clamor is again renewed.]

What, is this clamor as if men hailed a king? (Calls.) Is there
one without there? (ILANN enters.) Ah! returned from Alba with
the fugitives!

ILANN--King, we have fulfilled our charge. The sons of Usna are with
us in Emain Macha. Whither is it your pleasure they should be led?

CONCOBAR--They shall be lodged here, in the House of the Red Branch.
(ILANN is about to withdraw.) Yet, wait, what mean all these cries
as of astonished men?

ILANN--The lady, Deirdre, has come with us, and her beauty is a
wonder to the gazers in the streets, for she moves among them like
one of the Sidhe, whiter than ivory, with long hair of gold, and her
eyes, like the blue flame of twilight, make mystery in their hearts.

CONCOBAR--(starting up) This is no fading beauty who returns! You
hear, Druidess!

ILANN--Ardrie of Ulla, whoever has fabled to thee that the beauty of Deirdre is past has lied. She is sorrowful, indeed, but her sadness only bows the heart to more adoration than her joy, and pity for her seems sweeter than the dream of love. Fading! Yes, her yesterday fades behind her every morning, and every changing mood seems only an unveiling to bring her nearer to the golden spirit within. But how could I describe Deirdre? In a little while she will be here, and you shall see her with your own eyes. [ILLAN bows and goes out]

CONCOBAR--I will, indeed, see her with my own eyes. I will not, on the report of a boy, speak words that shall make the Red Branch to drip with blood. I will see with my own eyes. (He goes to the door.) But I swear to thee, Druidess, if thou hast plotted deceit a second time with Naisi, that all Eri may fall asunder, but I will be avenged.

[He holds the curtain aside with one hand and looks out. As he gazes his face grows sterner, and he lifts his hand above his head in menace. LAVARCAM looks on with terror, and as he drops the curtain and looks back on her, she lets her face sink in her hands.]

CONCOBAR--(scornfully) A Druid makes prophecies and a Druidess schemes to bring them to pass! Well have you all worked together! A fading beauty was to return, and the Lights of Valor to shine again in the Red-Branch! And I, the Ardrie of Ulla and the head of the Red Branch, to pass by the broken law and the after deceit! I, whose sole thought was of the building up of a people, to be set aside! The high gods may judge me hereafter, but tonight shall see the broken law set straight, and vengeance on the traitors to Ulla!

LAVARCAM--It was all my doing! They are innocent! I loved Deirdre, O king! let your anger be on me alone.

CONCOBAR--Oh, tongue of falsehood! Who can believe you! The fate
of Ulla was in your charge, and you let it go forth at the instant
wish of a man and a girl's desire. The fate of Ulla was too distant,
and you must bring it nigher--the torch to the pile! Breakers of
the law and makers of lies, you shall all perish together!

[CONCOBAR leaves the room. LAVARCAM remains, her being shaken with
sobs. After a pause NAISI enters with DEIRDRE. AINLE, ARDAN,
ILANN, and BUINNE follow. During the dialogue which ensues, NAISI
is inattentive, and is curiously examining the chess-board.]

DEIRDRE--We are entering a house of death! Who is it that weeps so?
I, too, would weep, but the children of Usna are too proud to let
tears be seen in the eyes of their women. (She sees LAVARCAM, who
raises her head from the table.) O fostermother, for whom do you
sorrow? Ah! it is for us. You still love me dear fostermother;
but you, who are wise, could you not have warned the Lights of Valor?
Was it kind to keep silence, and only meet us here with tears?

LAVARCAM--O Deirdre, my child! my darling! I have let love and
longing blind my eyes. I left the mountain home of the gods for
Emain Macha, and to plot for your return. I--I deceived the king.
I told him your loveliness was passed, and the time of the prophecy
gone by. I thought when you came all would be well. I thought
wildly, for love had made a blindness in my heart, and now the king
has discovered the deceit; and, oh! he has gone away in wrath,
and soon his terrible hand will fall!

DEIRDRE--It was not love made you all blind, but the high gods have
deserted us, and the demons draw us into a trap. They have lured
us from Alba, and they hover here above us in red clouds--cloud
upon cloud--and await the sacrifice.

LAVARACAM--Oh, it is not yet too late! Where is Fergus? The king dare not war on Fergus. Fergus is our only hope.

DEIRDRE--Fergus has bartered his honor for a feast. He remained with Baruch that he might boast he never refused the wine cup. He feasts with Baruch, and the Lights of Valor who put their trust in him--must die.

BUINNE--Fergus never bartered his honor. I do protest, girl, against your speech. The name of Fergus alone would protect you throughout all Eri; how much more here, where he is champion in Ulla. Come, brother, we are none of us needed here. [BUINNE leaves the room.]

DEIRDRE--Father and son alike desert us! O fostermother, is this the end of all? Is there no way out? Is there no way out?

ILANN--I will not desert you, Deirdre, while I can still thrust a spear. But you, fear overmuch without a cause.

LAVARACAM--Bar up the door and close the windows. I will send a swift messenger for Fergus. If you hold the dun until Fergus comes all will yet be well. [LAVARCAM hurries out.]

DEIRDRE---(going to NAISI)--Naisi, do you not hear? Let the door be barred! Ainle and Ardan, are you still all blind? Oh! must I close them with my own hand!

[DEIRDRE goes to the Window, and lays her hand on the bars NAISI follows her.]

NAISI--Deirdre, in your girlhood you have not known of the ways of the Red Branch. This thing you fear is unheard of in Ulla. The king may be wrathful; but the word, once passed, is inviolable. If he whispered treachery to one of the Red Branch he would not be Ardrie tomorrow. Nay, leave the window unbarred, or they will say the sons of Usna have returned timid as birds! Come, we are enough protection for thee. See, here is the chessboard of Concobar, with which he is wont to divine, playing a lonely game with fate. The pieces are set. We will finish the game, and so pass the time until the feast is ready. (He sits down) The golden pieces are yours and the silver mine.

AINLE--(looking at the board) You have given Deirdre the weaker side.

NAISI--Deirdre always plays with more cunning skill.

DEIRDRE--O fearless one, if he who set the game played with fate, the victory is already fixed, and no skill may avail.

NAISI--We will see if Concobar has favourable omens. It is geasa for him always to play with silver pieces. I will follow his game. It is your move. Dear one, will you not smile? Surely, against Concobar you will play well.

DEIRDRE--It is too late. See, everywhere my king is threatened!

ARDAN--Nay, your game is not lost. If you move your king back all will be well.

MESSENGER--(at the door) I bear a message from the Ardrie to the sons of Usna.

NAISI--Speak out thy message, man. Why does thy voice tremble? Who art thou? I do not know thee. Thou art not one of the Red Branch. Concobar is not wont to send messages to kings by such as thou.

MESSENGER--The Red Branch are far from Emain Macha--but it matters not. The king has commanded me to speak thus to the sons of Usna. You have broken the law of Ulla when you stole away the daughter of Felim. You have broken the law of the Red Branch when you sent lying messages through Lavarcam plotting to return. The king commands that the daughter of Felim be given up, and--

AINLIE--Are we to listen to this?

ARDAN--My spear will fly of itself if he does not depart.

NAISI--Nay, brother, he is only a slave. (To the MESSENGER.) Return to Concobar, and tell him that tomorrow the Red Branch will choose another chief. There, why dost thou wait? Begone! (To DEIRDRE.) Oh, wise woman, truly did you see the rottenness in this king!

DEIRDRE--Why did you not take my counsel, Naisi? For now it is too late--too late.

NAISI--There is naught to fear. One of us could hold this dun against a thousand of Concobar's household slaves. When Fergus comes tomorrow there will be another king in Emain Macha.

ILANN--It is true, Deirdre. One of us is enough for Concobar's household slaves. I will keep watch at the door while you play at peace with Naisi.

[ILANN lifts the curtain of the door and goes outside. The Play at chess begins again. AINLE and ARDAN look on.]

AINLE--Naisi, you play wildly. See, your queen will be taken. [A disturbance without and the clash of arms.]

ILANN--(Without) Keep back! Do you dare?

NAISI--Ah! the slaves come on, driven by the false Ardrie! When the game is finished we will sweep them back and slay them in the Royal House before Concobar's eyes. Play! You forget to move, Deirdre. [The clash of arms is renewed.]

ILANN--(without) Oh! I am wounded. Ainle! Ardan! To the door!

[AINLE and ARDAN rush out. The clash of arms renewed.]

DEIRDRE--Naisi, I cannot. I cannot. The end of all has come. Oh, Naisi! [She flings her arms across the table, scattering the pieces over the board.]

NAISI--If the end has come we should meet it with calm. It is not with sighing and tears the Clan Usna should depart. You have not played this game as it ought to be played.

DEIRDRE--Your pride is molded and set like a pillar of bronze. O warrior, I was no mate for you. I am only a woman, who has given her life into your hands, and you chide me for my love.

NAISI--(caressing her head with his hands) Poor timid dove, I had forgotten thy weakness. I did not mean to wound thee, my heart. Oh, many will shed hotter tears than these for thy sorrow! They will perish swiftly who made Naisi's queen to weep! [He snatches up a spear and rushes out. There are cries, and then a silence.]

LAVARCAM--(entering hurriedly) Bear Deirdre swiftly away through the night. (She stops and looks around.) Where are the sons of Usna? Oh! I stepped over many dead bodies at the door. Surely the Lights of Valor were not so soon overcome! Oh, my darling! come away with me from this terrible house.

DEIRDRE--(Slowly) What did you say of the Lights of Valor? That--they--were dead?

[NAISI, AINLE, and ARDAN re-enter. DEIRDRE clings to NAISI.]

NAISI--My gentle one, do not look so pale nor wound me with those terror-stricken eyes. Those base slaves are all fled. Truly Concobar is a mighty king without the Red Branch!

LAVARCAM--Oh, do not linger here. Bear Deirdre away while there is time. You can escape through the city in the silence of the night. The king has called for his Druids; soon the magic of Cathvah will enfold you, and your strength will be all withered away.

NAISI--I will not leave Emain Macha until the head of this false king is apart from his shoulders. A spear can pass as swiftly through his Druid as through one of his slaves. Oh, Cathvah, the old mumbler of spells and of false prophecies, who caused Deirdre to be taken from her mother's breast! Truly, I owe a deep debt to Cathvah, and I Will repay it.

LAVARCAM--If you love Deirdre, do not let pride and wrath stay your flight. You have but an instant to fly. You can return with Fergus and a host of warriors in the dawn. You do not know the power of Cathvah. Surely, if you do not depart, Deirdre will fall into the king's hands, and it were better she had died in her mother's womb.

DEIRDRE--Naisi, let us leave this house of death. [The sound of footsteps without]

LAVARCAM--It is too late!

[AINLE and ARDAN start to the door, but are stayed at the sound of CATHVAH'S voice. DEIRDRE clings to NAISI. CATHVAH (chanting without)]

Let the Faed Fia fall;
Mananaun Mac Lir.
Take back the day
Amid days unremembered.
Over the warring mind
Let thy Faed Fia fall,
Mananaun Mac Lir!

NAISI--Why dost thou weep, Deirdre, and cling to me so? The sea is calm. Tomorrow we will rest safely at Emain Macha with the great Ardrie, who has forgiven all.

LAVARCAM--The darkness is upon his mind. Oh, poor Deirdre!

CATHVAH (without)--

Let thy waves rise,
Mananaun Mac Lir.
Let the earth fail
Beneath their feet,
Let thy Waves flow over them,
Mananaun: Lord of ocean!

NAISI--Our galley is sinking--and no land in sight! I did not think the end would come so soon. O pale love, take courage. Is death so bitter to thee? We shall go down in each other's arms; our hearts shall beat out their love together, and the last of life

we shall know will be our kisses on each other's lips. (AINLE and
ARDAN stagger outside. There is a sound of blows and a low cry.)
Ainle and Ardan have sunk in the waters! We are alone. Still
weeping! My bird, my bird, soon we shall fly together to the
bright kingdom in the West, to Hy Brazil, amid the opal seas.

DEIRDRE--Naisi, Naisi, shake off the magic dream. It is here in
Emain Macha we are. There are no waters. The spell of the Druid
and his terrible chant have made a mist about your eyes.

NAISI--Her mind is wandering. She is distraught with terror of
the king. There, rest your head on my heart. Hush! hush! The
waters are flowing upward swiftly. Soon, when all is over, you
will laugh at your terror. The great Ardrie will sorrow over
our death.

DEIRDRE--I cannot speak. Lavarcam, can you not break the enchantment?

LAVARCAM--My limbs are fixed here by the spell.

NAISI--There was music a while ago. The swans of Lir, with their
slow, sweet faery singing. There never was a sadder tale than theirs.
They must roam for ages, driven on the sea of Moyle, while we shall
go hand in hand through the country of immortal youth. And there
is Mananaun, the dark blue king, who looks at us with a smile of
welcome. Ildathach is lit up with its shining mountains, and the
golden phantoms are leaping there in the dawn! There is a path
made for us! Come, Deirdre, the god has made for us an island on
the sea. (NAISI goes through the door, and falls back, smitten by
a spear-thrust.) The Druid Cathvah!--The king!--O Deirdre! [He dies.
DEIRDRE bends over the body, taking the hands in hers.]

LAVARCAM--O gentle heart, thy wounds will be more bitter than his.

Speak but a word. That silent sorrow will kill thee and me. My
darling, it was fate, and I was not to blame. Come, it will comfort
thee to weep beside my breast. Leave the dead for vengeance, for
heavy is the vengeance that shall fall on this ruthless king.

DEIRDRE--I do not fear Concobar any more. My spirit is sinking
away from the world, I could not stay after Naisi. After the Lights
of Valor had vanished, how could I remain? The earth has grown dim
and old, fostermother. The gods have gone far away, and the lights
from the mountains and the Lions of the Flaming Heart are still, O
fostermother, when they heap the cairn over him, let me be beside
him in the narrow grave. I will still be with the noble one.

[DEIRDRE lays her head on NAISI's body. CONCOBAR enters, standing
in the doorway. LAVARCAM takes DEIRDRE'S hand and drops it.]

LAVARCAM--Did you come to torture her with your presence? Was not
the death of Naisi cruelty enough? But now she is past your power
to wound.

CONCOBAR--The death of Naisi was only the fulfilling of the law.
Ulla could not hold together if its ancient laws were set aside.

LAVARCAM--Do you think to bind men together when you have broken
their hearts? O fool, who would conquer all Eri! I see the Red
Branch scattered and Eri rent asunder, and thy memory a curse after
many thousand years. The gods have overthrown thy dominion, proud
king, with the last sigh from this dead child; and out of the
pity for her they will build up an eternal kingdom in the spirit
of man. [An uproar without and the clash of arms.]

VOICES--Fergus! Fergus! Fergus!

LAVARCAM--The avenger has come! So perishes the Red Branch! [She hurries out wildly.]

CONCOBAR--(Slowly, after a pause) I have two divided kingdoms, and one is in my own heart. Thus do I pay homage to thee, O Queen, who will rule, being dead. [He bends over the body of DEIRDRE and kisses her hand.]

FERGUS--(without) Where is the traitor Ardrie?

[CONCOBAR starts up, lifting his spear. FERGUS appears at the doorway, and the scene closes.]

1901

NOTE TO THOUGHTS FOR A CONVENTION

I was asked to put into shape for publication ideas and suggestions for an Irish settlement which had been discussed among a group whose members represented ah extremes in Irish opinion. The compromise arrived at was embodied in documents written by members of the group privately circulated, criticized and again amended. I make special acknowledgments to Colonel Maurice Moore, Mr. James G. Douglas, Mr. Edward E. Lysaght, Mr. Joseph Johnston, F.T.C.D., Mr. Alec Wilson and Mr. Diarmuid Coffey. For the tone, method of presentation, and general arguments used, I alone am responsible. And if any are offended at what I have said, I am to be blamed, not my fellow-workers.

The author desires to make acknowledgment to The Times for permission to include an article on "The Spiritual Conflict."

The Codes Of Hammurabi And Moses
W. W. Davies

QTY

The discovery of the Hammurabi Code is one of the greatest achievements of archaeology, and is of paramount interest, not only to the student of the Bible, but also to all those interested in ancient history...

Religion   ISBN: *1-59462-338-4*   Pages:132
MSRP *$12.95*

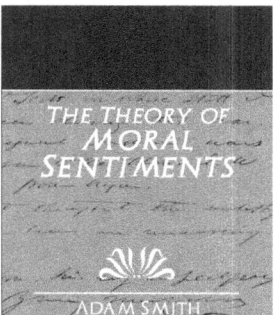

The Theory of Moral Sentiments
Adam Smith

QTY

This work from 1749. contains original theories of conscience amd moral judgment and it is the foundation for systemof morals.

Philosophy   ISBN: *1-59462-777-0*   Pages:536
MSRP *$19.95*

Jessica's First Prayer
Hesba Stretton

QTY

In a screened and secluded corner of one of the many railway-bridges which span the streets of London there could be seen a few years ago, from five o'clock every morning until half past eight, a tidily set-out coffee-stall, consisting of a trestle and board, upon which stood two large tin cans, with a small fire of charcoal burning under each so as to keep the coffee boiling during the early hours of the morning when the work-people were thronging into the city on their way to their daily toil...

Pages:84

Childrens   ISBN: *1-59462-373-2*   MSRP *$9.95*

My Life and Work
Henry Ford

QTY

Henry Ford revolutionized the world with his implementation of mass production for the Model T automobile. Gain valuable business insight into his life and work with his own auto-biography... "We have only started on our development of our country we have not as yet, with all our talk of wonderful progress, done more than scratch the surface. The progress has been wonderful enough but..."

Pages:300

Biographies/   ISBN: *1-59462-198-5*   MSRP *$21.95*

The Art of Cross-Examination
Francis Wellman

QTY

I presume it is the experience of every author, after his first book is published upon an important subject, to be almost overwhelmed with a wealth of ideas and illustrations which could readily have been included in his book, and which to his own mind, at least, seem to make a second edition inevitable. Such certainly was the case with me; and when the first edition had reached its sixth impression in five months, I rejoiced to learn that it seemed to my publishers that the book had met with a sufficiently favorable reception to justify a second and considerably enlarged edition. ..

Pages:412

Reference   ISBN: *1-59462-647-2*   *MSRP $19.95*

On the Duty of Civil Disobedience
Henry David Thoreau

QTY

Thoreau wrote his famous essay, On the Duty of Civil Disobedience, as a protest against an unjust but popular war and the immoral but popular institution of slave-owning. He did more than write—he declined to pay his taxes, and was hauled off to gaol in consequence. Who can say how much this refusal of his hastened the end of the war and of slavery ?

Law   ISBN: *1-59462-747-9*

Pages:48

MSRP $7.45

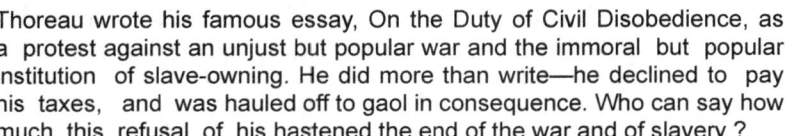

Dream Psychology Psychoanalysis for Beginners
Sigmund Freud

QTY

Sigmund Freud, born Sigismund Schlomo Freud (May 6, 1856 - September 23, 1939), was a Jewish-Austrian neurologist and psychiatrist who co-founded the psychoanalytic school of psychology. Freud is best known for his theories of the unconscious mind, especially involving the mechanism of repression; his redefinition of sexual desire as mobile and directed towards a wide variety of objects; and his therapeutic techniques, especially his understanding of transference in the therapeutic relationship and the presumed value of dreams as sources of insight into unconscious desires.

Pages:196

Psychology   ISBN: *1-59462-905-6*   *MSRP $15.45*

The Miracle of Right Thought
Orison Swett Marden

QTY

Believe with all of your heart that you will do what you were made to do. When the mind has once formed the habit of holding cheerful, happy, prosperous pictures, it will not be easy to form the opposite habit. It does not matter how improbable or how far away this realization may see, or how dark the prospects may be, if we visualize them as best we can, as vividly as possible, hold tenaciously to them and vigorously struggle to attain them, they will gradually become actualized, realized in the life. But a desire, a longing without endeavor, a yearning abandoned or held indifferently will vanish without realization.

Pages:360

Self Help   ISBN: *1-59462-644-8*   *MSRP $25.45*

The Rosicrucian Cosmo-Conception Mystic Christianity *by Max Heindel*   ISBN: *1-59462-188-8* **$38.95**
The Rosicrucian Cosmo-conception is not dogmatic, neither does it appeal to any other authority than the reason of the student. It is: not controversial, but is: sent forth in the, hope that it may help to clear...   *New Age/Religion Pages 646*

Abandonment To Divine Providence *by Jean-Pierre de Caussade*   ISBN: *1-59462-228-0* **$25.95**
"The Rev. Jean Pierre de Caussade was one of the most remarkable spiritual writers of the Society of Jesus in France in the 18th Century. His death took place at Toulouse in 1751. His works have gone through many editions and have been republished...   *Inspirational/Religion Pages 400*

Mental Chemistry *by Charles Haanel*   ISBN: *1-59462-192-6* **$23.95**
Mental Chemistry allows the change of material conditions by combining and appropriately utilizing the power of the mind. Much like applied chemistry creates something new and unique out of careful combinations of chemicals the mastery of mental chemistry...   *New Age Pages 354*

The Letters of Robert Browning and Elizabeth Barret Barrett 1845-1846 vol II   ISBN: *1-59462-193-4* **$35.95**
by Robert Browning and Elizabeth Barrett
Biographies Pages 596

Gleanings In Genesis (volume I) *by Arthur W. Pink*   ISBN: *1-59462-130-8* **$27.45**
Appropriately has Genesis been termed "the seed plot of the Bible" for in it we have, in germ form, almost all of the great doctrines which are afterwards fully developed in the books of Scripture which follow...   *Religion/Inspirational Pages 420*

The Master Key *by L. W. de Laurence*   ISBN: *1-59462-001-6* **$30.95**
In no branch of human knowledge has there been a more lively increase of the spirit of research during the past few years than in the study of Psychology, Concentration and Mental Discipline. The requests for authentic lessons in Thought Control, Mental Discipline and...   *New Age/Business Pages 422*

The Lesser Key Of Solomon Goetia *by L. W. de Laurence*   ISBN: *1-59462-092-X* **$9.95**
This translation of the first book of the "Lemegton" which is now for the first time made accessible to students of Talismanic Magic was done, after careful collation and edition, from numerous Ancient Manuscripts in Hebrew, Latin, and French...   *New Age/Occult Pages 92*

Rubaiyat Of Omar Khayyam *by Edward Fitzgerald*   ISBN:*1-59462-332-5* **$13.95**
Edward Fitzgerald, whom the world has already learned, in spite of his own efforts to remain within the shadow of anonymity, to look upon as one of the rarest poets of the century, was born at Bredfield, in Suffolk, on the 31st of March, 1809. He was the third son of John Purcell...   *Music Pages 172*

Ancient Law *by Henry Maine*   ISBN: *1-59462-128-4* **$29.95**
The chief object of the following pages is to indicate some of the earliest ideas of mankind, as they are reflected in Ancient Law, and to point out the relation of those ideas to modern thought.   *Religiom/History Pages 452*

Far-Away Stories *by William J. Locke*   ISBN: *1-59462-129-2* **$19.45**
"Good wine needs no bush, but a collection of mixed vintages does. And this book is just such a collection. Some of the stories I do not want to remain buried for ever in the museum files of dead magazine-numbers an author's not unpardonable vanity..."   *Fiction Pages 272*

Life of David Crockett *by David Crockett*   ISBN: *1-59462-250-7* **$27.45**
"Colonel David Crockett was one of the most remarkable men of the times in which he lived. Born in humble life, but gifted with a strong will, an indomitable courage, and unremitting perseverance...   *Biographies/New Age Pages 424*

Lip-Reading *by Edward Nitchie*   ISBN: *1-59462-206-X* **$25.95**
Edward B. Nitchie, founder of the New York School for the Hard of Hearing, now the Nitchie School of Lip-Reading, Inc, wrote "LIP-READING Principles and Practice". The development and perfecting of this meritorious work on lip-reading was an undertaking...   *How-to Pages 400*

A Handbook of Suggestive Therapeutics, Applied Hypnotism, Psychic Science   ISBN: *1-59462-214-0* **$24.95**
by Henry Munro
Health/New Age/Health/Self-help Pages 376

A Doll's House: and Two Other Plays *by Henrik Ibsen*   ISBN: *1-59462-112-8* **$19.95**
Henrik Ibsen created this classic when in revolutionary 1848 Rome. Introducing some striking concepts in playwriting for the realist genre, this play has been studied the world over.   *Fiction/Classics/Plays 308*

The Light of Asia *by sir Edwin Arnold*   ISBN: *1-59462-204-3* **$13.95**
In this poetic masterpiece, Edwin Arnold describes the life and teachings of Buddha. The man who was to become known as Buddha to the world was born as Prince Gautama of India but he rejected the worldly riches and abandoned the reigns of power when... *Religion/History/Biographies Pages 170*

The Complete Works of Guy de Maupassant *by Guy de Maupassant*   ISBN: *1-59462-157-8* **$16.95**
"For days and days, nights and nights, I had dreamed of that first kiss which was to consecrate our engagement, and I knew not on what spot I should put my lips..."   *Fiction/Classics Pages 240*

The Art of Cross-Examination *by Francis L. Wellman*   ISBN: *1-59462-309-0* **$26.95**
Written by a renowned trial lawyer, Wellman imparts his experience and uses case studies to explain how to use psychology to extract desired information through questioning.   *How-to/Science/Reference Pages 408*

Answered or Unanswered? *by Louisa Vaughan*   ISBN: *1-59462-248-5* **$10.95**
Miracles of Faith in China
Religion Pages 112

The Edinburgh Lectures on Mental Science (1909) *by Thomas*   ISBN: *1-59462-008-3* **$11.95**
This book contains the substance of a course of lectures recently given by the writer in the Queen Street Hail, Edinburgh. Its purpose is to indicate the Natural Principles governing the relation between Mental Action and Material Conditions...   *New Age/Psychology Pages 148*

Ayesha *by H. Rider Haggard*   ISBN: *1-59462-301-5* **$24.95**
Verily and indeed it is the unexpected that happens! Probably if there was one person upon the earth from whom the Editor of this, and of a certain previous history, did not expect to hear again...   *Classics Pages 380*

Ayala's Angel *by Anthony Trollope*   ISBN: *1-59462-352-X* **$29.95**
The two girls were both pretty, but Lucy who was twenty-one who supposed to be simple and comparatively unattractive, whereas Ayala was credited, as her Bombwhat romantic name might show, with poetic charm and a taste for romance. Ayala when her father died was nineteen...   *Fiction Pages 484*

The American Commonwealth *by James Bryce*   ISBN: *1-59462-286-8* **$34.45**
An interpretation of American democratic political theory. It examines political mechanics and society from the perspective of Scotsman James Bryce   *Politics Pages 572*

Stories of the Pilgrims *by Margaret P. Pumphrey*   ISBN: *1-59462-116-0* **$17.95**
This book explores pilgrims religious oppression in England as well as their escape to Holland and eventual crossing to America on the Mayflower, and their early days in New England...   *History Pages 268*

QTY

The Fasting Cure *by Sinclair Upton*
In the Cosmopolitan Magazine for May, 1910, and in the Contemporary Review (London) for April, 1910, I published an article dealing with my experiences in fasting. I have written a great many magazine articles, but never one which attracted so much attention... New Age/Self Help/Health Pages 164

ISBN: *1-59462-222-1* **$13.95**

☐

Hebrew Astrology *by Sepharial*
In these days of advanced thinking it is a matter of common observation that we have left many of the old landmarks behind and that we are now pressing forward to greater heights and to a wider horizon than that which represented the mind-content of our progenitors... Astrology Pages 144

ISBN: *1-59462-308-2* **$13.45**

☐

Thought Vibration or The Law of Attraction in the Thought World
by William Walker Atkinson   Psychology/Religion Pages 144

ISBN: *1-59462-127-6* **$12.95**

☐

Optimism *by Helen Keller*
Helen Keller was blind, deaf, and mute since 19 months old, yet famously learned how to overcome these handicaps, communicate with the world, and spread her lectures promoting optimism. An inspiring read for everyone... Biographies/Inspirational Pages 84

ISBN: *1-59462-108-X* **$15.95**

☐

Sara Crewe *by Frances Burnett*
In the first place, Miss Minchin lived in London. Her home was a large, dull, tall one, in a large, dull square, where all the houses were alike, and all the sparrows were alike, and where all the door-knockers made the same heavy sound... Childrens/Classic Pages 88

ISBN: *1-59462-360-0* **$9.45**

☐

The Autobiography of Benjamin Franklin *by Benjamin Franklin*
The Autobiography of Benjamin Franklin has probably been more extensively read than any other American historical work, and no other book of its kind has had such ups and downs of fortune. Franklin lived for many years in England, where he was agent... Biographies/History Pages 332

ISBN: *1-59462-135-7* **$24.95**

☐

Name	
Email	
Telephone	
Address	
City, State ZIP	

☐ **Credit Card**   ☐ **Check / Money Order**

Credit Card Number	
Expiration Date	
Signature	

Please Mail to: *Book Jungle*
PO Box 2226
Champaign, IL 61825
or Fax to: *630-214-0564*

ORDERING INFORMATION
web: *www.bookjungle.com*
email: *sales@bookjungle.com*
fax: *630-214-0564*
mail: *Book Jungle PO Box 2226 Champaign, IL 61825*
or PayPal *to sales@bookjungle.com*

Please contact us for bulk discounts

DIRECT-ORDER TERMS

**20% Discount if You Order
Two or More Books**
Free Domestic Shipping!
Accepted: Master Card, Visa,
Discover, American Express

www.ingramcontent.com/pod-product-compliance
Lightning Source LLC
Chambersburg PA
CBHW080903020726
47502CB00008B/2335